Praise for Ellie Alexander's Bakeshop mystery series

"Delectable."   —*Portland Book Review*

"Delicious."   —*RT Book Reviews*

"Quirky . . . intriguing . . . [with] recipes to make your
stomach growl."   —*Reader to Reader*

"This debut culinary mystery is a light soufflé of a book
(with recipes) that makes a perfect mix for fans of Jenn
McKinlay, Leslie Budewitz, or Jessica Beck."
                    —*Library Journal* on *Meet Your Baker*

"Marvelous."   —*Fresh Fiction*

"Scrumptious . . . will delight fans of cozy mysteries
with culinary delights."   —*Night Owl Reviews*

"Clever plots, likable characters, and good food . . . Still
hungry? Not to worry, because desserts abound in . . .
this delectable series."
          —*Mystery Scene* on *A Batter of Life and Death*

"[With] *Meet Your Baker,* Alexander weaves a tasty tale
of deceit, family ties, delicious pastries, and murder."
          —Edith Maxwell, author of *A Tine to Live,
                                    A Tine to Die*

"Sure to satisfy both dedicated foodies and ardent mystery lovers alike."
          —Jessie Crockett, author of *Drizzled with Death*

Chilled to the Cone

Ellie Alexander

St. Martin's Paperbacks

This is a work of fiction. All of the characters, organizations, and events portrayed in this novel are either products of the author's imagination or are used fictitiously.

First published in the United States by St. Martin's Paperbacks, an imprint of St. Martin's Publishing Group.

CHILLED TO THE CONE

For information, address St. Martin's Publishing Group, 120 Broadway, New York, NY 10271.

www.stmartins.com

ISBN: 978-1-250-21438-6

Our books may be purchased in bulk for promotional, educational, or business use. Please contact your local bookseller or the Macmillan Corporate and Premium Sales Department at 1-800-221-7945, ext. 5442, or by email at MacmillanSpecialMarkets@macmillan.com.

Printed in the United States of America

10 9 8 7 6 5 4 3 2 1

For many years now I've had the privilege of not only living in Ashland, but also using the Shakespearean hamlet and the surrounding Rogue Valley as my muse. The theme of community and connection runs strong throughout the series, and I often speak about how true that is in real life. Never has that been more so than this past year. I wrote *Chilled to the Cone* long before the pandemic upended our lives and before a wildfire would tear through Ashland and burn two neighboring towns. There has been unfathomable loss in this little corner of the world, as Jules would say. Yet, in the midst of total devastation, the effects of which will likely be felt for years to come, I've witnessed the truest outpouring of heartfelt community that words can never do justice to describe. In that spirit I dedicate this book to the people of southern Oregon, you have my whole heart.

Chapter One

They say that every journey starts with a single step. As of late, it felt like my steps were taking me in opposing directions. Fortunately, our little corner of southern Oregon wasn't too large. Ashland is nestled in the Siskiyou Mountains just north of California, giving us long, glorious stretches of sun, stunning vistas, and an abundance of fresh pine-scented air. Not only are we tucked between deciduous forests and gently rolling golden hills, we are also home to the world-renowned Oregon Shakespeare Festival. Throughout the year tourists came from near and far to take in a production of *The Tempest* in the Elizabethan, beneath a ceiling of stars, or experience an intimate performance of new works by innovative playwrights in one of the many theaters on the OSF campus.

When I had returned to my childhood home a while ago I hadn't been sure what to expect. I had thought my stop might be temporary, but Ashland captured me under her spell. I knew now that this was where I was meant to be. It was an exciting time to have a renewed appreciation for the place where I had grown up.

Maybe that was the gift of leaving. Distance and time away from my beloved hometown had made me want to embrace and experience all that the Rogue Valley had to offer. Thus far, I had barely scratched the surface. Ashland is known as the spot where the palms meet the pines. Leafy palms give rise to a conifer canopy of ponderosa pines, cedars, and white firs. Our temperate climate and fertile, organic valleys are ideal for growing pears, fruits, herbs, and grapes. Vineyards dot the hillsides throughout the region along with alpine lakes, pristine rivers, and hiking trails so remote that you can disappear into the forest and meander for hours without seeing another soul, except for the occasional black bear that might amble past.

From the healing Lithia waters to the wild deer that nibbled on lush green lawns to the constant bustle of activity on the plaza and the bevy of friends and family who had welcomed me in, I could finally declare with confidence that nothing could ever make me want to leave again.

That was especially true with Torte's latest endeavor. Our family bakeshop had been expanding. It happened organically. First, we learned that the basement space beneath the cozy bakeshop my parents opened thirty years ago had come up for sale. Mom and I couldn't pass up the opportunity, so we secured some grant money and city loans to break through the floor and build our dream kitchen, complete with a wood-burning pizza oven, a state-of-the-art kitchen, and a cozy seating area in the basement. The renovations meant that we had been able to expand our offerings with a kitchen twice the size as well as additional seating in the basement and a new and improved coffee bar and pastry counter upstairs.

My next venture had been a total surprise. My estranged husband, Carlos, at the urging of my best friend, Lance, had made us partners in Uva, a boutique winery just outside of town. I left Carlos on the ship where we had both worked, after I learned that he had a son, Ramiro, that he had never told me about. In hindsight, it might have been a rash decision, but leaving Carlos meant that I had returned home to Ashland, a decision I did not regret.

The bakeshop and winery should have been enough. I had plenty on my plate with managing Torte, growing our staff, and trying to figure out what to do with Uva. However, the universe had other plans for me. Sterling, my young sous chef, had been experimenting with a line of concretes—rich, custard-like ice creams with decadent and unique flavor combinations like lemon rosemary, dark-chocolate toffee, pear and blue cheese, and strawberry balsamic with toasted pecans. We had added a small cold case during the remodel to house our daily concrete offerings. They had become so popular that on busy days we sold out by early afternoon no matter the season.

In a twist of fate, my friend Laney Lee had called to inform me that a seasonal space in Ashland's up-and-coming Railroad District was available for lease. Laney owned a Hawaiian street food truck, Nana's. We had become fast friends after I had tried her passion-fruit lemonade one hot afternoon last summer. She had been keeping her eye on the outdoor space adjacent to where she parked her cart on summer days. The lot in question was attached to a ground-floor yoga studio with an apartment above. It had been used as a walk-up coffee kiosk, but the owner of the coffee shop had jumped ship and moved to Paris, leaving the space unexpectedly vacant. Laney had initially hoped that the garden, with its sweet outdoor counter and small covered area with a fridge, cooler, and sink, might serve as a permanent location for her food truck. Alas, it wasn't meant to be. The city wouldn't approve any upgrades for the site. Laney needed a stove and an oven to make her delicious fusion Kalua pork tacos and sweet and sugary malasadas.

She had called me a few days ago with the news that the seasonal space was about to go on the market. "Jules, you have to come take a look at this place. It's perfect for Torte Two."

"Torte Two?"

"Yeah, think about it. It's a perfect opportunity to expand. You could do walk-up coffee, even bring pastries over from the bakeshop. This area gets great summer traffic. With exorbitant rent prices on the plaza, I think we're going to see a lot more action here in the Railroad District."

"That's so nice of you to think of us, Laney," I had said. "But we just finished a major expansion. I'm not sure a second location is in the cards right now."

"Come take a look at the space," Laney had pleaded. "I've had my truck here for ten years and I want to be neighbors with something complimentary like Torte— you would draw customers into the area with your name recognition alone. That would be great for you and for all of us trying to build a new shopping destination. I don't want to see a big investor or corporate coffee take over. There are rumors swirling that a huge national chain is considering doing a build-out. They want to tear up the garden and turn the lot into a mega industrial coffee shop. We can't let that happen. If you are even a little interested, I can put you in touch with Addie. She owns the property and I know she'd give you a deal. Plus, the space is only open from May until September. It would be a great way for Torte to hit a new market, and it's really low risk."

I had hesitated on the call. "I don't know, Laney. We're already short-staffed. I'm not sure we can take on another project, even if it is seasonal."

"Opportunities like this don't pop up often in Ashland, Jules." Laney was nothing if not persistent. "You know that. Come by later this week. I'll show you around and introduce you to Addie. She's young and ambitious. Her yoga classes have attracted a lot of new faces to the Railroad District. She likes the idea of keeping the space a walk-up restaurant. No pressure, I promise."

Laney had been convincing. I agreed to stop by and take a look—more than anything to get off the phone, which is how I found myself making the short half-mile walk from Torte to the intersection of Fourth and A streets on a spring afternoon.

Downtown Ashland was extremely walkable, with relatively flat streets and sidewalks. I crossed Main Street, with Andy and Sterling in tow, and passed the blue awnings of the police station. To call it a station was an exaggeration. It was a contact point in the plaza, staffed by three officers and Ashland's park cadets who patrolled downtown and the surrounding parks on foot and by bike, handing out minor citations and alerting the police of any dangerous situations or criminal activity. The station looked more like a welcome center with its dish of water for dogs, stacks of maps, and window boxes with cheery germaniums. We continued along Water Street, paralleling Ashland Creek, which flowed heavy with snowmelt.

Andy was my resident barista who had recently opted to drop out of college in order to broaden his coffee knowledge. I wasn't thrilled with his decision to leave school, but if I had learned anything in my thirty-plus years it was that we all have to follow our own path. Andy's ultimate dream was to open his own coffee shop. Mom and I had assured him that we would support him in any way we could, from sending him to regional barista competitions and trainings to giving him a larger role in our vendor partnerships and more management responsibilities.

Sterling was in a similar position. Since he'd landed in Ashland, he had become an integral part of our team. His natural talent and willingness to learn made him a leader in the kitchen. Most days he planned our lunch menus. Customers raved about his specialty soups, charred flatbreads, and herb-infused salads and pastas.

I felt so grateful to have both of them on my team. However, I probably should have thought through bringing them to meet Laney. They both buzzed with eager excitement as we made our way past the lumberyard that smelled of pine and cedar shavings and the hardware store with its friendly staff who were always ready to direct customers to the light-bulb aisle or consult on paint colors. Next we passed Ashland Grange, a long tan warehouse with a green metal roof that sold everything from horse feed to festive terra-cotta pots.

"Boss, this could be so cool. I mean ice cream is hot right now. Ha ha, pun totally intended," Andy said, stepping to the side to allow a guy wheeling a cart of cans to recycle at the Co-Op across the street. "Me and Sterling have a ton of ideas for you."

"Don't get too excited," I cautioned, removing a pair of sunglasses from my purse. A drizzly morning had given way to a brilliant late-afternoon sun. "This is simply a tour. I'm not making any promises."

Andy's freckles looked more pronounced when he grinned at Sterling. "Told you she would say that."

Sterling unzipped his dark gray hoodie and tied it around his waist. "Don't worry. She'll cave once she realizes how great this could be."

"Hey, I'm still here, guys." I pretended to be insulted. In reality, I enjoyed the easy banter and rapport I had with my staff.

Laney's pink food truck, Nana's, was painted with yellow and white flowers. It stood out like a bright spot in the otherwise semi-industrial area as we approached the gated garden and vacant coffee stand. What once must have been an inviting and charming garden reminded me of something out of *Grimm's Fairy Tales*. Wood trellises sagged under gnarly twisted vines of ancient ivy. We entered through a weathered gate and were greeted with an assortment of rusting bistro tables and chairs and faded and broken sun umbrellas that were scattered throughout the overgrown garden. Cracked pots that may have once housed fragrant strawberries and potted herbs now sprouted weeds. No wonder a corporate coffee chain was interested in bulldozing the space. It was definitely in need of some TLC.

Laney sat at a rusty table with a young woman who looked vaguely familiar.

"Jules, so glad you made it." Laney stood to hug me. She was closer to Mom's age, with long dark hair, deep-set eyes, and a friendly smile. I recognized her hibiscus-flower apron. It was the same design that was painted on the side of Nana's truck. "This is Addie, who owns the building," she said as a way of introduction. "Have you two met?"

Addie stood to greet me. She was significantly younger than both of us. I wasn't always the best judge of age, but she couldn't be much older than Andy.

"I don't think so," I said, extending my hand.

Addie moved with the grace of a dancer. "Nice to meet you. I'm pretty new to town. I moved here from SoCal last year." She wore a pair of sleek aqua-blue yoga pants, a plush cashmere wrap, and Uggs.

"How are you liking the Rogue Valley?" I asked, after introducing Sterling and Andy.

"Great. It's such an awesome community. Everyone's been really open and welcoming and my yoga studio is thriving." She pointed behind us to the two-story building. A sign reading NAMASTE YOGA hung on the covered porch that led to the lower level. Tibetan prayer flags flapped in the slight breeze. "My parents helped me invest in the building. They were pretty concerned about competition because everyone in Ashland is into yoga, as you know, but my classes are packed. I've had to hire three instructors to keep up with the demand."

It was a bit of an exaggeration to claim that *everyone*

in Ashland practiced yoga. I did agree that as a whole Ashland's freethinking population was focused on health and wellness. Yoga, Pilates, meditation, Qi Gong, and Tai Chi classes were plentiful in our little artists' mecca. I enjoyed being part of a community that prided itself on health and well-being. Perhaps it was embedded in our DNA. The Lithia waters that flowed through the plaza had long been revered for their healing properties. Ashland offered abundant opportunities to unplug. I had come to realize that was because we were a part of nature, literally surrounded and embraced by mountains in every direction. It was common to spot black bears lumbering through the vast network of trails above Lithia Park or see flocks of wild turkeys strutting around a neighbor's front yard.

Addie stretched her limber arms. "Want to check out the kitchen?"

"Sure." We followed her to the back of the garden.

As Laney had mentioned on the phone, the prep kitchen wasn't more than ten feet long. It was covered by an overhang that, like the entrance, was wrapped in even more decades-old ivy. A walk-up coffee counter and a large chalkboard menu served as a barrier from the small outdoor kitchen with its row of cabinets, a prep space, a fridge, and a sink. The wood counter was rotting, with large splinters that could prove dangerous. The fridge had been tagged with purple graffiti and two of the cabinet doors were missing hinges.

How long had the place been empty?

"It's not much, but it also won't take a lot to make it prettier," Addie said, reaching into the waistband of her yoga pants and removing a single key. She proceeded to unlock a door next to the sink. "This is a storage closet for supplies. You and your staff will also have access to the bathrooms inside the yoga studio. I know it's not a full commercial kitchen, but it's perfect for coffee. Electric, water, and Wi-Fi are all included in the lease. The train is a nuisance, but you'll get used to it. It only passes through twice a day, and it's short cargo cars. I learned not to schedule yoga at noon because when it passes behind us it lets out a shrill whistle and shakes the building. No big deal—I pushed back our start time to twelve fifteen. It shouldn't be a problem for you, other than hearing the noon and five whistle."

She was talking as if the space was already ours.

"Basically, it's move-in ready now." She glanced up at the ivy-ensconced pergola that looked like it might collapse on our heads at any minute. "That should give you plenty of time to put your own spin on the space for a late spring or early summer opening." Her attention veered as a man wearing a long purple cape pedaled past us on a rusty bike.

I recognized him immediately. He was affectionately known around town as "the Wizard" due to his cape and wiry silvery hair and the trail of gold and green metallic streamers that flapped from his bike. As far as I knew, he was homeless by choice. He tended to travel in a radius throughout the Railroad District. I often spotted him in Railroad Park making figure eights on the paved bike path or holding court on his favorite bench, orating to no one in particular. The Wizard was famous for his elaborate balloon art. He delighted kids in the park with balloons shaped like monkeys and mermaids. Once he'd recreated the Elizabethan, our version of the Globe Theatre, out of balloons. It was so impressive that one of the local art galleries had put it on display for a month.

Addie muttered something under her breath that sounded like, "Stay away, crazy."

Laney waved to him. "Stop by the truck later, okay? I have a bento box saved for you."

The Wizard gave her a slight nod of acknowledgment and steered his bike toward the path that led to Railroad Park.

I wasn't surprised that Laney helped feed the Wizard. That was on par with the rest of the community. At Torte, we delivered day-old pastry and breads to the shelter and had an unspoken policy to cover the cost of hot coffee or a warm bowl of soup for anyone who might need it—especially during the cold winter months.

Addie didn't appear to share the same sentiment. "That guy creeps me out." She kept her eyes narrowed on him until he was out of sight.

"The Wizard?" Laney wrinkled her brow. Her golden-flecked eyes were filled with confusion. "He's harmless."

"Hardly," Addie scoffed. "You should try being here after my late-night hot-yoga class. He's always hanging around on the railroad tracks, just staring me down." She licked her thumb and tried to rub graffiti from the fridge. "I'm sure he's responsible for this damage, and I never walk to my car alone now."

I caught Laney's eye. She shrugged in confusion.

Addie pointed to the roofline of Namaste. "I've installed surveillance cameras in the front of the building and up there. I'm going to catch him in the act one of these days. Trust me, you're going to want to keep an eye out for him. I make one of my students come with me, because I'm waiting for him to attack."

"Attack?" Laney laughed, making her long braids shake. She wore her dark hair in braids tied with small pink hibiscus flowers. "I've known the Wizard for years. He's a gentle, tender soul. If anything, he's a bit of a free spirit. But dangerous—never."

Sterling, who had been quiet thus far, backed her up. "Yeah. I've run into him a few times and he seems like he's kind of in his own world, dancing to his own beat as they say, but I've never gotten a dangerous aura from him."

"That's because he's harmless," Laney insisted. She untied her raspberry sherbet–colored apron and folded it neatly.

"I totally disagree. He's weird." Addie scowled and rubbed the spray paint on the fridge harder. It was futile. Removing the graffiti was going to take more than scrubbing. An industrial cleaner was in order. "Anyway, what do you think of the space? Should we get an agreement put together?"

"Well, I don't know." I floundered. "I would have to discuss things with my mom, as she's a partner in the business, and run some numbers on the viability of opening a second coffee spot so close to the bakeshop."

"This isn't that close, boss," Andy chimed in. He had flipped his faded red baseball hat backward. Strands of auburn hair escaped from beneath it. "And it would be an awesome space for a summer ice cream shop. Am I right, Sterling?"

"For sure." Sterling's piercing blue eyes studied the space. I had a feeling he was making calculations in his head. "That back wall could be transformed into a larger menu. We could hang a Torte banner there." He pointed above us. "It definitely needs a deep cleaning and gutting, but there's potential here for sure."

"Yeah, and imagine if we string twinkle lights from the front gate to the awning," Andy added. "Boss, you've got to give this some real thought. This could be really cool. We could serve our signature concretes, ice cream sandwiches, and a very small line of coffees so that we're not competing with ourselves. I'm thinking cold brew, affagatos, and blended coffee milkshakes." His face lit up as he spoke.

"It's a good idea," Sterling said, using his hands to measure the counter space. "We could easily fit a cold case here. And, if you wanted to go crazy and offer cold sandwiches or pasta salads for summer picnic lunches, we could probably swap out this half fridge with a tall narrow one."

Laney smoothed out a crease in her folded apron, which she had set on the dilapidated counter. "Smart staff you have here, Jules. They're right. You can create an entirely new Torte experience. And coffee and ice cream would go beautifully with my teriyaki pork and fried jasmine coconut rice. Like I said on the phone, it would be great for business. Bringing the Torte brand to the Railroad District would give us real cachet."

Their excitement was contagious. I couldn't help but picture the garden courtyard tables filled with the sound of happy customers. I could almost see young kids sitting on the grass with dripping ice cream sandwiches and their parents sipping refreshing cold brew on a hot summer afternoon. "It would be fun," I admitted. "We'd have to make sure that our offerings were unique, and it is going to take some serious muscle to rip down the dead ivy and get this place sparkling again."

"We can do that, boss. No problem." Andy gave Sterling a fist bump. "Give us a day and we'll come up with a Torte Two menu for you."

I grimaced. "If we do this, we're going to need a better name."

Sterling closed his eyes for a minute. "I've got a couple ideas on that too."

"So, should we go put paperwork together?" Addie brushed her hands on her yoga pants.

"Not yet. Let me talk this through with Mom and the rest of our team. Can we have a couple days to think about it?"

Addie blew out a long breath, as if she was trying to center herself. "I guess, but don't take too long. There are a lot of other interested parties, but because of my yoga vibe, I'd like to keep the garden pretty chill. Laney highly recommends you, so if you want it, we can make it happen. But if you don't, I'm putting it on the market on Monday."

"Deal. I'll let you know one way or the other before Monday." I shook her hand.

We parted ways. Laney left me with a hug and a promise to stop by Torte and help brainstorm if we wanted any other input. Sterling and Andy chatted about concrete flavors and potential shop names all the way back to Torte. I did appreciate their enthusiasm and I could definitely see the potential, but I had to be realistic too.

Was I ready for another new venture? Things at Torte had finally started to feel settled. We had an easy routine and a highly capable staff. Did it make sense to disturb that balance?

And there was one more major issue that I hadn't voiced—Carlos. My husband had opted to take an extended leave from his work as head chef on the *Amour of the Seas*. He had been in Ashland for the past three weeks to give things a go. This was our last chance to try to figure out what we both needed from our relationship, or whether it was time to say goodbye for good. If I took on yet another project, would I be intentionally sabotaging any hope for a future with him?

Chapter Two

The last time I'd seen Carlos had been when he'd surprised me by showing up on Christmas Eve with his son, Ramiro, in tow. We had enjoyed a magical week of snowshoeing on Mt. A, skating at the ice rink across from Lithia Park, and staying up late eating Carlos's famous paella and playing board games with Mom and the Professor in front of a crackling fire. Our time together felt too short. Before I knew it, they were boarding a plane for Ramiro to return to Spain and Carlos to return to the ship. But Carlos had made me a promise as he kissed me at the gate. "Mi querida, I am coming again. It is arranged. I have four weeks of leave. I will come to Ashland. It is the only way. We must try, si?"

I couldn't argue with him. For nearly two years I'd been torn between two worlds—my life in Ashland and what I'd left behind on the sea. I knew that Carlos and I couldn't keep up this dance. Something had to give. It was time to make a decision once and for all. The problem was me. I couldn't give up Ashland. I didn't want to. And yet it wasn't fair to ask Carlos to do the same. He had sailed the oceans for decades, soaking in tropical waters, briny air, sandy beaches, and each port of call. His food was a reflection of his global travels. When he cooked, his passion came through in every bite. Watching him in the kitchen was like watching an artist layer colors on a canvas. I hated asking him to give up a life that I knew he loved.

He had assured me that he wanted to experience Ashland for a longer stretch of time. "It will be wonderful, you will see. I can cook at Uva and spend time pruning the vines and connecting with the dirt. I will embrace the land and the mountains. The Rogue Valley it is abundant with new tastes and flavors for me to savor. Do not worry, Julieta. I will do anything for you, my love."

I didn't doubt that he would. What I doubted was whether Ashland was right for Carlos. The nearest beach was hours away, accessible by a narrow winding road carved through the colossal redwood forests. While Ashland and the surrounding valley had a plethora of cultural activities, from the theater to music festivals, art shows, culinary retreats, and an eclectic dining scene, we were no Madrid or Paris. Torte's busiest day in the kitchen paled in comparison to a slow day in the ship's massive kitchens, with chefs shouting orders to their line cooks like drill sergeants barking out orders to their troops. It was hard to imagine Carlos settling into the slower pace of life I had come to cherish. What I worried about most was him putting on a show for me. If we were really going to make our relationship last, it had to be authentic for both of us, and I had a sinking feeling that even if he was miserable he wouldn't tell me.

True to his word, he arrived the third week of March,

shortly after I had finished moving into my childhood home, a two-story house tucked into the conifer canopy on Mountain Avenue. It didn't take long for us to fall into step. Carlos, like me, required little sleep. We spent the first few days together sipping glasses of Tempranillo and getting reacquainted until the wee hours of the night.

Our time apart hadn't diminished our desire. Curling up in Carlos's arms felt like coming home. His sweet accent lulled me to sleep every night. We eased into a comfortable routine. He would drop me off at Torte before the sun came up and spend the bulk of each day studying and shaping Uva's organic, fertile vineyards. He seemed happy enough. Our conversations in the evenings were filled with news of the first buds on the vine, his ideas for summer wine dinners, and ideas about potential partnerships with local restaurants and suppliers.

The Rogue Valley was located in what vintners referred to as the Goldilocks zone. Our latitude of forty-two to forty-three degrees put us on the same latitude lines on the map as the most revered growing regions in the world, like Argentina, New Zealand, and Southern Europe. Uva was a boutique winery with five acres of south-facing grapevines on the east side of town. The drive from my house at the top of Mountain Avenue to the winery took less than ten minutes, but it felt like a different world. Every time I steered the car in the direction of Uva, I drank in the magnificent views of a snow-capped Grizzly Peak and the rustic golden pastoral grasses where herds of cattle and sheep grazed. The two-lane road took me past rambling farms with free-range chickens, stacks of firewood, crumbling barns, and old Ford trucks—relics of years gone by. The pièce de résistance was cresting the hill and making a sharp right turn onto Pilot View Road, where the iconic Pilot Rock and Mt. A jutted up amongst the dark green ridgeline of the Siskiyou range.

We didn't produce enough wine to expand our reach outside of southern Oregon, but Carlos had grandiose plans. "Imagine, Julieta, if we could deliver our wine to San Francisco and Seattle. It would be wonderful, no? We must submit our Cab Franc and red blends to the *San Francisco Chronicle*. We will win gold for sure. It will be amazing for Uva. It will put us on the map."

"Sure, but that's a lot more work, and then there's the issue of Richard Lord," I had retorted.

"No, no. Do not give that man a thought. He is nothing. He is no problem, and not worth any of your time. We will be done with him soon. You will see." Carlos had sounded so confident as he swirled blackberry-colored wine in his glass.

I didn't share his optimism. Richard Lord, the vile owner of the Merry Windsor, who had been the one and only person in Ashland who had gone out of his way to make my transition home as miserable as possible, was a part-owner of Uva. My friend Lance, the artistic director for OSF, and I had been racking our brains for ways to buy out Richard. It would have been one thing if Richard actually cared about Uva. He didn't. He just wanted to make sure that neither Lance nor I had an opportunity to make the winery a success.

After my meeting with Laney and Addie, I didn't say anything to Carlos about the possibility of taking over the outdoor space. I told myself it was because he was already too wrapped up in Uva. I didn't want to burden him, but the truth was I needed to sit with the idea. Alone.

Did that mean something? Did normal couples keep things from each other? We'd never been a typical married couple. Our life on the ship didn't allow it, but now that Carlos was in Ashland, I kept trying to fit us in boxes that refused to close up neat and tight. Part of me wanted to believe that we were in the middle of figuring out a new path forward while the other part worried that keeping anything from Carlos was a sign that our future was doomed.

I slept on it. The next morning I woke with a new resolve that Carlos had to be part of any decision. If he was willing to give us a chance, I had to do the same.

After a quick cup of coffee, I got dressed and waited in the car for Carlos to drive me to the bottom of Mountain Avenue. From there I would walk to Torte and he would continue to Uva or return up the steep hill and go back to bed. Bakers' hours are torture.

"Julieta, you are quiet this morning," Carlos noted. He was dressed for a cold morning amongst the vines in a pair of jeans, leather ankle boots, a red-and-black flannel, and a black vest. His skin was naturally olive in color, his hair was dark, and his eyes constantly held a hint of mischief.

"You are starting to look like a true Oregon mountain man," I replied, flipping the collar of his vest down.

"Si. It is true. I have learned the value of layers, as you say." He winked.

After years on the ship, it had taken me a little while to adjust to Ashland's cooler springs with below-freezing temps in the morning and evening. Layering was key. This morning I wore a pair of leggings, a long-sleeve T-shirt, and a Torte sweatshirt that would likely come off before noon.

"Is something bothering you?" Carlos asked as he steered the car toward the sidewalk to park next to Southern Oregon University.

"Not exactly. There's something I want to talk to you about. A new opportunity that's come up." I stared out the window to the spawning front lawns of the SOU campus.

Carlos stopped me. "No, no. We do not need to talk about this now. I do not want you to worry."

"Worry?" It was still dark, so I squinted to try and read Carlos's face. "What do you mean?"

"The ship. It is nothing." He kept his hands on the steering wheel, even though we were parked.

"The ship?" I repeated. "I think we're talking about two different things. I was going to tell you about a new space for lease in the Railroad District that could make a great walk-up ice cream shop."

"That sounds wonderful." Carlos sounded a bit too eager to change the topic. "Tell me more."

I gave him a brief recap of my meeting with Addie. When I was done, he was full of enthusiasm. "Si, this is a wonderful idea. Why would you not try it? Two shops will bring in more revenue."

"And more work," I countered.

"True, but you like a good challenge, Julieta. You get bored easily—this project will invigorate your spirits. What does Helen say?"

"I haven't discussed it with Mom yet. I'm going to share the proposal with her this afternoon."

"Good. Good." Carlos looked at the clock on the dash. "I will drive you to Torte this morning. It is getting late."

Late was relative, but I didn't refuse his offer. "What about the ship?" I asked as he pulled away from the curb and turned onto Siskiyou Boulevard.

"The ship? It's always something. They want me to call and speak with the chef. Apparently, there is drama in the kitchen." He made a gesture with his right hand. "What can you do? You know chefs. They can be very demanding, and it seems that my replacement he is not so fun in the kitchen. I will take care of it."

I got the sense there was more that he wasn't saying. Was he considering returning to the ship already? Could that be why he was being evasive? I decided not to press it for the moment. I had enough to think about.

"Julieta, let me know what Helen thinks of the ice cream shop, okay?" He left me at Torte with a kiss. "I will see you later, si?"

"Of course." I kissed him back, letting our lips linger for a moment. Then I went to unlock the bakeshop.

The early hours before we opened served as my morning meditation. The leisurely process of warming ovens, kneading bread dough, and mixing vats of cake batter calmed my mind. Carlos was right about the fact that I tended to thrive with multiple pots on the stove so to speak. While I added bundles of applewood to the built-in fireplace and got it started, I thought through the logistics of two spaces. The garden wasn't far. My staff could easily walk, and with some careful scheduling we should be able to manage with hiring a few extra part-time workers. It was going to come down to the numbers. I needed to pencil out hard costs for revamping the garden, supplies and equipment, and salaries.

That could wait. Duty called. I rolled up my sleeves and tied on a fire-engine–red Torte apron. We liked to serve a hot breakfast dish along with our signature pastries and sandwiches. I had set aside a few loaves of brioche and knew exactly what I wanted to bake—a wood-fired French toast served with fresh berries and mascarpone cheese.

I went to the walk-in and returned with heavy cream, eggs, butter, and berries. Instead of individually grilling each slice of brioche, I cut the day-old bread into cubes then set them aside. Next I whisked eggs, heavy cream, honey, fresh lemon juice, and vanilla until the mixture was light and frothy. I added a pinch of cinnamon, nutmeg, and salt. Then I layered the cubes of bread in an oven-safe baking dish and poured the egg mixture over the top. I slid the French toast into the wood-fired oven to bake for twenty to thirty minutes. My goal was to create a nice crunchy crust with a gooey center, almost like a bread pudding.

While the casserole baked, I added a container of Mascarpone cheese to one of the electric mixers. Then I slowly incorporated honey, vanilla, and fresh orange and lemon juice and zest. I whipped the cheese until it was lush and silky. I dipped my pinkie into the cream for a taste. The slight tang of the Mascarpone paired beautifully with the hints of citrus and vanilla. Once the

French toast baked, I would serve a heaping scoop with a dollop of Mascarpone cream and berries.

Soon the kitchen was bursting with activity as everyone began to arrive. Sterling took command of the stove, searing beef for a lunchtime stew. Marty, a jovial San Francisco transplant in his mid-sixties, managed bread production. Not only did we bake enough bread to keep the pastry case stocked, we also delivered to our wholesale accounts on the plaza. There was rarely a moment when the bread racks weren't stacked with loaves of rising sourdough, honey wheat, rosemary olive, and our classic white.

"Hey boss, can you come up here?" Andy called from the top of the stairs shortly before it was time to open. "I have drink samples for everyone."

We had a tradition at Torte to taste any specials before they went up on our chalkboard menu. Before we opened the bakeshop's doors to our customers we would gather around the coffee bar or in the basement kitchen and dive into a delectable spread of garlic herbed butter rolls, beef stew, pistachio shortbread, and Andy's coffee drink of the day.

Marty brushed his hands on his already floured apron. "Can't pass up an offer for a morning cup of joe."

I chuckled and followed him upstairs with tasting plates of my French toast bake. The entire team was huddled at the pastry case. Andy balanced a tasting tray of milkshakes. "I'm calling this the brain freeze. It's a double shot of espresso hand blended with Sterling's coffee concrete. Topped off with whipped cream, a drizzle of dark chocolate, and chocolate espresso bean shavings." Andy winked at me as he passed around the drinks.

"That's a coincidence," Sterling said in jest. "I went with an ice cream theme today as well." He proceeded to open the cold case next the pastry counter after shooting me an impish look with his bright blue eyes. "These are Bethany's molasses cookies sandwiched with a lemon cream concrete." He handed out the ice cream sandwiches.

"Am I missing something?" Marty asked, biting into the soft ice cream sandwich. "Is it already summer? You guys are in an ice cream state of mind."

"Tell them, boss," Andy encouraged, offering me one of his blended creations.

"These two are outnumbering me." I tried to wink as I took a sip of the frothy milkshake. Winking has never been my forte. I usually ended up scrunching one side of my face in a weird half smile. "The three of us went to look at a space yesterday that has the potential to be a summer walk-up for coffee and concretes." I went on to tell my team about the meeting. When I finished, everyone jumped on the ice cream bandwagon.

"We should totally do it, Jules," Bethany said, twisting her bouncy curls around her index finger. As usual she wore a punny T-shirt. Today's read, GOOD THINGS COME TO THOSE WHO BAKE.

A truer statement could not be found in my opinion. I passed around samples of the wood-fired French toast.

"Think of the social content we could create," she continued. "Have you seen some of the amazingly inventive ice cream sundaes that some of the fancy shops in New York are doing?" She paused to pull out her phone to show us pictures of overflowing milkshakes with scoops of ice cream piled on top along with whole slices of cake, sprinkles, mounds of whipped cream, chocolate straws, and bright red cherries.

"Those aren't just crazy shakes and sundaes," Steph noted, taking Bethany's phone for a closer look. She tucked her violet hair that had been recently cut in an angular bob behind one ear. "They defy architecture."

"And gravity," Marty added, peering over Steph's shoulder. He took a bite of my breakfast casserole. "This is out of the world, by the way. That slight char on the top is perfection and the Mascarpone melts in your mouth."

Everyone agreed.

"It's like a French toast party in my mouth." Bethany returned her attention to the crazy shakes and looked at me with eager eyes. "Wouldn't they be so fun to make? I mean, obviously with our own Torte spin. But, they would definitely draw in a young crowd."

I took a sip of Andy's blended coffee. It was creamy and perfectly balanced with a subtle sweetness from the coffee ice cream and rich notes of espresso. "This is delish."

Sequoia, one of our newest hires, ran a slender finger sporting a mood ring around the rim of her molasses lemon ice cream sandwich. "I'll leave the wild sundaes to you," she said to Bethany. "I'm in agreement about an ice cream sandwich line. I'd love to do an oatmeal cookie with a matcha concrete. Or, what about a chocolate black-bean banana cookie with an avocado ice cream?"

The addition of Sequoia to the team had given us a very alternative Ashland slant, which I appreciated.

"Brilliant." Sterling gave her a nod of approval.

"My mother used to make churro ice cream when I was a kid," Rosa offered. She was the most soft-spoken member of the team. I relied on her calming aura in the kitchen and enjoyed that she was closer to my age then the rest of the team. It was nice to have her and Marty lend some of their wisdom and life experience to our young staff.

"Oh, yay! Churro ice cream sandwiched between real churros. Count me in!" Andy shot Rosa an air high five.

"I love your enthusiasm, but there are a ton of things to consider," I said, resting my coffee shake on the counter. "For starters, the stress on all of you. We would have to have at least two staff plus a couple of floaters managing the new space."

"Sure, but you could hire a few high school or SOU students looking for summer work," Sterling suggested.

"True. That's certainly a possibility, and something I've been sketching out in terms of budgeting. You and Andy would likely be gone from Torte for the bulk of the busy season though. We'd have to hire replacements for you."

"Well the deal's off," Andy announced. "We can't be replaced, can we, Sterling?"

Everyone chuckled.

Marty raised his index finger. "I have a suggestion. If we are primarily selling ice cream and cold coffees at the walk-up shop, what would the hours be? Would it make sense to open that space at noon through late evening?" He paused to dab a drip of the coffee shake from his round cheeks. His good-natured grin and white beard always made me think of Santa when he smiled. "Maybe Sterling and Andy can start their mornings here, and you hire a few SOU and Ashland High students to take up the slack."

They raised valid points. "Good thoughts, everyone. I'll talk it over with Mom. If you have other suggestions in the meantime, please feel free to share them."

For the rest of the day, thoughts of waffle cones and Neapolitan banana splits kept popping into my head. The more I considered the idea, the more I wanted to call Addie and say yes. By the time Mom showed up after lunch, I had nearly convinced myself.

"What do you think?" I asked her as we reviewed the paperwork Addie had sent over. We shared a pot of French press and a plate of pistachio shortbread.

"Honey, it sounds like a perfect fit." Mom leafed through the rough menu I'd put together. "It would give Andy and Sterling some autonomy and I don't think it would compete with Torte. From what you're saying, the spaces would complement each other. What about cost?"

Addie had sent over a breakdown of the lease terms. It was shockingly affordable. Considering the state of the garden, she couldn't charge the exorbitant rent that some property owners tried to get away with charging on the plaza.

"This looks very reasonable," Mom said, placing her reading glasses on the tip of her nose. "Although it makes sense, since there's no physical building and up-keep has to be minimal. What do you think? Are you leaning one way?"

"I think I want to do it. The risk seems low. We could give it a shot for this summer, and if it's too much extra work, we simply wouldn't renew the lease for next year."

"I agree. What does Carlos say?"

I was quiet for a moment. Only a moment, but Mom knew me too well.

"You don't want to do this because of him?" Concern flooded her walnut eyes.

"No. It's not that. I mean, not exactly. I guess it feels like starting this project might take away from working on our relationship."

"Do you think that's true?" Mom's voice was gentle. "If part of Carlos being here is experiencing what it's really like to live here, it seems like you owe him a chance to see the real you—the Ashland you."

"True."

"Honey, this is between the two of you, but I'll leave you with this." She paused to break off a bite of pistachio shortbread. "Since you've returned home, you've had a new spark. A joy that radiates out from you in every direction. You're filled with light and it's contagious. People want a part of your inner light that shines so bright, and in return for sharing that, the universe continues to show you new opportunities. Thus far, you've embraced each new thing that's crossed your path—the basement expansion, Uva, expanding Torte's catering line, special events. If this is something that fills your heart, you should follow that. Carlos is a grown-up, he can handle you taking up more space in the world. From what I've observed, I'd say that you stepping into your power is one of the many reasons he loves you."

Her words stuck with me long after our conversation. I had never considered my return to Ashland as stepping into my power. She was right. Ashland had grounded me. After cocooning myself in, I had emerged with renewed confidence in my abilities as a pastry chef and as a person. Carlos wasn't a threat to that. At least not unless I made him one. If I continued to shut him out, that might change.

Chapter Three

The next afternoon, I caved to the pressure (both internal and external) and signed the lease with Addie. It didn't take her long to draft a contract. We had agreed on a six-month trial. Our lease would start immediately and take us through September. If we were happy with sales and our ability to staff two locations, we could renew in October.

"Congratulations," Addie said, handing me the keys and my copy of the lease. "You can get started as soon as you're ready."

"That will likely be now," I replied.

Our goal was to open Torte Two, or whatever the new ice cream shop was to be called, by the premiere of *The Count of Monte Cristo* at the Elizabethan in late May. It would be perfect timing to coincide with the return of outdoor shows at OSF. The festival boasts one of the longest-running seasons on the West Coast. Productions begin each March in the indoor theaters on campus and continue through the end of October every year. Outdoor performances at the Lizzie (as the Elizabethan is affectionately known to locals) commence in May when late spring evenings turn warm.

There was plenty of work to do to prepare our new pop-up ice cream shop for a bustling summer. For starters we needed to land on a name, design a logo, and create an outdoor dining experience complementary to Torte. I was glad that Addie had gotten the paperwork together quickly. We had no time to waste. The project list of everything that needed to be done seemed to be growing by the minute. We needed to rip down the ivy, sand and stain the coffee counter, clean and paint the bistro tables, repair the cabinets, weed the planters and pots, and give the grass a long overdue mow.

After signing the paperwork, I headed straight for the hardware store and called the team to come meet me at the new space.

A half hour later I found myself standing in the ailing garden holding an assortment of rakes and shovels. "Who's ready for this?" I asked Carlos, Sterling, Mom, and Andy who had joined me to survey the space and begin sketching out formal plans.

"To new adventures," Carlos exclaimed, uncorking a bottle of champagne and passing around glasses. Fortunately, he had thought to bring along a bottle of sparkling cider for Andy and Sterling.

"In two weeks I'll be able to join you in an official toast," Andy noted eyeing the champagne bottle. "I can't believe I'm finally going to be of age."

Mom raised her glass. "To your almost birthday."

"You're hardly the partying type," Sterling said to Andy as he sipped his cider. Sterling had struggled with addiction in the past and I appreciated how open and honest he was about some of his early challenges. "It's not all it's cracked up to be."

"Nah, I know. I don't care about that," Andy replied. "It's such a pain not to be able to pour customers a glass of wine or help serve drinks at our Sunday Suppers, though. I'm looking forward to that and maybe not being known as the kid anymore."

"Don't get any ideas about that. You'll always be kids in my eyes." Mom ruffled his hair. Then she turned to Sterling to make it clear she was including him in the "kids" category.

"I do not understand these American customs. It is much easier in Spain," Carlos offered. "We do not make such a big deal about a sip of wine or champagne. It is part of our culture. I remember when Ramiro was six or seven we would give him a half glass of wine at Christmas or parties. I think this is a better way to introduce alcohol, si?"

"Absolutely, I couldn't agree more." Mom's brown eyes twinkled with delight. She and Carlos shared a mutual respect for one another. I was happy that their relationship was evolving too. When Carlos and I had gotten married on a spontaneous weekend escape in Marseilles, there hadn't been time to invite her. It was one of my biggest regrets. Not that it wasn't a dreamlike experience to tie the knot at such a romantic port of call, but in hindsight having Mom stand by my side while I professed my love might have been worth waiting a bit.

"So should I pour you a glass for a toast?" Carlos asked Andy.

Andy shook his head and held his palm over his glass

to block Carlos. "No way. Mrs. The Professor is married to a detective. I'm not about to start breaking the law now, especially when I'm so close to becoming a full-fledged adult."

We all laughed. The Professor was Ashland's resident detective and Shakespeare aficionado. He could recite a quote from the bard for nearly any occasion. My parents and Doug, aka the Professor, had been friends since I was a young girl. I had recently learned that he had secretly loved Mom for many years. It wasn't until she had healed from losing my dad that he declared his admiration and proposed. Their wedding last summer had been nothing short of magical.

Mom raised her glass. The afternoon light danced off the trellis built into the fence with its sweet-smelling honeysuckle vines. Cherry trees lining the sidewalk were just beginning to bud. The grass was still dewy, and the umbrellas and bistro tables damp. In a few weeks, as the sun continued its rotation, the dew would give way to an abundance of spring blooms and warming skies.

"It's been a while since I've been here. I had forgotten what a pretty space this is. And the view." Mom pointed toward the railroad tracks. The golden hills in the distance were flecked with the first flush of color.

"Mrs. The Professor, you're right. Ashland is a Bob Ross painting in real life." Andy gave her a lopsided grin.

"The view was one of the many reasons I couldn't resist Addie's offer." I matched his smile.

"To views and ice cream." Mom raised her glass.

I followed suit. Once everyone had enjoyed a celebratory sip, Andy clapped twice. "Enough chatting—we have some serious plans to firm up." With that, he pulled out a spiral notebook he had rolled and stuffed into the back pocket of his jeans and motioned for Sterling to come closer to him. "We've been plotting names, flavors, pricing, and everything in between. Isn't that right, Sterling?"

Sterling leaned over Andy's shoulder. "The kid is correct."

Andy punched him. "No way, that is not sticking. You can call me a lot of things, but not kid. And you're only a few years older than me anyway."

"We tease because we love." Sterling patted him on the back. "But Andy's come up with some great stuff. I've been focused on pricing and I think the preliminary numbers we originally came up with are going to yield an even higher profit margin. I've found a new dairy supplier, Dean. He owns an organic farm in Talent out by the hemp fields and he's going to offer us fifteen percent less than the other vendors we spoke with."

"What about his product? I don't want to sacrifice quality," I interrupted.

Mom shot me a nod of approval. I could tell she agreed. I was committed to giving Andy and Sterling more responsibilities and autonomy, but they both had a lot to learn. When I had attended pastry school in New York, I spent my first summer interning at a French pastry shop and the chef had told me repeatedly that the only—absolutely only—way to perfect my baking prowess was through trial and error. That was the philosophy I tried to pass on to my staff. If one of Andy's latte creations bombed, so be it, but I wasn't sure I was ready to hand over the reins when it came to quality control.

"Told you she'd say that," Andy snickered.

Sterling protested. "Give us a little credit, Jules. You've taught us well. We have a meeting set up with Dean later. He's going to drop by some samples. The farm is certified organic and the cows are completely free range. I haven't seen it, but Dean has the gold seal on his milk and said we could visit anytime."

"Very good. They have done their research." Carlos topped off my champagne. His dark eyes lingered on mine for a moment. I'd never been able to resist his seductive smile. Although lately I'd noticed a subtle shift in him. His usual playfulness was lacking ever so slightly. I doubted that anyone else had picked up on the change but it had me wondering if he was holding something back.

"Plus, we made samples for you. We want to do a blind tasting." Andy pointed to a cooler resting on a nearby table.

"Now?" Mom asked.

"It's up to you. We can go over our ideas now and do the tasting last, or vice versa. Whatever you say, Mrs. The Professor." Andy had affectionately called Mom "Mrs. C." for years until she and Doug married. Now his term of endearment for her was "Mrs. The Professor."

"I'd love to hear your thoughts about the space and setup." Mom said, turning to me. "What about you?"

"You read my mind." I motioned to the stack of garden tools. "We need to figure out what to demo and what to keep. The little free library has to stay." One of the most unique things about the funky garden was its many nooks and crannies. A little free library in the shape of an A-frame had been built into the corner of the fence. Lush bamboo planted in wooden garden boxes on the opposite side of the garden served as a green barrier between the walk-up shop and the Grange next door. Three trellised gates allowed for multiple points of access. If we could breathe new life into the existing structures, the space could be incredible.

Before they could start to show us their ideas, a commotion broke out across the street.

"Hey! Get outta here!" a man's voice thundered.

We turned our attention to the corner to see the Wizard spinning in wild circles in front of Cyclepath, the bike shop catty-corner from us.

"I told you to take your crazy somewhere else, old man!" Hunter, the owner of the bike shop, stood on his stoop. "I know you've been vandalizing and stealing my bikes." He held a bike wrench in one hand and yielded it like a weapon. "I'm calling the police again and if they refuse to arrest you, I would steer clear of here because I'm ready to take matters into my own hands."

Hunter was an intimidating guy *without* the wrench. He was well over six feet tall with a muscular build and shoulder-length black hair. Cyclepath dealt in high-end bikes. A collection of road bikes, commuters, and expensive electric bikes were loosely chained together outside the shop. The shop itself was painted a pale shade of yellow. Two bay windows flanked each corner. Both had showpiece bikes on display.

The Wizard continued to spin in circles, the streamers flapping from the rear of his banana seat like kite tails catching the wind. He shouted back at Hunter, but in gibberish I couldn't understand.

Three teenagers raced out of the bike shop. Each had a longboard tucked under his arm, and they were dressed in matching rolled-up cargo pants, flat-soled tennis shoes, and graphic T-shirts.

"Yeah, get out of here, old man!" One of them tossed something at the Wizard. I couldn't tell what it was. Maybe a wadded-up paper towel or a receipt.

The Wizard lunged at the teen.

"Hey, Lars, knock it off!" Hunter bellowed to the skater kid. Then he shook the wrench at the Wizard again. "If you lay a finger on my son, I'll kill you. You hear me? I'll kill you!"

"No. This is not okay." Carlos jumped up and went to intervene.

"I'm calling Doug." Mom had already pulled out her cell phone.

Andy and Sterling followed me toward the entrance of the garden.

Carlos used his Spanish accent to his advantage, stretching out his syllables and enunciating a faint lisp. "What is the problem?" He spoke with his hands. "Is there something we can do to help?"

Hunter brushed him off. "Stay out of it. This is between me and the old man." He narrowed his eyes at the Wizard.

Lars, the skater kid, thrust out his chest. "Yeah, get moving, old man."

Laney came out from her food truck. "Leave him alone!"

Hunter yanked Lars away from the Wizard.

Laney wiped her hands on the floral apron tied around her waist and approached the Wizard. Her voice was calm and gentle. "Come with me and have some iced tea. I made a fresh batch—coconut and pineapple—your favorite."

The Wizard flung his long purple cape to one side and stopped the bike so quickly it made a screeching noise and left a skid mark on the street. Laney ran toward him, as he almost fell over. He recovered, planted one bare foot on the pavement, and swiveled his head toward Hunter. "I see things, you know. I see things!"

Hunter threw his hands around his chest. "Sure you do, crazy."

The skater kids snickered.

"I know who did it! I see things!" the Wizard repeated. "I see things!"

Laney reached out her arm and tried to steer him toward the food truck. "Come with me. Let's have a glass of iced tea and take a little break."

He threw her arm off of him. "I know what's happening! I see things!"

Sterling looked to me. "Is he okay?"

I shook my head. "I don't know."

Hunter retreated into his shop, dragging the group of skaters with him, but not without a final warning. "I don't care what you think you've seen, you crazy lunatic. Stay away from my bikes." He smacked the wrench on the metal handrail. A ringing sound reverberated. Other shop owners had come outside to see what the commotion was all about.

The Wizard tucked his cape underneath him so it wouldn't get caught in the spokes, did a half circle around us, and sped off screaming. "I'm watching! I'm watching you!"

Laney let out a long sigh as we returned to the garden. "Hunter needs to stop. It just agitates him."

"What do you think he meant by 'seeing things'?" I asked.

She twisted the strings on her apron. "Who knows? He has some serious mental-health issues. I wish he would accept help. There are so many social services available that he could connect with, but he refuses. Trust me, I've been trying to get him help for years."

I knew that was a common theme amongst Ashland's small homeless population. Thomas, my longtime friend and lead detective, had often talked about his frustration with trying to solve the problem and getting people off the streets. "It's complicated, Juliet," he had once said. "Ashland is unique in that we have many more alternatives than other towns our size, but the problem is that if someone doesn't want help, we can't force it."

"I understand," I said to Laney as we approached her cheerful food truck, painted pale lemon yellow with raspberry pink hibiscus flowers. "Let us know if there's anything we can do."

"You'll see a lot of the Wizard around here," she said, staring at the bike path. Her face had splotched to match the raspberry color of her food truck. My instincts told me that she was angry, yet her words were filled with concern. "It would be great if you could make sure that your staff understands he's not a threat, and of course, I try to save leftovers for him."

"We'll do the same." I nodded to my team.

Mom squeezed Laney's hand. "We'll take good care of him. That's what community is all about."

Laney gave her a half-hearted smile and returned to her truck. The rest of us reconvened in the garden except for Carlos. I wasn't sure if he was trying to mollify the situation or if in the process of trying to calm Hunter down he had he gotten a sales pitch for an electric bike. Carlos had had his eye on an electric bike for a while. They were a necessity with Ashland's steep, hilly terrain.

We reconvened around a bistro table in desperate need of freshening up.

"Well, shall we talk strategy?" Mom asked, trying to change the tone. "I want to hear your brainstorms."

Andy pushed two of the bistro tables together. We sat around them as Sterling dished up samples of his newest concrete creations—smoked tart cherry, peach and maple crumble, toasted white chocolate almond brittle, and dark-chocolate sea salt. Each flavor melted in my mouth.

"While you're tasting, take a look at these sketches." Andy passed around colorful drawings. "Steph did these for us. You'll see that we moved the bistro tables to the east side of the lawn. We'd like to create a stone path here." Andy pointed to the middle section of the overgrown grass. "That way we can contain flow for customers who want to grab a coffee or concrete to go, and leave the west side of the lawn for a play area. We were thinking we could build a sand table and keep bubbles and beach balls on hand."

"This is lovely," Mom noted. "Stephanie did a beautiful job."

It was true. Stephanie's artistic vision of what the new space could look like filled me with eager anticipation.

Dividing the space into unique areas made sense. The raised garden beds on the far left could definitely be salvaged. I could almost smell the fresh mint and strawberries we could grow to use in our concretes.

Andy continued. "We'd like to buy red-and-teal umbrellas to match with Torte's branding, but otherwise we'll use everything on hand. The coffee bar could use a new paint job, and so will these tables and chairs. The perimeter fence and gates are also going to need sprucing up." He pointed to the right side of the garden where two booths had been built into the fence. Each had an outdoor candelabra hanging above it. "The booths are so cool and the candleholders have to stay. We're going to string lights in a zigzagging pattern from the perimeter. Otherwise, the only other thing we'll need to invest in is new signage and menus."

"Speaking of signage"—Sterling took over—"we've come up with a few initial name ideas. Tell us what you think of Triple Torte, Cream and Custard, and last but not least, Scoops."

"Possibilities," Mom said with her eyes focused on the coffee bar.

"Hmmm. I'll have to think on them, but I love the direction you're going in. My first instinct is Triple Torte because I can picture an ice cream cone with three scoops."

Andy ribbed Sterling. They shared a laugh. "Funny you should say that, boss." He reached into his bag and handed us cutouts of ice cream cones with three scoops and the words TRIPLE TORTE written in the same fleur de lis font we used at Torte. "Stephanie designed this as a mock-up logo."

"It's great." I was impressed with how much thought they'd put into their presentation. "But, I kind of love Scoops too. It's simple and sweet."

"Just like you, boss." Andy made a goofy face.

Carlos came up behind us, taking the empty chair next to me. He placed his arm around my shoulder. His brow was damp and he had taken off his vest. "What did I miss?"

I handed him the ice cream cutout. "We're talking about possible names." I lowered my voice. "How was Hunter? Were you able to help him chill out?"

He scowled. "No. I tried to calm him down. I did not like the way he was treating that man. Those boys too. If Ramiro ever behaved like that to one of his elders, I would be absolutely furious and I would know that I had not done my job as a father." He matched my tone. "It is obvious that the Wizard—is that what you call him?"

I nodded.

Carlos's dark eyes were severe. It took a lot to rattle him. "He is in need of help. Not people screaming and shouting at him like this. Did you see that? Those kids threw things at the poor old man. It is terrible. The boy who was antagonizing him, Lars, he is Hunter's son and Hunter does nothing to stop him. Unbelievable."

My eyes drifted across the street. The skater kids had come outside again. They took off on their longboards in the direction of the park. I hoped they weren't heading after the Wizard to harass him more.

"Julieta, I have a bad feeling about him. I think it will be important that you keep your distance. I do not trust him. He has a terrible temper." Carlos glanced across the street toward Cyclepath. "It worries me to have you and your young staff across from him."

"I'm sure it will be fine," I replied. "He was probably upset and got worked up."

"Maybe." Carlos didn't sound convinced. "Still, I think it will be better if you stay away."

We turned our attention to Andy as he poured us samples of his cold brew. Carlos' warning was too late. I had already signed a lease. Whether we wanted to or not, we were about to become neighbors with Cyclepath—and avoiding Hunter was out of the question.

Chapter Four

For the next few days Sterling, Andy, and I spent the bulk of our time at Scoops. We had put the list of potential names to a vote, and Scoops was the clear winner. It was good timing to be away from the bakeshop as we had a few weeks before things would start to ramp up once the Oregon Shakespeare Festival officially launched its new season. For the moment the theater was in previews, which drew a loyal following in Ashland, but the rush of the tourist crowds would begin in earnest in April and May and continue through the heat of the summer.

I arrived at the new space on a cool but crisp late March morning. Knowing that today's task was sanding and staining the coffee bar and staining the fence, trellises, and gazebo, I had dressed for the occasion in a pair of well-worn jeans, tennis shoes, and an old sweatshirt from my cruise ship days. It was azure blue—the signature color of the *Amour of the Seas* where Carlos and I had met and fallen in love—with the words *Seas the Day* written in white scroll across the chest. Crew members had received the sweatshirts as part of a team-building exercise. *Seas the Day* had been our staff motto thanks to an overzealous cruise director who loved a good pun.

The Railroad District was much quieter than the plaza. It was nearly ten o'clock. When I had left Torte there wasn't an empty table in the bakeshop. The same couldn't be said for our new digs. Workers stacked empty pallets at the Grange and a few locals wandered into the antique and pet shops directly across the street. Nana's food truck pumped out intoxicating smells of sweet onions and garlic, but it wouldn't open until noon. Otherwise the neighborhood was empty, except for three kids with skateboards hanging out in front of Cyclepath, one who I recognized as Lars, Hunter's son. I wondered why they weren't in school.

Andy and Sterling were down the street getting paint supplies at the hardware store. That was one of many benefits of living in a small town. We rarely had to go far for supplies. The Grange was on the opposite side of the garden. And the hardware store and lumberyard were just past that. The organic pet store sat across the street in a converted cottage. I watched as a young woman stopped to allow her two corgis to drink from a fountain designed for furry, four-legged friends.

While I waited for the guys to return, I started pulling weeds. It felt good to get my hands dirty. The calming sound of gentle music floated from Addie's yoga studio as I snipped and trimmed the border. A handful of morning yoga-goers streamed past me on their way to class at Namaste. They were dressed in similar attire to Addie—stretchy yoga pants, slip-on shoes, and loose, free-flowing tops. A woman I recognized as a regular at Torte stopped to say hello. She toted a rolled-up yoga mat and a water bottle under one arm.

"I heard a rumor that Torte was going to open a second shop here. This might be dangerous for my post-workout routine," she joked.

"Technically speaking we won't be doing any baking here, if it's any consolation." I went on to explain our concept for Scoops.

"That's great! I'll be able to get my coffee fix." She grinned. "I can't imagine smelling your delicious bread and pastries baking while trying to concentrate on Warrior Two."

"No need to worry. Everything we serve here will be cold." Maybe we should add teas and smoothies to the menu for the post-yoga crowd.

She left with a promise to return for our grand opening. I went through the side gate and around the yoga studio entrance to the back of the building that sat directly across from the railroad tracks. Addie had told me that she would leave us garbage, recycling, and yard debris bins.

The businesses ended at the tracks. To my right an alleyway offered access to parking for Cyclepath and a lawyer's office. The alleyway turned into a bike path farther down at Railroad Park. A six-foot-high chain-link fence served as a barrier to the open grassy fields on the other side of the tracks.

I spotted a herd of deer bedded down in the reedy grasses. The flaxen mountains in the distance were dusted with snow. I could definitely get used to these views, I thought as I found a forest-green yard-debris can. The backside of the yoga studio and Hunter's bike shop across the street had been tagged in the same purple spray paint as the fridge in our new kitchen. There were broken bottles near the train tracks and what looked like a makeshift tent erected with a blue tarp and some plywood.

Is that where the Wizard slept?

I didn't have time to get closer because a man's voice rang out on the tracks. "Get back here!"

I turned to see two men barreling their bikes down the path directly at me. I recognized the Wizard from his cape and retro bike. The other bike looked like it had been ridden through a mud pit. Layers of caked dirt and grime covered the spokes and handlebars.

They were coming at me so fast that I froze.

Behind them a younger man, riding a bike with a trailer attached, shouted for them to stop. "I know you stole my product! Stop!"

The Wizard made a sharp left turn to avoid running into me. His counterpart slammed on his brakes and steered to the right. That took him over the gravel berm above the tracks. His bike screeched to a halt and catapulted him over the handlebars. I let go of the yard-debris can and ran to help him.

"Are you okay?" I bent down next to him on the gravel.

He moaned. The guy was much younger than the Wizard, probably mid-twenties or early thirties.

"Are you hurt? Should I call an ambulance?" I asked.

The Wizard flipped his bike around and rode over to us. "NO! No police."

"Okay." I threw up my hands. "I won't call the police, but your friend might need an ambulance."

The man who'd been chasing them rolled up on his bike and screeched to a halt next to us. His loose baggy pants were knotted with rubber bands at the ankles to keep them from tangling with his spokes. He skidded one foot along the gravel. "Karma sucks, doesn't it? Stop stealing from me!"

The Wizard's hands flew up in the air. "You stop! You stop!"

"Touch my product, and you'll regret it." He didn't bother to check to see whether the guy on the ground was okay before speeding off toward town, with his black bike trailer rattling behind him.

The guy on the ground flipped onto his back. His right palm was badly cut and bleeding. "No cops," he grunted, trying to sit up.

"Take it slow," I cautioned. "What's your name?"

"Sky." His hands were as dirty as his bike. Blood seeped from the gash on his hand.

"Let me run into the yoga studio. I'm sure Addie has a first-aid kit."

The Wizard yelped. "No! She's a bad woman." He got off his bike and rocked back on forth on his heels while tapping his temples.

I glanced around for anything clean that we could use to apply pressure to the wound. There was nothing. The man's ragged clothing was grimy and stained. It was evident that he'd been sleeping outside for a while by the twigs and branches embedded in his dreadlocks and his lack of personal hygiene.

I tugged off my sweatshirt, glad that I had layered my

clothing for the day. "Here, wrap this around your hand. I'm going to find a first-aid kit. Are you sure you don't want me to call an ambulance? That might need stitches."

He followed my directions and pressed the sleeve of my sweatshirt onto his injury. "No. Like the Wizard said, we don't want to see the cops. They'll make trouble for us."

What was their resistance to the police? Did it have to do with the guy who'd been chasing them? Maybe they had stolen from him. But if they had, there was no need for Sky or the Wizard to worry about the police. I had witnessed firsthand how the Professor and Thomas interacted with Ashland's homeless population. They were nothing but kind and worked diligently to find solutions and support for the unhoused versus tossing them in jail for panhandling.

"I'm not going to call the police," I said, standing. "But we need to take care of your hand."

"No! Don't listen to her," the Wizard shouted, waving his hands wildly. "They'll come and they'll try to take us, Sky. Don't do it!"

I wasn't about to hang around and argue the merits of Ashland's police force. "Keep an eye on your friend," I said to the Wizard. "I'll be back in a minute."

The Wizard followed my command. I headed for Addie's yoga studio. I took the stairs to the small wraparound porch two at a time. A reception area with a single desk and shelving for expensive yoga gear was empty. Calm bluish lighting and the gurgling sounds of an indoor water feature gave the entryway a tranquil feel. A class schedule hung behind the desk. According to the calendar, Addie was currently teaching Gentle Yoga for beginners.

I didn't want to riffle through the reception area, so I walked down the hallway and carefully opened the studio door. The open room had natural pine-wood floors and an abundance of natural light thanks to two skylights. About twenty students were positioned on floor mats in Child's Pose.

When I opened the door, every head popped up.

Addie shot me a nasty look.

"Sorry to interrupt." I approached her, keeping my voice barely above a whisper. "There's been an accident outside and I was wondering if you have a first-aid kit."

"An accident?" She stood on her tiptoes to see out the side window. A flash of disgust clouded her face. "For him—the freak show? No way. I'm not helping him. He's probably faking it to try and get inside my studio. He's not allowed in here."

Everything about Addie was in contradiction. Why would she refuse to help? I wasn't asking her to perform surgery. I simply needed a first-aid kit.

Two of her students moved to get up. Addie snapped her fingers. "Child's Pose, now!"

The class acquiesced. Everyone returned to the positions I'd found them in. "It's not for the Wizard. A man flipped over on his bike. I think he might need stitches, but I won't be able to tell until I can clean the wound."

She huffed and pointed to a cabinet in the far corner of the studio. "Fine. The first-aid kit is over there, but don't say I didn't warn you. That guy is crazy and super dangerous. I wouldn't get involved if I were you."

I retrieved the first-aid kit while she instructed her class in their next move and got out of there before she changed her mind. Outside I found the Wizard sitting next to Sky.

"How's the patient?" I asked, putting on a pair of disposable gloves and removing antiseptic wipes from the first-aid kit. Professional kitchens can be quite dangerous. Burns, cuts, and falls are all hazards of the job, so ever since culinary school I had maintained my first-aid and CPR certification and insisted that my staff do the same.

"It stings." Sky pulled my sweatshirt from his hand, revealing a two-inch cut straight down the midline of his palm. He must have snagged it on something when he fell.

"Can I clean it out for you?" I knelt next to him.

He closed his eyes and thrust his hand toward me. I took that as a yes.

The cut oozed as I carefully wiped gravel and dirt from his hand. He winced and stabbed his free hand into his thigh as I methodically disinfected the gash, wrapped it in gauze, and sealed it with medical tape. "You're good to go," I said, tugging off my gloves. "But you should keep an eye on that. If it bleeds through the gauze you probably need to go to the hospital and get stitches."

"Nah. I'm good. I don't feel a thing now." He wiggled his fingertips. His muted blond dreadlocks hung below his shoulders. Two black gauge plug earrings the size of quarters encompassed his earlobes.

"You didn't hit your head or anything, did you?" I assessed him as he tried to stand. "Are you dizzy?"

"No. Feeling good after the Wizard gave me this." He took a drink from a silver flask he pulled from his back pocket.

"Let's go, Sky." The Wizard stared into Addie's studio. He pulled his friend up to his feet. Sky rocked to the left and then the right. Did he have a concussion? That had been a nasty fall. It had happened so quickly that I didn't remember if he'd smacked his head on the pavement, but from the way he was swaying, he was either concussed or drunk. Given that it was just ten in the morning, I hoped that it wasn't the latter.

"Are you sure?" I asked. "I can get someone to give you a ride to the hospital."

Sky took another long slug from the flask. "Nah. Thanks, nurse." He straddled his bike and started to hand me my *Amour of the Seas* sweatshirt. "You want this back?"

"No, please keep it."

The Wizard gave me a formal bow. "Thank you."

"You're welcome. Be sure to keep an eye on your friend's cut. It can get infected easily." I reached for the first-aid kit and pressed antibiotic ointment, gauze, and tape into his hand.

He positioned his bike and flung his cape behind him. Before he rode off with Sky he made an obscene gesture at Addie's studio. What was the deal with the two of them? Addie made it sound like he was dangerous, but from what I had just witnessed I wasn't sure that I agreed with her. The Wizard had appeared genuinely concerned for Sky. I hoped that we weren't putting ourselves in the middle of drama. Between the altercation I had witnessed with Hunter and the Wizard yesterday,

Addie's reaction to him this morning, and the mystery man who'd been chasing them, it was almost as if my fellow business owners in the Railroad District had a vendetta against the homeless man.

Chapter Five

I returned the first-aid kit to the studio. Addie was still teaching class, so I left it on the reception desk. Sterling and Andy arrived carrying three gallon buckets of paint and stain, brushes, and a large drop cloth at the same time I rounded the corner dragging the yard debris bin behind me.

"You missed the action," I said, dumping a pile of weeds into the bin.

"What's that, boss?" Andy balanced two gallons of paint in each hand.

I told them about the Wizard and Sky.

"It's weird, isn't it?" Sterling asked, setting down the drop cloth and a can of stain. "It's sort of out of character for Ashland. Why harass a homeless guy? Unless he really is vandalizing things and stealing bikes. But what's his beef with a yoga studio?"

"Exactly." I glanced toward Addie's studio. "She keeps insisting that he's dangerous, but I don't get it."

"Because no one does," Andy added.

Sterling arranged a variety of different-size paint-brushes on one of the bistro tables. "A wise woman once told me to trust my instincts."

"Mom," I said with a nod.

"No." Sterling scowled. "You, Jules."

"Did I say that?" I wrinkled my nose. "That was very wise of me."

"And she's so humble," Sterling said to Andy.

I dropped the subject as we mapped out our strategy for painting.

Andy would paint the fading trim around the coffee bar while Sterling and I concentrated on staining the fence and trellises. We had opted for a dark walnut stain with red undertones. The darker stain should cover any flaws in the wood and give the garden new life.

"Before we get started, Dean, the new milk vendor, is going to drop by with samples," Sterling said, rolling up the sleeve of his hoodie to reveal a black sports watch. "Speak of the devil. He's right on time."

To my surprise I looked up to see the guy who'd been chasing the Wizard and Sky. "You?"

Dean stared at Sterling, who had gotten up to open the gate and then at me. "Do I know you?"

I thrust my thumb over my shoulder. "I just saw you. I was helping the guy who fell on the tracks."

"Oh right." Dean darted his eyes toward the railroad tracks. "I thought you looked familiar." He carried a plastic cart with an assortment of glass milk bottles.

"What were you doing?" I caught Sterling's eye as he followed behind Dean.

"Huh? Oh, that. That was nothing. Do you mind if I set this down?" He didn't wait for my answer. "I'm tired of those homeless guys stealing my product. I find my milk bottles shattered all over the tracks. I'm going to have to get a lock for my trailer."

He began taking bottles of milk, heavy cream, and chocolate milk out of the crate.

Sterling ran his fingers through his jet-black hair. "I guess you've sort of met. Jules, meet Dean. Dean, meet my boss, Jules."

One of the bottles slipped from Dean's hand and landed sideways on the table. "Sorry about earlier," Dean said, standing the bottle up. "You know how it is as a small-business owner, you can't be too careful about the bottom line."

"Have you talked to the police about the theft?" I asked. Chasing two homeless guys on bikes didn't seem like the most productive solution.

"Nah. It's no big deal. Don't want to bother the cops with petty theft. Like I said, I'll get a lock for my trailer. It's frustrating more than anything. I give away free product all the time. That's part of being here in the Railroad District. We see people in bad shape. I'm constantly offering samples and product that's nearing its expiration to the homeless guys who hang around the tracks. It makes me crazy when they trash my stuff." He sighed and poured thick, creamy milk into glasses. "Enough on that. Who wants a taste?"

I couldn't get a good read on Dean. He didn't strike me as an organic farmer. More like a computer nerd posing as a farmer with his gangly frame, baggy pants cinched at the ankles, and tucked-in button-down shirt. I could understand his frustration with giving away free samples only to have his product stolen. It gave me new insight on his interaction with Sky and the Wizard.

"My girlfriend runs the farm," Dean said, passing around samples. "We're purely organic. Our property is on the other side of I-5. Over by the hemp farms."

That would explain the faint whiff of hemp I kept smelling.

Andy climbed off a ladder. He had taken down the two security cameras Addie had installed so that we didn't damage them while staining the pergola. "Where do you want these, boss?" He held the white cameras in the palm of his hand.

"Maybe put them on top of the fridge for now. I'll ask Addie later."

"Cameras?" Dean untwisted the cap on a glass jug of milk. "High tech."

"They're not ours. Addie had them installed," I replied.

"Got it." Dean passed around more samples. "We do everything in small batches. Our cows are grass fed and free range, and that shows in the milk. Drink up. Give it a taste and let me know what you think. Once people try our milk they can't go back to anything that's been mass-produced. You'll taste fresh grass in every sip." He encouraged us to try the samples.

I didn't pick up on notes of fresh grass, but his milk was good.

"Since we're new to the game, we're giving you and a few other businesses our exclusive introductory rate. As you're tasting, with this quality product you're getting a steal of deal." Dean went into a sales pitch that wasn't necessary. Mom and I had already agreed to a three-month trial.

"Keep the samples." Dean pushed bottles of milk at me. "Let me know when you want deliveries to start. Should I work with you or Sterling on that?"

"Sterling will be your point of contact." I stood and shook Dean's hand.

After he left, Andy put the milk samples in the fridge. Sterling and I prepped the fence for staining.

"Sorry about that, Jules. I had no idea he was the guy who was chasing the Wizard."

"How could you? It's not your fault, and in all fairness to Dean, I have no idea what the story is behind what happened on the tracks earlier."

"What do you think? Should we scrap the idea of working with him?" Sterling covered the gate hardware with blue painter's tape. "I don't want to force you into a business partnership you're not comfortable with."

"I appreciate that. You don't need to worry about me. His pricing is beyond reasonable for local, organic milk. In fact, I wonder how he can be making any profit with those prices. Let's give it a try and see how it goes." I knew that I had a soft spot in my heart for the Wizard and Sky. Mom had always teased that from the time I could walk I would collect strays. From lost cats to a baby deer that got separated from its mama, animals and people in need tended to gravitate toward me. It wasn't fair to end our newly formed relationship with Dean. I had no idea if Sky and the Wizard really were stealing his milk and smashing the used bottles on the tracks. If it was true, it would explain his earlier outburst.

Not that I approved of his methods, but I could understand his frustration.

"Okay, I'll keep an eye on him." Sterling lugged buckets of stain to the fence.

"I'd appreciate that."

Sterling and I quickly developed a system. He painted one slat a time and I followed, wiping up any drips and filling in missing spots. It was tedious work, but it felt good to be outside in the pleasant spring air. It was a good thing we were outside because the strong fumes of the stain would have been overpowering in an enclosed space.

"Jules, can I ask you something?" Sterling asked, dabbing his paintbrush into the bucket of stain.

"Of course. You can ask me anything." I was glad that I had worn a short-sleeved T-shirt underneath the sweatshirt I had given to Sky. As was typical in springtime in Ashland, the morning had warmed to the low seventies. Tiny pink blooms budded in the trees nearby. The scent of cherry blossoms mingled with the heavenly smells of Nana's street food. I noticed a line had started queuing up in front of her truck.

"It's about Stephanie." Sterling tucked a lock of his dark hair behind his ear, and rolled up the sleeves of his hoodie, revealing a beautiful hummingbird tattoo that ran the length of his forearm. "I know that you're discrete, but I want to keep this between us."

"Absolutely." I motioned as if I was zipping my lips shut. "Whatever you need to talk about will go no further." I paused for a minute. "Wait, please don't tell me that she's quitting."

I had come to rely on Stephanie's immense talent,

especially when it came to design. She had an innate eye for color combinations and was meticulous with a piping bag. Buttercream was her natural medium. Our requests for custom-cake designs had tripled in the past year, thanks to Stephanie's artistry.

"No. Nothing like that." He ran his brush along a slat of wood. "You know what housing is like in Ashland. It's been a nightmare to find a decent place that doesn't cost a couple grand a month."

I nodded.

"A guy I know from the skate park gave me a heads-up on a new complex that his grandfather is developing in that empty lot across from the high school. I guess they already broke ground. They're building three-story townhouses and according to my friend they're going to be rent controlled." He paused for a moment as a group of yoga students who had finished class stopped to take note of our progress.

"That's great." I used a rag to dab excess stain from the top of a fence post.

"Yeah. It's about time. I love Ashland. I've found my people here, but lately I've been wondering if I can afford to stay in the Rogue Valley."

"Sterling, no! Do not say that." I dropped the rag and reached for the sleeve of his gray hoodie. "If you need a short-term loan, Mom and I will help. We'll do anything to keep you. You're such a valuable member of our team. What would I do without you?"

"Chill, Jules." His brilliant blue eyes flashed with his smile.

"What about my house? I have plenty of space. In fact, I've been thinking about offering up one of the spare rooms to a college student. I'd be happy to have you stay with me for however long you need." The thought of losing Sterling made me ill. Of course I hadn't broached the subject of leasing our rooms with Carlos. If things didn't work out with us, that was my backup plan.

Stop, Jules, I scolded myself. You can't think like that.

"Thank you for the offer, Jules, really. I appreciate it, but I want my own place, and these new townhouses sound perfect. Not to mention, you have a lot going on right now with having Carlos around. I think it would be pretty weird to have one of your staff move in."

I started to protest, but he cut me off.

"Here's the deal—I want to ask Stephanie to move in with me. She only has one more year left at SOU and she's tired of living in the dorms. I think if we moved in together we could afford one of the townhouses."

I smoothed out a streak of stain, buying myself a minute to respond. Sterling and Stephanie had been dating for over a year and they seemed like a well-matched couple, but moving in together was a big step. A step that in my opinion shouldn't be taken because of finances.

"What do you think Steph will say?" I asked.

Sterling held his paintbrush in his right hand and met my eyes. "Look, Jules, I can tell by your face what you're thinking. You're pretty transparent."

I tried to keep my cheeks and brow as neutral as possible. "How so?"

"You're thinking I want to move in with her to save money. It's not that. I swear. You know what Ashland is like. I could post an ad on Craigslist for a roommate and have a dozen offers within a couple minutes. I don't want a roommate. I'm in love with Stephanie. She's the one." His eyes were filled with emotion. "I want to marry her, Jules."

"Sterling." I pressed my hand to my chest. "You're going to make me tear up."

"Don't get mushy on me." Sterling nudged me with his elbow.

"What's the issue, then?"

He sighed. "It's a lot of stuff. Stephanie's family is pretty strict. I don't know that they'll be okay with her moving in with me, and I don't want her to think that me asking her is motivated by money. I'm going to propose eventually, but she's made it clear she doesn't want to get married anytime soon. She wants to finish school and thinks that there's no need to rush."

"So you two have talked about this?"

We returned to staining as we talked. "Yeah, we've talked about it. She told me the only way she'll ever get married is if it can be a Halloween wedding."

"That would be cool and that sounds like Steph. Plus can you even imagine the costumes and food we could come up with for a Halloween wedding?" I crossed my fingers on both hands.

"There's no question in my mind. She's the perfect match for me. We balance each other out, you know? And, I want to take some more writing classes at SOU. The townhouses are only a couple blocks away. We could both walk to campus and to Torte. With taking on more responsibility here and with the nice raise you and your Mom gave me, I can afford them. It's just that . . ." He trailed off.

"I'm confused, what are you worried about? It sounds like you have a plan and you've thought this through."

"I can already hear Steph's parents telling her that we're too young and it's a rash move. They're paying for her college and I don't want to put her in a position to jeopardize that or her relationship with them. My dad and I have slowly been trying to rebuild trust after everything that went down when my mom died. I don't want to see Stephanie go through what I've gone through. But at the same time I know that we're ready for this step. I know that we would both be happy living in the townhouses and not have to worry about rent, money, or transportation."

I appreciated that Sterling had put thought into the decision and that he was looking out for Stephanie's best interest.

"I'm hardly suited to give you advice on making rash decisions on love. I've told you about marrying Carlos on a whim, right? Sterling, we're hopeless romantics. Mom would say that's a good thing. It lends itself to passion and poetry, but speaking from experience, sometimes feeling deeply also means opening yourself up to heartbreak and loss." I thought back to my whirlwind wedding with Carlos in Marseilles. I didn't regret my decision to marry him on the spot. Nor did I regret leaving him on the ship two years ago when I learned that he had a son he had never told me about. I realized now that I had to leave. If I hadn't, I might have stayed stuck. Stuck in a life I didn't know was wrong for me. Even with the sadness and confusion I'd caused both of us, I was thankful that a string of events had sent me in a new direction. Blame it on my name, but my heart had always led me—for better or for worse.

Sterling shooed away a fly. "That's the thing that I keep coming back to. Isn't love supposed to be rash? Isn't that what every love sonnet is about? I don't want to wait to start my future with Stephanie. I learned that from losing my mom young. We're not promised forever. That's a lesson that will stick with me. If I love Stephanie now, why should I wait to be with her?"

"I think you have your answer." I gave him a knowing look.

Andy hollered from the other side of the garden. "Hey, can one of you come help me with the ladder?"

"On my way," Sterling called. Then he handed me his paintbrush. "Thanks for listening, Jules. I'm going to think on it some more."

"I'm honored that you trusted me with this, and anytime you want to talk, I'm always happy to listen." He went to help Andy. I moved on to the next section of fencing. Love was complicated enough without the external pressure of parents and other people's expectations. I didn't envy him. Having Carlos in Ashland had been equally wonderful and confusing. If you had asked me on that magical day in Marseilles if I would be considering whether or not we had a future together today, I would have been speechless. I could imagine myself laughing at the mere thought that Carlos and I wouldn't have a picture-perfect future. But like the ever-changing tides, our lives had ebbed and flowed in different directions. Maybe if I had stayed. Maybe if I hadn't steered my ship home. Maybe we'd be bobbing blissfully on some tropical sea instead of trying to fig-ure out how—or if—we fit together on land. Or maybe I would have been entirely miserable.

Hearing Sterling sound so sure of his love and devo-tion for Stephanie rattled me. I enjoyed having Carlos in Ashland, but if he hadn't insisted on coming, would I have continued to let things drag out indefinitely be-tween us? Yes, I had missed him, but was that enough? If there was one thing I was sure of it was that we both deserved to be happy, and I couldn't shake the feeling that Carlos wasn't being entirely truthful with me.

"Jules, Jules," Andy's voice shook me back into reality.

"Huh?" I glanced around the garden to see Sterling steadying the ladder while Andy hung a red-and-teal banner above the coffee and ice cream counter. Like Steph's original sketch, the logo was in the shape of an ice cream cone with a scoop each of chocolate, vanilla, and strawberry ice cream with scoops dripping from one side of the cone.

"I was asking if this looks level to you."

"Move it a little higher on the left," I said, walking closer and shaking myself free from thoughts of Carlos.

Andy shifted the banner. "Like that?"

"Perfect." Between the bright banner, the fresh coat of paint, and the matching red-and-teal barstools we had purchased, the space was beginning to take shape.

Andy fastened the banner and climbed down from the ladder.

Suddenly voices echoed behind us. It sounded like they were coming from the railroad tracks.

"HELP! HELP!" A woman screamed as the sound of a train whistle blared. I glanced at my watch. The train came through Ashland twice a day.

We dropped everything and raced out of the garden gate and to the backside of the building toward the tracks.

The shrill blows of the train whistle mixed with the high-pitched screams of Laney Lee, who was standing in the middle of the tracks.

It took me a second to process what was happening.

The noon train was barreling toward Laney.

"Laney, move!" I yelled.

She turned her head. Her eyes were wild with fear. Then she pointed at her feet.

I gasped. The Wizard lay sprawled out across the tracks.

"What do we do?" I turned to Sterling and Andy as panic welled inside me. "We've got to get him off the tracks."

Andy began waving at the train, which fortunately looked to be slowing. But was there time?

Sterling ran to help Laney. I followed, kicking gravel as I sprinted toward the tracks. The Wizard was passed out cold. Sterling grabbed his feet. "Support his head," he said to Laney. That seemed to snap her out of a fog of disbelief.

"Jules, lift his torso," Sterling commanded. "On three."

We tugged his body, but his purple cape was caught in the tracks.

"Stop! Stop!" Andy continued to wave and yell at the train, which was now only about fifty feet away.

The train conductor applied the brake. An ear-piercing screeching sound reverberated as the tracks shook.

"Try again," Sterling yelled over the sound. He had managed to rip the Wizard's cape.

I flexed my muscles, thankful for the many hours I spent kneading dough and lifting heavy bags of flour.

"Ready?" Sterling didn't wait for an answer. "One, two, three."

We heaved the Wizard from the tracks just as the train came to a halt two feet from where we'd been standing.

I let out a long sigh. That was close. Too close.

"Jules, Jules." Sterling sounded panicked.

My heart rate spiked. I turned, half expecting to see the train barreling toward us again.

"Jules, look." Sterling held out his hands. They were covered in blood.

"Oh no, are you hurt?"

He shook his head, staring at his bloody hands and then at the Wizard. "This isn't my blood."

I looked down and realized that the Wizard hadn't been passed out. He was dead.

Chapter Six

This couldn't be happening. I had just seen the Wizard a few hours ago. My head felt fuzzy, like I was watching everything unfold on a movie screen.

"Someone call the police!" Laney wailed. She cradled the Wizard's head in her arms. "Call the police! We need help!"

I sprang into action, grabbing my phone and dialing the Professor. "It's Juliet. There's been an accident on the railroad tracks," I blurted out the minute I heard his deep baritone voice on the other end of the line.

His tone was calm. "Is an ambulance required?"

"Yes, but"—I hesitated as I looked at the Wizard, whose lifeless body was limp in Laney's arms—"I think he's dead."

The Professor talked me through protocol, promising he was on his way and would be there shortly. "When we hang up, I want you to call nine-one-one dispatch and tell them everything you've told me. I'm in the plaza and will be there in less than five minutes."

I followed his instructions. The 911 operator had

me stay on the line until help arrived. In a blur, an ambulance with a shrill siren and flashing lights zoomed
down the alley and blocked the pathway, followed by the
Professor's sedan and a white police SUV with Thomas
and Detective Kerry.

Sterling, who typically kept his emotions in check,
was visibly shaken. He was sitting crossed-legged next
to the Wizard's body, staring at his bloody hands. I
pulled him away from the railroad tracks as EMS workers raced toward us carrying medical bags. "Let's go sit
down." I pointed to the garden.

Andy, who was standing nearby, shot me a thumbs-
up. "I was thinking the same thing, boss. We should give
the police some space."

Without being prompted, he wrapped a muscular arm
around Sterling's shoulder and guided him to the garden. I recognized the signs of mild shock. It was under-
standable. Sterling had witnessed death close up. There
was no escaping an emotional reaction to that.

Andy helped Sterling sit in one of the bistro chairs.
I went to get him a towel for his hands and a glass of
water. If only we had pastries or coffee on hand. A hit
of sugar or espresso never hurt in a situation like this.

"How are you doing?" I asked, handing Sterling a
damp towel. "Here, wipe off your hands."

His eyes were glassy. "I feel kind of lightheaded." He
wiped the blood from his hands, staring with disbelief
at the towel that was turning red.

"That's normal," I reassured him.

Members of Addie's yoga class had spilled out into the
street to see what the commotion was about. Hunter,

his son Lars, and a bike mechanic had come out of Cyclepath as well.

"Is he dead?" Sterling dropped the towel on the grass. "He's dead, isn't he?"

"I think so." I handed him a glass of water. "Try to drink something."

The ambulance had silenced its siren, but its flashing lights bounced off Namaste. Something smelled like it was burning. I wondered if it was from the train coming to a screeching stop or if in her rush to help, Laney had left something on the stove.

Andy turned to me. "Hey boss, I could use a coffee. Do you mind if I run over to Torte and bring back a pot of espresso? Maybe some sandwiches or cookies?" He caught my eye. I could tell he was trying to speak in code.

"Good idea." I shot him a look of gratitude. "I think that would be great."

I turned my attention to Sterling. "I've been in your position before and I know how unsettling it is to say the very least."

"I didn't realize when we were lifting him off the tracks that he was already gone. It wasn't until we set him down that I looked at his face and could see that there was nothing in his eyes." He clutched the glass, but it shook so hard that water spilled from the top.

"I know." I placed my hand on his knee. "I know."

We sat together in contemplative silence while activity blurred around us. I knew the best thing for Sterling and for myself was to take a few minutes to breathe and try to center ourselves. Shock was a real concern. Sterling's ashen face, the bluish tint to his lips and fingernails, and his shallow rapid breathing had me ready to call the paramedics over.

"That was his blood." Sterling stared at his quivering hands.

"Yeah." I nodded. "Try inhaling through your nose, nice and slow." I modeled breathing for him.

He followed along, inhaling deeply, holding his breath for a moment, and then releasing it slowly.

"Good. Keep focusing on each inhale and exhale." I watched his attention shift from his hands to his breathing. "There was nothing else you could have done."

Sterling reached for the water again, his hands still trembling. "I couldn't get his cape free. If only I could have gotten him free sooner."

"No. He was already dead. The fall must have killed him. You did everything you could, Sterling. You were amazing."

He blew out a long stream of air. "Was he already dead? It feels like a weird nightmare."

"I'm sure of it." How had the Wizard died? And what was he doing on the tracks? Had he had an accident like Sky? I pictured the scene in my mind, but couldn't recall seeing his bike anywhere.

The smell of smoke grew stronger. I looked to my left and noticed gray smoke billowing from Laney's food truck.

"Are you okay for second?" I asked Sterling, pointing to Nana's Street Food.

Sterling took another drink. His hands were a bit steadier, which I took as a positive sign. "I'm feeling slightly better. I'm just going to sit and keep breathing for a while though."

"Good. You're going to be fine. Like I said, it's totally normal. You have more color now. Keep breathing, and I'll be right back." I left him and ran to the food truck.

The minute I opened the door, a huge black cloud of smoke engulfed me. I coughed and covered my mouth with my sleeve.

My eyes stung as I waved smoke from my face and surveyed the tiny galley kitchen. Sure enough a pot of rice had been left on the stove. The water had evaporated, leaving a blackened mess searing on the bottom of the pan. The smoke was thick. I flipped off the burner, found some pot holders, and took the burning pot outside.

As I stepped out of the truck, Laney approached me.

"Oh no! Thank you, Jules. I totally forgot that I had food going in the midst of all of this." She motioned behind her to the railroad tracks. "Is the truck on fire?" She coughed and fanned smoke from her face. Like Sterling, her hands were coated in dried blood.

"No, the truck is okay. Smokey but fine."

"Thank you." Laney wiped tears from her eyes with her sleeve. She looked worse than Sterling. Her skin was sallow, her pupils were huge, and sweat beaded on her forehead. "I can't believe this is happening. I can't believe he's dead."

I placed the pot on the sidewalk as smoke continued to billow. "Did you see what happened?"

She tried to brush her hands on her apron. "I have no idea. I got here about an hour ago to start lunch prep. I was in the middle of chopping fresh herbs for my daily salad special when I heard something out back. It sounded like fighting. I went to see what was going on and found the Wizard on the tracks."

"Did you see anyone else?"

She tapped her forehead with her index finger, trying to retrieve a memory. "I think so. Everything happened so fast, but I'm pretty sure I saw a guy speed away on a black electric bike. It could have been a biker already on the path, though I'm not sure."

"Were there any signs of trauma on the Wizard?"

"Yes. Look." She held out bloodstained hands. "I think he'd been hit in the back of his head. There was a huge bump and so much blood. I told the police about it. . . . Do you think he fell? Do you think he felt any pain? I hope he went quickly." Tears poured from her again.

"He could have fallen," I said as much for my sake as for hers.

"Maybe. But where was his bike? I didn't see his bike anywhere. He's never without that bike. He was alone on the tracks."

But faceup, I thought. If he had been hit on the back of the head how could he have fallen faceup?

"Someone killed him, I'm sure of it." She wiped her eyes with her apron.

"How do you know?"

She turned her head toward Cyclepath. "Because I've been paying attention. Hunter has had it out for the Wizard for months. You saw his outburst. He's been harassing and threatening him daily. Same for Lars. That punk kid is always in trouble. I don't know why Hunter's gotten it in his head that the Wizard had anything to do with missing bikes and vandalism. If I were him, I'd be looking close to home.

"The only thing the Wizard ever did was ride his bike back and forth on the street and pathway. That irked Hunter. Why? I have no idea. The Wizard never would have stolen a bike. His bike was his most beloved possession. I think it was his only possession and he wouldn't have parted with it. The fact that his bike is missing makes me sure that Hunter's involved. Hunter probably stole it from him or made Lars do it. They hated him."

"Do you really think so?"

"Yes!" Her tone was forceful. "Hunter didn't like the fact that the Wizard wasn't classy enough for this area. That's why he kept trying to run him off. It didn't have anything to do with stolen bikes. I know he wanted the Wizard dead. I saw Lars harassing him the other night. He and his buddies were chasing after him on their skateboards, throwing rocks and pine cones at him. I bet you anything that Hunter put them up to it."

"That's a big accusation, Laney." I wondered if she was simply upset and in shock, like Sterling.

"It's not an accusation. He's been threatening the Wizard for weeks now. I've told the police about it, but they said there was nothing they could do unless the Wizard agreed to talk with them. He wouldn't. You know what he's like—what he was like." She buried her face in her apron.

"Oh Laney, I'm so sorry." I hugged her.

She gulped back tears. "He was a wonderful man, Juliet. He had a heart of gold. I can't believe Hunter killed him. Why? Why? Just to make sure that his fancy bike shop attracted rich tourists?"

I let her vent.

"I told the police this dozens of times. Now, maybe they'll look into Hunter's shady practices. They could have stopped this though. They could have saved the Wizard. I blame them as much as I blame Hunter." She broke down.

I felt terrible for her. I knew how disturbing it was to see someone come to harm. "It sounds like you really cared for him. He was lucky to have you as a friend."

My words didn't appear to bring her any comfort. That comment made her cry harder.

"He was a tortured gentle soul who didn't deserve to die. Not like this." She looked in the direction of the tracks.

I was about to suggest that she come sit down with Sterling in the garden, but Detective Kerry came up to us. She was tall and thin with long red hair and wide green eyes. Unlike Thomas and the Professor, who tended to dress casually, Kerry wore tailored black slacks, a matching black jacket, and heels. "Can I have a word, Juliet?"

"Sure." I turned to Laney. "Are you good?"

Laney brushed tears from her eyes with her apron again. "No, but there's nothing more I can do. I need to go wash my hands and clean up. I guess I might as well get lunch prep finished. Not that I want to cook, but at least it will give me something to do. And I'm going to need to air out the truck before customers start to arrive."

"I'll check in once I'm done chatting with Kerry," I promised, giving her another hug.

Detective Kerry pulled me over to the side of the half-stained fence. "Doug wants me to take your statement. I know you already spoke with him on the phone, but we need to get it written down."

"Of course." I told her everything I remembered.

She took notes on a legal notepad, meticulously surveying the space around us while I relayed the chain of events.

When I finished, I glanced to the tracks where the ambulance was pulling away. "Is it true that he was murdered?"

Detective Kerry kept her face neutral. "I'm not at liberty to answer that, but I can tell you that we will be pursuing multiple leads."

Was that code for yes?

I knew it was futile to press her. She was a locked vault. It was one of the many reasons that the Professor had hired her and was preparing her and Thomas to take over the department in the coming years. I couldn't blame Detective Kerry for doing her job, but I was more than curious to know if Laney was right about Hunter and Lars. Was his death an accident or could someone have killed him?

Chapter Seven

By the time I returned to the garden, I found Sterling and Andy nursing coffees and eating club sandwiches. "You look better," I said to Sterling.

"Yeah, this guy always has my back." Sterling gave Andy a weak smile.

"Don't thank me. This is from Marty," Andy said offering me a sandwich. "I gave everyone a brief recap and Marty immediately packed up sandwiches. He told me to tell you and Sterling that stress burns calories and the best way to counteract that surge of adrenaline and to feel normal is with a protein sandwich like this club. It's got layers of turkey, ham, cheese, bacon, lettuce, tomatoes . . . and Marty's secret sauce. He also wanted me to tell you that everything is under control at Torte and not to worry."

I sat down and took half of the giant sandwich. Never had I been more grateful for my staff. Not only was Marty's sandwich the fuel I needed, but worrying about Torte hadn't crossed my mind. It was such a gift to know that the bakeshop was in capable hands.

"What's the word, boss?" Andy asked. "Thomas took

my statement, but unfortunately there wasn't much to tell. We only saw the aftermath. Was the guy already dead?"

"They're not saying at the moment." I poured myself a cup of steaming coffee.

"That's standard procedure, right?" Sterling asked. His lips had lost their bluish tint and his hands were much steadier as he poured himself a refill. "I talked to Thomas too. He made it sound like they knew the guy was already dead."

I wasn't surprised that Thomas might have been more forthcoming than Detective Kerry. "Yeah, I'm sure they have to play things close to the chest until they get the official report from the coroner."

"How do you think he was killed?" Sterling ripped off a hunk of his sandwich.

"I don't know. Laney told me she felt a lump and a cut on the back of his head. I'm guessing that's where the blood came from. But I can't figure out the mechanics of that unless he fell backward onto the tracks."

"Or was pushed off his bike, maybe?" Andy offered.

"Yes, but where's the bike?" I sipped the coffee, tasting delicate notes of cherries and chocolate.

"Good question." Andy adjusted his faded red baseball cap and looked around us, as if expecting to see the Wizard's banana-seat bike propped against the gate.

"What about his friend?" Sterling asked, taking another bite of the massive stacked sandwich. "Sky, was that his name? The guy who fell this morning. What happened to him?"

"Another good question." I seconded Andy's statement. How long had it been since I'd seen Sky and the

Wizard? Three hours? What had occurred in that short stretch of time to cause someone to murder the Wizard? If it was murder. And the bigger question was, what was the Wizard's story? He had a name, a past, maybe even a family.

"Does anyone know who he actually was?" Sterling asked.

Had he read my mind? "I was wondering the same thing," I said, cradling my coffee in my hands. "Laney seems to be the most connected to him. Once the shock of the morning wears off, I'll try to talk to her again and see if I can find out anything more. She is really shaken up, understandably."

Emergency lights flooded the garden as the ambulance and two police cars left the scene. A few minutes later, the Professor unlatched the side gate and walked toward us. He wore a pair of khaki slacks, a pale blue and green button-up shirt, and his signature tweed jacket. In one hand he held a Moleskine notebook and in the other a mangled set of handlebars secured in a large plastic evidence bag.

"Sorry to interrupt," he said with an attempt at a smile that didn't reach his eyes. "As the Bard would say, 'Discomfort guides my tongue and bids me speak of nothing but despair.'" He placed the notebook on the bistro table and nodded to an empty chair next to Andy. "May I?"

"Of course," I replied.

"Can I pour you a coffee, Mr. Professor?" Andy offered, reaching for the thermos.

"That would be much appreciated." The Professor set the bag with the twisted handlebars on an empty bistro table next to him.

"Are those from the Wizard's bike?" I asked.

Andy handed him a cup of coffee and passed him a sandwich.

"Many thanks." The Professor ran his finger along the plastic evidence bag. "We do believe these belonged to the deceased. Although, it's puzzling. They were found at Railroad Park. Not anywhere near the scene of the crime. At the moment we have found nothing more of his bike, but Thomas and Kerry and the rest of the team are searching a wide perimeter as we speak, in hopes that more will turn up."

"Do you think he crashed?" I asked.

The Professor took a long sip of his coffee and exhaled. "Doubtful. The trauma to his head isn't consistent with that kind of a fall. It appears more in line with blunt force. We'll have to wait for confirmation from the coroner, but I suspect he was bludgeoned on the back of his head with a heavy, solid object, like a baseball bat . . . or even these." He looked to the handlebars.

"You think he could have been killed with his own handlebars?"

"Not necessarily, but at this point we have to pursue every angle."

I let his words sink in. "So you suspect that someone killed him?"

Creases formed in the Professor's eyes as his lips pressed together. "Indeed." He paused. Everyone went quiet.

"Who would kill him?" Andy voiced what I knew we were all thinking. "He was just a lonely homeless guy."

"I agree." The Professor gave him a solemn nod.

"Murder is always an intolerable act in every circumstance, but given the Wizard's state of living and the fact that the only thing he could be accused of was bringing joy in the form of his rambling rants and sharing balloon art with children in the park, it seems incomprehensible to us that someone should wish to end that life. And yet that's the line of work that has called to me for these many years. I fear that with the passing of time, I'm able to stomach the thought less and less." He pushed his plate away.

I knew that the Professor had been yearning to retire for a while, partly due to his relationship with Mom. They had talked of traveling more. The job had worn on him. In the past months, I had noticed a shift. His resolve to bring justice to our community hadn't faltered, but the emotional burden of carrying the weight of such horrific losses had begun to take a toll. I hoped that Thomas and Kerry were ready to take over soon.

"Do you know anything more about the Wizard?" I asked.

"Most likely as much as you do. He's been a fixture in town for many, many years. Thomas and Kerry will be doing their due diligence. The coroner may be able to provide us with some answers as well. If the Wizard was ever in our system, we'll potentially be able to match prints or dental records, but we won't know for a while." He flipped open his notebook. "That's one of the reasons I wanted to stop by. I know that each of you has already provided a statement—thank you for that—but I wondered if any of you happen to know more about the Wizard. Take a moment and think about it. At this stage even the slightest clue might be helpful. Consider where you've seen him around town, people you may have witnessed him interacting with, and so forth."

We considered his words for a moment.

"He used to come by Torte," Andy said. "I used to see him in the mornings when I'd open. Sometimes I'd give him samples of our daily specials. He'd kind of hang around the plaza by the Lithia Fountain. I think a lot of the restaurants looked out for him. I'd see him getting pasta from the Green Goblin and leftover sandwiches from Puck's. The only person who ever harassed him was Richard Lord."

I wouldn't mind seeing Richard Lord behind bars.

"Yeah, now that you mention it, I used to see him at the skate park," Sterling added. "He hasn't been around there for a while, but last summer he would bike around the park. Most of the skaters were pretty cool with him. Except for Lars." Sterling glanced across the street to Cyclepath.

"You know Lars?" I asked.

"Not really." Sterling was thoughtful for a moment. "He hangs around the skate park a lot. I'm trying to remember when this was. Probably a month or so ago, Lars and a couple of his friends were really cruel to the Wizard one night out there. They were calling him terrible names and throwing stuff at him. Skaters get a bad rap, but a bunch of us banded together and kicked them out. It's not cool to torment anyone."

Sterling's recollection matched what Laney had said.

The Professor took note of Andy and Sterling's observations.

"It's the same for me," I said. "The Wizard has been

a fixture around town. It wasn't until we started this renovation project that I've seen him more frequently." I went on to tell him about my conversation with Laney and her insistence that Hunter from Cyclepath was involved, as well as about Dean's interaction with the Wizard and Sky earlier, and Addie's refusal to help.

When I finished, the Professor made a final note and closed his leather notebook. "Very informative as always. I must bid you adieu for now, but if our discussion triggers any other memories, please be sure to reach out right away." He picked up the journal and evidence bag and left with a half bow.

"What now, boss?" Andy was halfway through his second club sandwich. I'd barely been able to eat more than a few bites.

I looked around the garden at the partially stained fence. "It's totally up to you two. I think I'm probably going to stick around and finish staining, but you are more than welcome to go home or do whatever you need to take care of yourselves." It felt strange to continue our project as if nothing had happened and yet I knew that if I sat and stewed it would only make things worse. Color had returned to Sterling's cheeks. Between the coffee, the sandwich, and our chat with the Professor, I was feeling slightly more relaxed too.

"I could move. I think I need to do something productive." Andy jumped up and began clearing our dishes. It was interesting to observe how everyone handled stress differently.

"Do you want to take off early?" I asked Sterling, taking a final sip of coffee. "Andy and I can finish."

"No. That would be worse. I need to do something

too." He gave me a knowing look. "I can remember a few times that you've come into the kitchen saying that you 'need to bake.' I get it now."

"It's true." I walked my coffee mug to the sink, where Andy was washing dishes. "One more for you." I handed him my mug, then I dropped my voice. "Thank you for getting coffee and sandwiches. That was just what the doctor ordered."

"Boss, no worries. I've got you covered. And, I'm going to keep an eye on our poet boy." He scrubbed the dishes with force.

"How are *you* doing?" I asked, studying his face.

"Fine. I think." He plunged a coffee cup into soapy water. "I don't think it's really sunk in yet, so I'm just going to go with the flow for the moment."

"Okay. Remember I'm here if you need to talk, and you don't need to stay." I wanted to wrap him in a hug, but instead I shot him a smile and returned to staining. The afternoon had warmed with the sun. Locals spilled into the neighborhood for afternoon bike rides, jogs, and leisurely walks. They were likely to be surprised by the sight of yellow caution tape and an active police presence.

The energy in the Railroad District was different than in the plaza. I recognized many familiar faces, some of whom stopped to ask what had happened when they passed by. Moms wheeling wagons filled with toddlers, bubbles, and snacks headed for play dates at Railroad Park. Businesspeople headed to lunch at the swanky Italian bar across the street from Cyclepath. Three doors down in the opposite direction I could smell litti chokha, Indian soul food, grilling at Kha. It was strange to see people going about their normal day when a gruesome death had occurred nearby.

A team of police officers in blue uniforms performed a methodical search of the area, as the Professor had mentioned they would. They emptied the dumpsters behind Cyclepath and stopped to question business owners and people passing by. Bright yellow evidence markers were placed strategically on the street. Every so often our work would be disrupted by shouts from one officer to another to get a better look at potential clues.

A long line had formed at Nana's. I had a feeling it wasn't only the scent of barbecued beef and Kalua pork that had attracted the crowd.

"You ready for second lunch?" Sterling caught me staring at the food truck.

"My rumbling stomach says yes." I nodded at the line. "I'm going to bet that Nana's is booming today so that people can get a closer look at the police activity."

"I'm sure you're right."

"I can wait for a while." We moved from section to section of the perimeter fence. The physical act of staining wasn't as cathartic as baking, but I worked up a sweat as the afternoon progressed. Once we had finished the inside section of fencing, we gathered our gear and went to work on the exterior. Sterling laid a drop cloth on the sidewalk and covered the fence hardware with blue painter's tape.

I had just begun staining the front gate when I spotted Hunter darting behind the dumpsters on the backside of Cyclepath. He didn't notice me, but I kept close watch on him as he lifted the heavy green lid on the dumpster and tossed something inside. Before returning along the sidewalk to the front entrance of his bike shop, he glanced around in every direction to make sure no one was watching. Then he ducked his head and hurried back inside.

"Did you see that?" I whispered to Sterling, who had finished taping the hardware.

"No. What?"

"Hunter," I hissed. "He dumped something in the garbage." I pointed to the dumpster.

"So?" Sterling looked confused.

"Never mind. I'm sure I'm being way too paranoid. My mind is playing out crazy scenarios, like Hunter dumping the murder weapon."

Sterling stared at the green receptacle. "There's one way to find out."

"I think I'll leave it to the police. We've had enough drama for one day."

My mind raced, though. Was I being unrealistic to wonder what Hunter was up to? Between Laney and Sterling, it sounded like Lars had been tormenting the Wizard. Why? Was he a kid in need of parental guidance or had Hunter been the driving force behind Lars' treatment of the Wizard? And, could the violence have escalated? If Lars and his friends had thrown rocks and pine cones at the poor old man, what would have stopped them from doing more?

Chapter Eight

We finished staining the fence by late afternoon. The result was transformative. Scoops was starting to look warm and inviting with the red-hued stain, Andy's fresh coat of paint, our banner, and the newly stained fence. We had made great progress. But there was still plenty of work ahead of us. For one, getting rid of the massive pile of ivy and weeds sitting in the middle of the garden.

If things progressed at this rate we'd be ready to open sooner than expected. Of course, there was still the matter of getting our permits approved by the city, finalizing a menu, and doing a bunch of test runs with our new equipment. To generate buzz, we had decided that we would give away free coffee and custards to anyone passing by during the renovation process. There was no point in wasting product. Plus a little free advertising never hurt.

"Not bad, boss," Andy said, standing back to appraise our work. "It's starting to look like Torte, only different."

I chuckled. "That's what we were going for, right?"

"Absolutely." His jeans and hands were splotched with red-and-teal paint. "Anything else we should do before we call it a day?"

"No. Thanks for your help today, with everything."

"Cool. I'll take this stuff back to Torte." Andy picked up a box with a coffee carafe and extra cups and plates.

"Thanks. Tell everyone I'll be by later this evening to order supplies for this location and to check in."

Andy turned to Sterling. "You coming, man?"

Sterling tucked his longboard under his arm. "Nah, I think I'm going to skate over to the high school and meet a friend."

"Okay. See you guys tomorrow." Andy left with a wave.

"Are you going to check out the townhouses?" I asked Sterling.

"Yeah, but do you want a hand with that other project before I go?" He motioned to the dumpster across the street.

I shot a look at the corner of the bike shop. Two police cars were parked on the street. Caution tape was stretched from Addie's yoga studio to the alleyway. As tempting as it sounded to take a peek at what Hunter had thrown in the trash, the police were on the case and I was probably overreacting. "No, go ahead."

"You sure?" He stacked empty buckets of the stain next to the kitchen.

"Yes, don't tempt me." I plunged our brushes into a bucket of paint thinner.

"Okay. If you're sure." Sterling hesitated. "I'll swing by the skate park after I walk through the condos and ask around about the Wizard."

"Good idea, and take it easy tonight. I know it's been horrible, and I know that you've been through loss before, but this is different, so please let me know if you need to talk more, okay?"

Sterling gave me a one-finger salute and skated away.

I dug through my bags and found my notebook. Then I sat at one of two booths built into the side of the fence and began making a list of everything we needed to outfit the new outdoor kitchen. That included coffee cups, glassware for milkshakes and affagatos, small plates and bowls, serving spoons, a small espresso machine, industrial blenders, and more. The list grew rapidly as I walked myself through a typical day at Scoops. We intended to open at the noon hour and stay open until dusk—potentially later during the height of summer. Our small menu would focus on our concretes, but we needed to prepare for grab-and-go items like sandwiches and pasta salads. That meant adding Earth-friendly recycled boxes to my list.

I had started on a second page when I heard a familiar voice calling my name, "Juliet, darling!"

I looked up to see Lance standing at the gate. He wore a pair of slim gray slacks, a matching jacket, and a skinny pale pink tie. "Well, don't be rude. Are you going to invite me in?"

"Come in, please, please." I swept my hands in front of me.

"What kind of greeting is that, for yours truly?" He

strolled over to the booth. His lanky frame moved with an elegant confidence. He smoothed a stray strand of his dark hair and blew me air kisses before sitting across from me.

"I wasn't aware I had to roll out the red carpet."

He narrowed his eyes. "A red carpet is always a good idea. Always."

"Noted." I pretended to make a note.

Lance leaned back and surveyed the garden. "So the rumors are true. I'm last to know. Painful, darling. Painful."

"You're not the last to know. The space came up for lease and I jumped on it."

"Smart move." He gave me a nod of approval. "This is taking shape nicely. Color me impressed. It's so quaint and quite charming, I must say."

If Lance wasn't a dear friend, I might have thought he was being condescending, but I knew he was sincere.

"Thanks." I smiled. "It's nuts that I'm doing this, but I agree that it's starting to feel like Torte."

"You've never been one to shy away from a challenge, Juliet. Why start now?"

I wanted to mention the fact that Carlos was here to give our relationship one last shot, but decided otherwise.

"Enough of the small talk, darling. Let's cut to the chase. I think you know why I'm here." He raised one eyebrow.

"To give me a pep talk?" I asked hopefully.

He fumed. "You are the last person I know in need of a pep talk. No, my dearest. To discuss our latest case."

"Case?" I wrinkled my brow.

"The murder." He directed a bony finger over his shoulder to the railroad tracks.

"How did you hear?" News spread fast in Ashland.

"Please." He rolled his eyes. Then he scooted forward and pressed his fingertips together. "Dish. Tell me *everything* you know."

I gave him a brief recap of the morning and then told him about my conversation with Laney Lee and the Professor.

"There must be more. I can tell by the way you're sucking in those glorious cheekbones that you're holding something back." He tilted his head to one side.

"Well, there is one thing, but you have to promise that if I tell you this, you'll keep your derrière on the bench."

"Me? Darling, you know that I'm a vault. Whatever you tell me will never leave these lips." He threw a hand over his mouth with a flourish.

"I'm not worried about you blabbing. I'm worried that you'll race out of here and try to find the item I'm going to tell you about, and you cannot do that. Understood?"

"Oh ye of little faith. Understood." He clapped twice. "Out with it!"

I sighed. Then I proceeded to tell him about seeing Hunter sneaking around the dumpster and disposing of something. "The police already searched the dumpster. I can't help but wonder if Hunter waited until after they were done to dispose of whatever he threw away."

Lance gasped. "Darling, you know what this means, don't you?"

I was afraid to ask.

"It means that we must investigate." He cracked his knuckles. "It's obviously too light at the moment, but tonight we will rendezvous here and figure out what nefarious acts that psycho—sorry, slip of the tongue—Cyclepath is up to."

I hesitated. "I don't know. What about Carlos? We're supposed to have dinner later."

"What about him? Bring him along if you want. He's easy on the eyes and that accent, swoon." Lance fanned his face.

"If we do this, and I'm not saying that I am . . ." I paused and waited for a group of yoga students to pass by.

"Uh-huh." Lance mocked me.

"As I was saying, if I participate in sleuthing through the trash with you, I'm not looping Carlos into this."

"Fine. Suit yourself. Leave the dreamy Spanish specimen at home. I'll meet you at my office at sunset. Wear black. All black."

"Lance, you are incorrigible."

"And that's why you love me, darling. You know you want to go dumpster diving. I'm simply your accessory to crime." He stood. "Now that it's settled, let's sync our watches. See you tonight. Ta-ta!"

He danced away before I could protest.

The truth was that he was right. I did want to rifle through the trash to find out what Hunter had tossed out. Was the Wizard's murder yet another sign that I didn't have space for Carlos in Ashland? I had been telling myself that I was worried that Carlos wasn't right for our small town, but the more I pondered it, to the more I wondered if the problem was me. Carlos likely wouldn't approve of Lance and me sneaking around at sunset, digging through dumpsters. Then again, why would he?

Chapter Nine

I didn't stay long after Lance left. I returned to Torte to find Marty and Bethany closing up the bakeshop for the evening. Everyone else had gone home.

"How was the day?" I asked Marty, who was folding a set of dish towels.

"Good. We had a nice steady crowd, but it was manageable. Word has already gotten out about your day. I'm so sorry to hear what happened."

"About the murder?" I asked without thinking.

Marty's eyes widened. "Murder? I hadn't heard it was murder."

"Technically, I don't know that it's official, but the Professor is convinced it wasn't an accident."

Bethany wiped down the marble countertop at our decorating station. "Yeah, every time I went upstairs to refill the pastry case, Sequoia and Rosa were fielding questions about the Wizard. They were fine because they didn't know anything, but it was definitely the topic of the afternoon. It's so sad. I can't believe he's dead. He was such a sweet man. He would hand me a heart balloon anytime I rode by him in Railroad Park."

"I know. It's heartbreaking."

Marty finished stacking the towels. "Andy mentioned that you saw it happen. That must have been terrible."

"It was disturbing." The thought of lifting the Wizard's lifeless body from the tracks made my throat swell.

"Sorry to bring it up." Marty must have noticed the shift in my face. "We're here for you if you need to talk. I'll tell Sterling and Andy the same tomorrow."

"Thanks." I gave him a genuine smile. "I know they'll appreciate that."

Bethany snapped the lid shut on a tub of buttercream. "We told Andy earlier that Team Torte is ready to rally."

I chuckled. "You guys are the best. We're all fine, I promise. It was a shock and I know it's something that is going to stick with us, but I have a feeling getting back to a normal routine is going to be the most helpful."

They finished prepping the kitchen so it was ready for another marathon day of baking tomorrow. Once they were done, I followed them to the basement door and locked it behind them.

A sense of calm washed over me, knowing that I had the kitchen to myself. I knew what I had to do—bake.

Carlos and I had planned to meet at Torte in about an hour. He closed the tasting room at Uva at five, but then liked to wander through the vines and check on their progress. Grapevines reconnect in the spring. The swelling buds surge to life after a winter of dormancy. Carlos had been completely captivated by the vine's transformation, giving me daily progress updates.

I decided to make dinner while I waited for him. The morning's event had left me with a hankering for comfort food, so I opted to make chicken curry pasties. The savory meat-filled pies were one of Carlos's favorites.

I started by making a buttery pastry crust. I grated cold butter into a large glass bowl, then added hot milk, flour, and a touch of salt. I worked the dough by hand. There was nothing as cathartic as kneading dough. The pastry formed into a smooth round ball. I covered it with a dish towel and started on the filling.

I went to the walk-in fridge and returned with an armful of chicken breasts, onions, cilantro, and peppers. I lit one of the burners on the gas stove and added a healthy glug of olive oil to a cast-iron skillet. Then I finely chopped the onion and cilantro stalks, saving the leaves for later. Tossing them into the skillet sent an aromatic fragrance through the kitchen. I breathed it in as I blanched them and incorporated chopped peppers. After chopping the chicken, I browned it with the veggies and stirred in coconut milk, curry paste, and chicken stock. I let the mixture simmer on low and returned to my pastry dough.

One of my tricks when it came to making pasties was to roll the crust out in cornmeal instead of flour. It would give the hand pies a lovely crunchy exterior, which should blend seamlessly with the butter pastry. I sprinkled cornmeal on a cutting board and rolled the dough into a large circle. Then I used a six-inch round biscuit cutter to make the individual pies.

Once the filling had thickened I tossed in sliced almonds, cilantro leaves, and a splash of cream. I scooped a heaping cupful of curry in the center of the first circle, then I folded the edges together to make a half-moon. I crimped them with my fingers, brushed the top with an egg wash, and set it on a parchment-lined baking sheet. I repeated the process until I'd made a dozen curry pasties.

The oven had come up to temp, so I slid the baking tray inside and set a timer for thirty minutes. While the pasties baked, I tossed together a simple green salad with toasted almonds, shredded carrots, and shallots, with a cilantro dressing.

My thoughts veered back to the Wizard. Who was he? If I could figure out more about him—his name, his past—maybe I'd be able to make sense of his death.

The other thing that kept bugging me was what Hunter had tossed in the garbage. What could it be? Hopefully, he wasn't planning on returning to the dumpster to retrieve whatever he'd thrown away before Lance and I had a chance to check it out later tonight.

Could Laney know more about the Wizard then she was letting on? Her reaction had been so visceral. And what about Addie? She had been so cold and callous when I had asked her for help this morning. Dean had been equally apathetic. Granted, if the Wizard had been stealing from him, especially if he'd been giving away his product, he had a reason to be frustrated. But that still didn't dismiss his behavior. Lastly there was Sky. Where had he disappeared to? He and the Wizard seemed to be connected, but could Sky have killed him and taken off?

Why would anyone want to kill a homeless man?

And what about Lars? Images of Hunter's son flashed through my mind. Could he and his group of skater friends have taken their taunting too far?

I shuddered at the thought.

There had to be something more at play. Could the Wizard have seen something that put him in danger? Or was his outward appearance a sham? Maybe he'd been involved with shady things going down on the railroad tracks.

Ashland was a very safe place to live, aside from occasional cougar sightings in Lithia Park and run-ins with black bears scavenging through neighborhood trash cans. The Railroad District, however, had been notorious for minor criminal activity—petty theft and graffiti. Thomas had told me the police station received more calls to break up fights in the Railroad District than anywhere else in Ashland.

The sound of the basement door unlocking brought me into the moment. "Julieta, what smells so wonderful?" Carlos came inside. The sight of his dark hair, bronzed skin, and dazzling smile still made my knees quiver. He had a bottle of wine tucked under one arm and a stack of papers under the other.

"Curry pasties. Your favorite." I pointed to the oven.

Carlos shifted the bottle of wine into one hand so he could hang his vest on the coatrack near the door.

"How was Uva?" I flipped the oven light on to check the pasties. They were a pale yellow. A few more minutes and they should turn golden brown.

He set the paperwork on the counter then walked straight to a drawer near the pantry and retrieved a bottle opener. It hadn't taken him long to get aquatinted with Torte's kitchen, which was especially impressive given that he spent the majority of his time at the vineyard. I chalked it up to his training as a professional chef. We tend to geek out over kitchens. Organization is critical in a commercial kitchen. Over the years Carlos and I had learned many of the same tricks: never storing food in cabinets that get hot, like above the stove; or having a safe place for sharp objects, like a knife dock or a magnetic strip; or reserving different cutting boards for sweets and savories.

In culinary school I had learned the term "mise en place," meaning everything in its place. That motto rang out in every kitchen I'd ever worked in, especially at Torte. Having a place for everything meant that we could bake more efficiently, effortlessly, and enjoyably.

Carlos uncorked the deep burgundy Cab Franc and poured us two glasses. There was an unfamiliar strain on his face. Carlos tended to sway upbeat. His way of dealing with the stress of managing a massive kitchen on the ship was to pull pranks on his staff and crack jokes.

"Is everything okay?" I asked when he handed me a glass and gave me a long, lingering kiss.

"Si, it was a long day. Nothing eventful." He released me.

"Are you sure? Usually you love spending long days at Uva." Or was I mistaken? Had Carlos been putting on an act? What if I was reading the situation wrong? Was he really miserable?

"It's true, mi querida, I do love the vineyard. It is so beautiful now. Every day the vines they teach me something new. It is like watching Mother Nature's miracle in action. The budding grapes, the deepening color of the leaves, and the views of the valley feed my soul. This morning as I was walking through the vines I saw a bobcat, a hawk, and a fox. It is so surprising. It is like nothing I ever experienced on the ship."

This sounded more like Carlos.

My timer dinged. He waited for me to remove the pasties from the oven. As expected, the cornmeal crust had crisped into an inviting butterscotch yellow. I slid them off the baking tray and onto cooling racks. "Why was today long, then?"

Carlos swirled the wine in his glass, holding it above his head to catch the light. He didn't answer right away. "It is nothing. I do not want to burden you."

"What?"

He tilted the glass and made a circular motion with his hand. "Richard Lord came by this afternoon. He is not happy about how things are working at the vineyard and is threatening to sue us."

I started to respond, but Carlos put a finger to lips. "Shhhh. It is okay. I will fix it. I do not want you to worry about this, Julieta. You have much going on with Torte and the new shop, and the staff. Uva was my decision. Not yours. I must fix this, okay?"

"Carlos, you don't understand what Richard can be like. I don't know that this is a battle we want to fight."

He closed his eyes and sipped the wine. Once a chef, always a chef. Despite the topic of a potential lawsuit, he took a moment to savor the essence of the wine. "Si, I understand, but it is not for you to worry. I will take care of this."

I wanted to say more, but his eyes were firm with resolve. If it were up to me, I would rather give up our shares in Uva than engage in a legal fight with Richard. It probably wasn't the wisest idea from a business perspective, but I didn't want to do anything that would threaten the life I had carved out here. Richard could easily make things very difficult for me. He was also the one person in Ashland who was a direct threat to finding a space for Carlos.

Carlos set his wineglass on the counter and rubbed my shoulders. "Let's sit and eat and talk of other things."

He plated the salad and pasties while I brought our wineglasses and the bottle out to the small seating area adjacent to the kitchen. On my way I noticed that the stack of papers he'd brought with him had the *Amour of the Seas* seal on the top.

"What's this?" I asked.

Carlos swooped over and ushered me into the seating area. "Nothing. I want to know about the new space. How did it go today?"

I wanted to know what the *Amour of the Seas* had sent him. Or maybe I didn't. I could make an educated guess that what was in the folder was a new contract. Was Carlos negotiating a new deal?

I dropped it, and told him about our progress as I bit into the tender pasty. The crust was soft and buttery and the curry filling hit all the right notes of spices mingled with the creamy coconut.

"This is wonderful." Carlos devoured his pasty. "I must make these . . ." he trailed off.

We both knew what words he had left unfinished. He was about to say "on the ship."

I concentrated on my wineglass, not wanting to make eye contact. Not wanting the words to be true.

"I mean, you must teach me how to make these." He took another pasty.

It wasn't until we had finished dinner that I brought up the subject of the Wizard's murder.

"Why did you not tell me this right away?" Carlos sounded hurt.

"Richard Lord." I grimaced.

Carlos reached for my hand. His touch ignited a tingling sensation through my body. "I am so sorry you had to go through that. Doug and Thomas, they must be on the case, si?"

"Yeah, we talked to them earlier." I left out details about my conversation with Lance, and gave Carlos a very condensed version of the day's events.

"You must be tired," he said with concern when I finished. "We should go home. You can take a bath. I will make you some tea."

"Thanks, that sounds wonderful, but I promised Lance I would swing by the theater for a few minutes." I felt terrible lying to Carlos.

His phone buzzed. Carlos reached into the pocket of his jeans. He stared at the screen but didn't answer it. Instead he silenced the call. "You go with Lance. I will clean up, and then I must return this call. I will meet you at home. I would like to stretch my legs. It is a luxury to walk so much here. Seeing the shops and the mountains makes my heart happy."

I protested.

"No, go. I will finish here."

If I waited any longer I would lose my resolve, so I left Carlos with a kiss and walked through the plaza to the Shakespeare stairs that led up to the OSF complex.

Lance was waiting for me outside the Bowmer

Theater. He was dressed in a black trench coat and matching black cap.

"Where did you come up with that outfit?" I asked.

"Costume department, darling." A bag lay at his feet. He opened it and handed me a matching trench coat and hat.

"Go ahead, put it on."

I didn't bother trying to protest. "You realize that we stand out more in these costumes, right?"

Lance waved me off. "We must look the part." He offered me his arm. "Shall we?"

What was I getting myself into?

Chapter Ten

The warm afternoon had given way to dusk. Lance and I walked down Pioneer Street toward the Railroad District, drinking in the sunset. Unicorn-colored clouds in blushing pinks, hazy blues, and the palest of purples erupted from the bluffs.

A handful of locals made their way to restaurants. A three-piece band strummed upbeat melodies on the patio of the Water Street Bar where people were huddled around outdoor fire pits.

"Stay in the shadows, Juliet." Lance pushed me to keep me from walking beneath a streetlamp.

"Lance, this is ridiculous." I slowed. "We're blocks away from Cyclepath."

"Shhhh. Trust me. We have to be discrete." He raised a finger and placed it to his lips. "What did you tell that dreamy husband you were up to tonight?" Lance asked, changing the subject. "I want to make sure that we keep our stories straight. Just in case."

I ribbed him with my elbow. "Hey, you're the one who got me into this. Now you have me telling white lies to Carlos."

"Ha! I barely had to twist your arm. Admit it. You are equally as invested, if not more so, in sleuthing out who killed the poor, innocent Wizard."

There was no way I was giving him the satisfaction of agreeing with him, so I changed the subject. "Carlos told me that Richard Lord stopped by Uva this afternoon. Apparently, he's threatening to sue us."

Lance kept his head up and alert. "As if. Richard Lord is full of hot air. Let him blow off some steam. He'll never go through with it."

"I don't know, Lance. Carlos looked worried. And Carlos isn't a worrier by nature." We passed by a group of high school students wearing red-and-white Grizzly gear on their way to a basketball game.

"Don't let Richard get under your skin. That's what he wants. He thrives on lording his self-imposed power around town. Ignore him and he'll go away."

I wasn't so sure. Richard had been upset about Lance and me owning shares of Uva since the beginning. He had been trying to undermine Torte, steal our ideas, recipes, and customers for as long as I'd been home— and even before then. I didn't trust him. He wasn't above using less-than-ethical tactics to get what he wanted. Case in point, he had tried to sign a deal with Mom that would have ultimately given him total control over Torte. If I hadn't returned home when I did, Torte might not belong to our family.

We were less than a block away from Cyclepath when Lance threw out an arm and whispered. "Stop."

I froze. "What?"

He squinted and nudged me next to the side of a

brick building that was home to one of Ashland's old-est hotels. "Look, I think someone has beaten us to the punch." Lance pointed toward Cyclepath at the opposite end of the block.

"I can't tell." Darkness had crept in. A sprinkling of stars danced overhead.

He popped the collar on his trench coat and yanked me forward. "Let's cross the street and see if we can get closer."

We crept onward.

Lance came to a halt at the organic pet shop. "This is close enough," he whispered. "Look."

I followed his finger, which was pointing at the open dumpster next to Cyclepath. A figure was bent over the large garbage bin. We watched in silence as the figure tossed trash on the ground. It was too dark to see who it was. Like us the figure was dressed in dark clothing, and he was halfway inside the dumpster.

I wrapped my arms around my body—not just because the sinking sun had dropped the temperature, but because I must have been right about Hunter. If someone else was digging through the dumpster, there must be something inside worth finding.

"Should we confront them?" I asked scooting closer to Lance.

Lance's spine was rigid. "No. Not wise. What if it's the killer? They could have a weapon."

"Good point." A chill came over me. I rubbed my hands together.

"We wait. Over there." He tugged me behind a mature Japanese maple tree on the median. The scent of apricots and freesia hit my nose. It couldn't be from the blooming maple tree. The sweet fragrance must have been wafting from another plant nearby.

I looked around us. The Railroad District was a ghost town. Cyclepath was dark, as was the lawyer's office next door, the hardware store, the Grange, and Namaste. There was no sign of police activity either. The caution tape had been removed and the police cars were gone.

The person continued to rifle through the trash, throwing garbage everywhere. They were obviously looking for something.

We waited for what felt like an eternity, although it was probably more like a matter of minutes. A group of bikers zoomed around the back alley. Their bright white helmet lights cut through the darkness.

The dumpster lid slammed shut with a loud thud, making me jump.

Lance threw his hand over my mouth to silence me.

The hooded figure who'd been going through the dumpster booked it in the other direction.

Meanwhile the bikers laughed and talked as they breezed by us.

"Let's go." I started to cross the street once the bikers were out of sight, but Lance grabbed my arm. "Give it a minute. Let's make sure whoever was sifting through the trash is really gone."

He wasn't usually this reserved. It was as if our roles had swapped.

We waited another few minutes before venturing across the street. Once we were close to the dumpster,

Lance covered his nose with the back of his hand. "The smell is horrific."

I coughed. It was true. The unpleasant scent of rotting garbage hit my nostrils. Quite the opposite of the sweet-smelling spring blooms we'd been hiding by.

"Do you see the black trash bag?" Lance used the flashlight on his phone to illuminate the mess on the ground.

There were three black trash bags scattered on the street. The bikers must have scared our criminal away. "Yeah, but where to start? Do we go through each of them?"

Lance reached into his coat pocket and removed two sets of disposable rubber gloves. "I believe we're going to have to get dirty."

The thought of opening the smelly bags made me want to gag, but we'd come this far. I stretched a pair of gloves over my hands. Lance did the same.

"Ladies first, darling. I wouldn't want to be ungentlemanly."

"Thanks. So thoughtful."

Lance held the light so I could untie the first trash bag. It was filled with nothing more than food scraps. The next held more of the same.

"This is so gross." I tried to push the smell from my nose by fanning my hands. That just made it worse.

"Chin up."

"Easy for you to say. You're holding the light. You're not reaching into these slimy bags." My hands felt clumsy as I worked my way through the garbage. A quivering feeling filled my stomach. What if whoever had been going through the trash was the killer? What if they came back?

"Trust me, the smell is just as overpowering from my vantage point." He made a face to prove his point.

I opened the last bag and let out a gasp.

"Lance, look!" I pulled a bike wrench out of the bag. It left a residue on my gloves. "Hold up the light. Is that blood?"

He positioned his phone so that we could see the tips of my gloved fingers. There was something dark and thick on them.

Lance cleared his throat. He blinked twice. "I think that may be, my dear. It just may be."

"I think this is the wrench I saw Hunter with when he threatened the Wizard. Do you think this could be the murder weapon? We have to call Thomas."

Shockingly Lance agreed. He took away my light and made the call. "Good evening, deputy detective, it's yours truly and I'm with my partner in crime. We have uncovered some startling evidence that I'm sure you'll want to see right away."

I could tell from Lance's impatient sneer that Thomas must be asking what prompted us to go dumpster diving. "That isn't the point, detective. Don't question our motives. We have been nothing if not diligent in our search."

Lance threw his hands up in an "I give up" gesture. "Yes, we have actual evidence. Come see for yourself. We'll be waiting."

He hung up the phone, drew in a breath, and released it before speaking again. "That man can be so exasperating. Asking about our motives rather than thanking us for going above and beyond our civic duty."

I stifled a grin. Before I could reply, a woman's voice broke the silence.

"Hey! Who's there! Get out of the garbage!"

Lance and I turned to see Addie standing on the front porch of her yoga studio. She held a flashlight in one hand.

I shielded my eyes from the beam of light. "It's Jules."

"Jules? What are you doing?" She pointed the light at her feet and took the stairs two at a time.

"Don't say anything," Lance cautioned.

I hid the wrench behind my back.

"What is that smell?" Addie wrinkled her nose. She opened and closed her mouth as if trying to find the right words. "Were you going through the garbage?"

"Us?" Lance tapped his chest. "Never. Juliet was asking my professional opinion on evening lighting options." He swept his hand against the star-steeped sky. "As I was saying darling, what do you think of twin floodlights on each corner? That should give the garden a dramatic effect, and you absolutely must backlight the water feature."

Addie tipped her head from one side to the other, weighing Lance's words. Her face tightened. "Why is there trash everywhere?"

"I don't know. Kids maybe?" I lied. "Addie, have you met Lance? OSF's artistic director?"

Lance broadened his chest. He started to extend a hand, but must have remembered his gloves because he quickly looped his arms behind his back. "Delighted.

Juliet tells me you own the charming yoga studio, Namaste. Is that correct?"

Addie's eyebrows drew together. "Are you wearing gloves?"

"Guilty as charged." Lance pressed his gloved hands together. "Hydrating hand mask. Working in the theater is so taxing on one's hands. As a director I would be nothing without these beauties."

There was no way Addie was going to buy that story. Thomas and Detective Kerry would be here any minute. I wondered if we should tell her the truth, but I wasn't convinced that she was totally innocent in the Wizard's death, given her outward distain.

Lance had other plans. He swept his hand across the sky as if directing a scene. "I would absolutely love your input. What if we add a touch of lighting on this side of the garden? A few mood lights. A spot. Perhaps something soft and golden to illuminate your studio."

"Sure. Sure." Addie sounded rushed.

In the distance a man's voice called for Addie. "Hey, Addie! Are you coming?"

Addie blew Lance off. "Sure, whatever you think. I have to go." With that she raced away, running toward the railroad tracks and vanished in the darkness.

"What was that?" I asked Lance. "A *hand mask*?"

"Improvisation, darling. Improvisation." He gave me a playful grin. "She seems skittish. Which is odd if you ask me. I thought that yoga instructors were supposed to be the model of calm."

It was a good thing that Addie had run off because Thomas and Detective Kerry arrived in their SUV with red-and-blue lights blazing a few minutes later.

"Do I even want to know what you two are going to say?" Thomas asked with a frown as he got out of the vehicle. He removed a heavy-duty flashlight from his uniform belt.

Kerry wore a thick blue police jacket over her pantsuit. Her red hair was twisted in a tight bun.

"It's probably better that we leave it at mere happenstance that Juliet and I stumbled upon what may be critical evidence in your case." Lance shared a gleeful look with me. "Our evening walk took us by this dumpster and seeing that there was garbage strewn about we took it upon ourselves—as any good law-abiding citizen would—to do our civic duty and tidy up."

"'Law-abiding citizen,' huh? Where?" Detective Kerry looked around us.

Lance's eyes glittered with impish delight. "Standing right here. Reporting what could become late-breaking evidence in your murder case, of course. I'll accept your deepest thanks after you've had a chance to examine our discovery." He gave her a grand sweeping bow.

She threw her head back and laughed.

If anyone could crack her stony exterior, it was Lance.

"Let's have it," Thomas said, tugging on a pair of blue plastic gloves.

I pulled the wrench from behind my back and handed it to him.

"A wrench?" Thomas gave the wrench a flat glaze.

"Yeah, do you think that's blood?" I showed them the tip of my gloves.

Detective Kerry leaned in for a closer look, then held out an evidence bag for Thomas. Neither of them responded.

"Hunter tossed something in here earlier. It was after your team finished searching this area. That can't be a coincidence, can it?" I tried to explain what I had seen. "Do you think this is what he was trying to get rid of? Maybe he hit the Wizard with the wrench and the Wizard staggered over to the tracks?"

"We'll have to examine it for prints." Thomas said. "At least you two had the wherewithal to put on gloves."

Kerry made a scolding sound under her breath.

"Not that we condone this kind of behavior." Thomas pursed his lips. "You realize we could arrest you for meddling in an official police investigation."

Lance laid on his most somber tone. "But of course. That's why we contacted you immediately. We didn't want a poor, innocent bystander to happen upon this mess and accidently destroy critical evidence."

I took off the rubber gloves. They were making my hands sweaty and my fingers itch.

"Thanks for being such outstanding citizens," Thomas said with sarcasm. "We'll take it from here."

"That's our cue, darling. Shall we finish our evening meandering?" Lance offered me his arm. "Keep up the stellar work, detectives."

We headed for the nearby bike path. Moonlight cast an eerie glow on the empty pathway.

"Well done, Juliet," Lance said once we were out of earshot. "I'm sure they bought our story."

"Yeah, right. They definitely did not believe a single word that came out of your mouth."

"I beg to differ." Lance scooted us to the side of the path as a biker wearing a black baseball cap approached. "They're none the wiser."

The biker swerved on the path, zigzagging from side to side.

Was the biker drunk?

Lance pushed me out of the way at the last minute into a patch of wild blackberry vines wrapped along a chain-link fence. Pain shot up my left arm.

The biker sped by so fast that I couldn't even see the spokes on the bike's tires. I could hear the biker's heavy panting and feel a gust of wind from the wake.

"Hey, stop!" Lance tried to flag the biker down.

The biker didn't stop. They pedaled faster.

I got to my feet. Thank goodness for the trench coat, I thought, yanking sharp blackberry vines from my arm.

We both stared down the path. The biker was almost to the intersection of the alleyway behind Cyclepath. I couldn't be sure, but the biker's build and height made me wonder if it was Sky. I squinted to try and get a better look, but the bike vanished into the darkness.

Chapter Eleven

I had barely recovered from the near miss with the first bike, when another one sped toward us. The biker's single bright light created a halo on the path.

"Stop!" Lance called, waving his arms in the air.

This time the biker slowed their pace. They came to a halt two feet from us.

I was shocked to see it was Dean, our new milk vendor.

"Dean?" I could hear the questioning surprise in my voice.

"Oh, hey. Yeah, is that you Jules?" He rested one foot on the ground. I noticed that his delivery cart wasn't attached to his bike tonight. His helmet light was so bright it blinded my eyes. Earlier he hadn't worn a helmet.

I threw my hand over my forehead to shield the light.

"Sorry." Dean got off his bike and adjusted his helmet light so it wasn't directly in our faces. His chest heaved from exertion. He knelt over and grabbed his knees.

"Are you okay?" I asked.

Dean held up a finger. "Give me a sec. I—uh." He

sucked in air through his nose. "Just have to catch my breath."

"Were you following that other bike?" Lance voiced what I had been thinking.

"What?" Dean forced the zipper of his reflective yellow jacket up and down. "What bike? I was finishing the last of my deliveries, and had some product that didn't sell. I came down this way to give it away and am heading for my truck. Addie lets me park it behind the studio."

He was finishing deliveries—without his cart? At this hour? That didn't make sense, but I wasn't going to accuse him of lying.

"I should keep moving. Have to get home to feed the cows. You know what they say: happy cows, happy customers." With that, he stretched a leg over his bike, clamped his foot on the pedal, and rode off.

"It's an odd hour for milk deliveries, isn't it?" Lance noted as we took the pathway through Railroad Park and up to A Street.

"Exactly. We get our milk delivery first thing in the morning. I've never heard of an evening delivery, and did you notice that his cart wasn't attached to his bike? He had to be lying. What if he was following after the biker who almost ran us over?" If my theory was correct and the first biker had been Sky, what could Dean want from him? Could it be connected to the Wizard's murder or to Sky's earlier accident?

"That's the spirit." Lance egged me on. "The question is why. Why would Dean be in the Railroad District at this late hour? I'm not a farming expert, but I have to image that his cows should already be fed and put to bed by now." He stopped and chuckled. "Sorry for the rhythm. Sometimes I can't help myself."

"Ha!" I gave him a mock laugh. I didn't want to jump to conclusions. Dean could have honestly been giving away unsold product, but it was strange that he didn't have his cart and was out at this late hour.

Lance fanned his face. "Whew. My, what an aroma there is on this moon-drenched evening. Let's play one of my favorite games. Skunk or pot?"

"Yeah. Dean smelled like pot earlier. Apparently his farm is next door to a hemp field." An undeniable odor hung in the air. In recent years, southern Oregon's enviable growing climate had been sought out by the burgeoning hemp and marijuana industries. There had been much discussion amongst the community on the pros and cons of farmland being bought up by out-of-state investors. One of the ongoing complaints was about the stench the fields generated. Recently a local elementary school neighboring a hemp field had to shut down because the fumes were making students and teachers sick.

"Do you think Dean could be involved? Admittedly, I haven't spent much time around here, but it's quite a remarkable coincidence that Dean and Sky—if that was Sky—would both be riding on the path at this time of night isn't it?" I didn't wait for him to answer. "Something feels really off."

"Agreed. But what we're missing is a connection." Lance tapped his index finger on his lips. "What was Dean's connection to the Wizard?"

"I'm not sure. I know they had a big argument over spilled milk—literally. Dean accused the Wizard of stealing his milk. He found a bunch of broken bottles

scattered along the tracks and accused the Wizard and
Sky of stealing from him. I can't imagine that stealing
a few bottles of milk would be motive for Dean to kill
him."

"Unlikely." Lance agreed.

We made it back to the plaza in less than ten minutes. Lance walked me to the front of Torte, where a soft
overnight light barely illuminated the inside of the cozy
bakeshop. Next door, empty aluminum tins in front of
A Rose by Any Other Name awaited a new day to be
filled with beautiful blooms. Music pulsed at Puck's
Pub, and a handful of teenagers huddled on the brick
benches in the center of the plaza.

I was about to call it a night when a tall, attractive
man approached us. His bald ebony head reflected the
glow of the streetlamp. He wore Southern Oregon Raid-
ers gear from head to toe.

"Lance, how's it going?" He greeted Lance with a
one-armed hug.

"Arlo, nice to see you." Lance's voice sounded jittery.
"Fancy meeting you here."

Was it my imagination or was the ever-composed
Lance flustered?

"I don't think we've met." Arlo extended a hand to
me. "Arlo. I'm the interim managing director at OSF and
part-time assistant softball coach at SOU."

"Great to meet you." I returned his handshake, which
was firm and confident. "Welcome to Ashland."

"Thanks. It's a charmer." His eyes drifted above us
to the Black Sheep, a British-style pub with giant ornate
oval windows and the Union Jack flying from the top of
the roof. "I've never lived anywhere quite as charming

and where I've felt welcomed from day one. I think I had five pies waiting for me on my front porch before I had even unpacked a single box."

"That's Ashland," I said with a laugh. "Interim director. Does that mean your stay will be temporary?"

Arlo looked to Lance, who was fiddling with the top button on his trench coat. "For now. This is what I do. I go into theaters in transition and help with structural changes. As I'm sure you know, you have one of the best and most innovative artistic directors in the world, with Lance."

Lance's cheeks flamed with color. I'd never known him to blush at a compliment.

"My role will be to run the search for a permanent managing director, grow the board, and basically ensure that Lance is free to fully realize the grand visions he has not only for the company and patrons but for the community at large."

"That sounds like a big role."

Lance still hadn't spoken.

"True, but it's one that I'm excited about. The passion this community has for the arts is stunning. That's one huge hurdle we won't have to face. Often times, my first order of business is working on community buy-in, but that's not going to the case here." Arlo gave Lance a knowing smile. "Thanks in large part to this guy."

"Uh—ah," Lance sputtered to find the right words. "You're too kind."

Arlo had correctly assessed the festival's role. Ashland and OSF were synonymous. Without the theater, Ashland would be a pretty little town tucked in the Siskiyou Mountains with beautiful vistas and picture-perfect hiking trails. The festival was the lifeblood of Ashland's economy. And without that revenue, the thriving business community, abundant shops, restaurants, and bed and breakfasts would take a big hit if we lost thousands upon thousands of returning theatergoers each year.

"How do you and Lance know each other?" Arlo sounded genuinely interested. "And are you twinning?" He noted our matching trench coats.

"I run Torte." I pointed to the bakeshop's red-and-teal awning behind us. "Lance and I have been friends for years now."

"Oh, Torte!" Arlo gave himself a playful smack on the forehead. "I should have made the connection. I've heard nothing but good things about your baking. Lance raves about you and your pastries. What do you call her, Lance? Your pastry muse?"

"Juliet is my pastry muse." Lance tapped my chin. "But, don't you agree that with these cheekbones she should grace the stage?"

Arlo leaned his head back and let out a deep laugh. "Given that death stare she's shooting at you, I'm going to say that's a hard no."

"I think you and I are going to be great friends," I said to Arlo.

"For sure, and I can't wait to stop by to taste these famous pastries." Arlo paused as a group of coaches wearing SOU softball gear rounded the corner. He gave them a wave and then turned his attention back to us. "Hey, a bunch of us are heading to Puck's for beers. Do you guys want to join us? I'd guess there's a great band playing tonight."

I waited for Lance to say something, but he stood frozen.

"Thanks for the offer, but I'll have to take a rain check." I pointed to Torte. "Bakers' hours means that I'm already up past my bedtime."

Arlo grinned. "How about you, Lance? You up for a beer?"

Lance didn't respond.

I nudged his waist.

"Sorry. Sorry. I was—uh—lost in thought for a moment." He stumbled over his words. "Did you say a beer?"

Arlo nodded. "It's me and the other coaches."

"Excellent. A beer sounds absolutely divine." Lance clapped.

Lance hated beer.

He kissed my cheeks. "Good night, darling. We'll reconvene tomorrow?"

"Sounds good. Enjoy the evening." I took off the trench coat and hat and handed them back to Lance, and headed south on Main Street. In the time I had known Lance, he had never mentioned much about his love life or lack thereof. We had commiserated on the fact that we were both hopeless romantics, destined to a life of longing. Had Arlo's arrival changed that? If I didn't know better, I would guess that Lance was smitten.

The happy thought fueled my drive home. When I entered the front door, the house smelled of lavender and roses. Pale pink rose petals lined the stairwell. A note rested on the banister that read FOLLOW THE ROSES.

I climbed the stairs. At the top, the trail of petals led to the bathroom, where Carlos had lit two dozen votive candles. A steaming bath with dainty petals awaited me, along with a hot mug of tea, a book, and a small vase of fresh cut roses.

"Julieta, you're home." Carlos appeared behind me. He wrapped his arms around my waist and kissed the base of my neck.

His lips on my skin sent a rush of emotion to my head. "This is beautiful. Thank you."

"It is nothing. You deserve to be pampered. You need to relax." He reached to the hook on the door and handed me a plush towel. "I do not want to see you for an hour. I will check on you to see if you need anything, but otherwise this time it is for you, mi querida." With that he kissed me, then shut the door behind him.

The fragrant scent of roses mingled with the rosemary bath bomb Carlos had added to the warm water. Before I knew it, I slipped into a deep state of relaxation. When Carlos came to check on me an hour later, the bath had gone cold and I was fighting to keep my eyelids from closing.

"Come, come, let's put you to bed." He roused me from the tub.

I was too tired to protest. The minute my head hit the pillow I was out. I slept through the night, waking to the sound of my alarm sometime after four. Carlos snored lightly. I snuck from beneath the covers and tiptoed to the bathroom to get ready for the day. My morning routine usually involved a quick splash of cold water to the face, followed by plenty of moisturizer and a little lip gloss, then tying my hair into a ponytail. Baking before the sun was up didn't require spending hours applying makeup, and for that I was thankful.

I tugged on a pair of jeans, a long-sleeved T-shirt, and a fleece sweatshirt. I left Carlos sleeping and headed downstairs to the kitchen to brew a pot of strong coffee. Early mornings weren't Carlos's style. On the ship we had had opposite schedules. I would wake early with the purple light, baking in the quiet morning hours. Carlos would start his day sometime after noon and cook until the stars came out. We would often find a way to share a glass of wine or tropical cocktail between shifts and sneak away for a bite. There was no need for him to get up at this ungodly hour, so after I savored a cup of coffee, I left him a note and opted to walk to Torte.

As I stepped outside, a blustery wind made me suck in my breath. I tucked my hands in my pockets. Torte was a mile and a half away from my house. It was a steep descent down Mountain Avenue past sleepy Southern Oregon University and then a straight shot to the plaza. The only light to guide my way came from streetlamps every few hundred feet and the crescent moon overhead. Otherwise, Ashland was deep in slumber.

I passed a family of deer munching on low-lying tree branches. Their ears perked up as I walked by, but they continued eating. The breeze rattled the budding trees that lined Mountain Avenue. The silence made my breathing steady. I thought about the ugly turn of events, and was more determined than ever to find out who had killed the Wizard.

A car drove along Siskiyou Boulevard when I reached the bottom of the hill and turned toward town. It was a newspaper carrier, tossing bundled newspapers on front porches. Even Main Street was deserted at this hour. I used my walk to try to think through motives. If I could figure out why someone wanted the Wizard dead, that would likely lead to figuring out who had killed him.

Hunter certainly seemed capable of violence. As did his son, Lars. If Carlos hadn't intervened, he might have hurt the Wizard. He was first on my list, especially because Laney was so certain he'd had it out for the Wizard. Then there was Sky. He appeared to be the Wizard's steadfast ally, but why had he disappeared? Could he be in danger too, or had I misread their friendship?

What about Addie? She had been insistent that the Wizard was dangerous, and she was reluctant to help when Sky had crashed on his bike. I wasn't sure about her. There was something I didn't trust, but I couldn't pinpoint what. Then there was Dean. What had he been doing on the bike path last night? He definitely hadn't been delivering milk. So why lie to us?

I had gone over a mile. The top of Ashland's only "skyscraper"—Ashland Springs Hotel—came into view. I walked past the three-story library, a record store, and my favorite dress boutique. The plaza was a hub for small family-owned businesses. It was no wonder Carlos had mentioned how much he enjoyed walking through town. The Tudor-inspired storefronts each with unique displays brought a smile to my face. I loved being part of such a creative community. At London Station dozens of colorful umbrellas dangled from the front windows with SPRING SHOWERS BRING MORE FLOWERS written in bright chalk. The wine bar featured a "locals only special" on Monday nights with a tasting flight, pasta and meatballs, Italian chopped salad, and tiramisu for twenty dollars. I'd have to remember that for a date night with Carlos.

Aside from Torte, there were only a couple restaurants that opened early for breakfast. It would be hours before the plaza was buzzing with life, and I liked it that way.

I continued down the hill and made it to the Merry Windsor. The Shakespearean-themed hotel owned by Richard Lord had an impressive façade with wrought-iron balconies, dark half timbers, and arched windows. The fake veneer didn't fool me. I knew that the interior of the hotel was in dire need of updating. Richard liked to boast about being Ashland's most authentically English hotel, but in reality the aging building was crumbling. Richard might outfit his staff in tights and tunics and display fake busts of the Bard throughout, but no amount of cheap Shakespearean reproductions could mask the smell of mildew or distract guests from the green shag carpet and cheap, stale-muffin breakfasts.

I noticed Dean's bike parked in front of the hotel. The cart was attached this morning and packed with pretty glass milk jugs. I couldn't believe that Richard would splurge for organic milk deliveries. His kitchen was much more inclined to shop in bulk at Costco.

As I stepped off the sidewalk to cross the street to Torte, Dean came out from the hotel lobby. "Jules, we meet again!" Two empty milk jugs clinked together when he placed them in a crate.

"You're up bright and early," I noted. "You were doing deliveries last night. I had no idea there was such a demand for milk." I watched his response.

"Duty calls. You know how that goes. I'm up with the cows and on my route before the sun even thinks about making an appearance." He made a checkmark on the clipboard attached to his cart.

"The Merry Windsor is a client?" What was Richard plotting?

Dean shuffled his feet. "I don't know if I'm supposed to say anything, but Richard is branching out into ice cream, did you hear?"

Internally I fumed, but to Dean I plastered on a smile. "No, really?"

"I guess so." He tapped his pencil on his clipboard. "Richard has big plans for the summer season. He's going to have a stand out here on the porch for the spring and summer. They're doing ice cream cones, shakes, that sort of thing."

"Go figure." I glanced at Torte. Leave it to Richard Lord to copy us. This is exactly what I had meant when I told Carlos that Richard couldn't be trusted.

"I'll get some more sample product for you down in the Railroad District a bit later if you want." Dean rearranged a few bottles in the cart.

"I think we're good for the time being. We're in renovation mode."

"Let me know if you change your mind. I'm down that way all the time." He tightened a rubber band around his left ankle and hopped on his bike. "See you around."

I watched him ride away. Dean had to be lying. It made me want to reconsider our partnership. What had he really been doing on the bike path last night?

"Juliet Capshaw," Richard's voice boomed. "Well, well, well. Come to spy, have you?" He folded his beefy arms across his chest.

"Good morning to you too, Richard." I took a step backward.

"Speaking of mornings, I opened a special gift this morning—my eyes. You should try it. You might learn a few things about this town and what's going on." He threw his head back and let out a nasty chuckle. As usual Richard was dressed in an outrageous outfit. His plaid orange-and-green golf pants were one size too small. A snug neon orange V-neck sweater and a checkered cap completed the look.

"You sniffing around for dirt?" He bent his fingers in a motion for me to come closer.

"Nope. On my way to work." I started to walk away.

"Not so fast, young lady!" Richard snapped both his fingers. "I think we have some things to chat about, don't we?"

"Like what?" I rubbed my shoulders to keep warm. "You copying us yet again?"

"*Me*? Copy *you*? Ha!" He removed a cigar from the pocket on his sweater. "What, you're worried about a little friendly competition?"

I didn't bother to respond.

"I'll have you know that I had the idea for Shakescream months ago." He ran the cigar under his nose.

"Shakescream?" I couldn't hide the sarcasm in my tone.

"That's right. Our ice cream stand opens next week. We'll be serving ice cream ode to Coneo and Juliet."

Classic.

I wanted to ask him if he was planning to serve scoops of whatever was on sale in the freezer aisle at the grocery store, but instead, I forced a smile. "Good luck, Richard. It sounds perfect for the Merry Windsor."

"Hey, I'm not done with you." Richard clenched the cigar between his teeth. "Where's your errand boy?"

"I have no idea what you're talking about." That was the truth.

"Your husband. You've got him running around town doing your dirty work."

What?

"Richard, I don't have time for this. I need to get to the bakeshop." I turned and walked away.

He said something under his breath I couldn't hear. Then he yelled, "Do your own dirty work, Capshaw."

I ignored his attempts to engage me in a debate. Instead I squared my shoulders and headed for Torte.

Richard Lord had no shame. He blatantly copied everything we did at Torte. Ice cream? Well, let him try. I knew that at the end of the day he cared more about his bottom line than the quality of his product. If he was going to steal our ideas, it was all the more motivation to make sure our concretes and custards were top notch. But what did he mean about Carlos doing my dirty work?

Chapter Twelve

I pushed away my thoughts of Richard Lord trolling our ideas as I prepped the kitchen for the morning. It started with heating the ovens, lighting a fire in the wood-burning pizza oven, and taking butter and eggs out of the walk-in fridge so they could warm to room temperature. Next, I reviewed our custom cake orders and did a quick inventory of the pantry and walk-in fridge, making note of what we referred to as "FIFO"—first in, first out. We constantly rotated stock of what had been recently purchased so that the oldest products were used first in order to eliminate waste.

Andy breezed in as I was labeling bunches of fresh herbs. He tossed his puffy jacket on the coatrack and made a beeline for upstairs. "I have lots I want to talk about this morning, boss, but first, coffee."

He would get no argument from me. While he tempted me with aromas of toasted coconut and pome-granates, I began whipping butter and powdered sugar together in a mixer. As they creamed into a smooth mixture, I added a touch of salt, flour, and cornstarch.

The roses Carlos had sprinkled in my bath last night had given me inspiration for a special cookie. I would make meltaways—soft, buttery, melt-in-your mouth cookies—and decorate them with pale spring buttercream roses.

I divided the dough into three batches and added a different extract to each—vanilla, almond, and lemon/orange. Then I covered the dough and placed it in the fridge to chill for thirty minutes. The earthy scent of applewood smoking in the wood-burning pizza oven made my stomach rumble. Mom and I hadn't been able to believe our luck when the crew working on basement renovations had unearthed the fireplace. It had become the center point of the kitchen, and had elevated our baking game. There was nothing like the deep flavor of a slightly charred flatbread or a skillet mac and cheese baked in a wood-burning oven.

Andy came downstairs holding two mugs of coffee. "Here you go, boss. Give this a try."

I took the coffee from him. A faint hint of citrus hit my nose. Upon closer inspection the light layer of whipping cream on top appeared to have a ribbon of lemon curd and thin swirls of lemon peel. "Is this a lemon coffee?"

"Don't judge." Andy held his coffee to his nose. "Smell. Take in the aroma. Just like you taught me."

"I'm not judging. The citrus is really coming through." I used my hand to waft the steam closer.

"Okay. Good. Good." Andy gave a serious nod of approval. "Go ahead and take a sip."

I lifted the coffee to my lips.

"But wait! Make sure you get a bit of everything—

the whipped cream, the lemon zest, the curd, and the latte." He demonstrated by tilting his mug at an angle and taking a slow sip.

I did the same. The taste was unlike anything I had tried in coffee form. Bright notes of the tangy lemon mingled with a light vanilla latte. The result was nothing short of mouthwatering. Andy's creation was like a sip of spring in my mouth.

"This is incredible," I said, taking another taste.

"You like it?" His eyes were hopeful. "I had a dream about it last night. I couldn't sleep. That's what I wanted to talk to you about. I think it was because of the Wizard. I guess it kind of messed me up, too."

"That's normal, Andy," I tried to reassure him. "If you weren't feeling a little unsettled after seeing a man die, I would be concerned."

He set his coffee down and then opened the top drawer of the decorating station and began organizing our massive collection of sprinkles, lining up each container in a tidy row as if he was trying to distract himself. "Yeah, it's weird because I felt really calm in the moment. I knew that Sterling was freaking and I could tell that you were pretty out of it too, so I guess I just kind of took over, but man, when I got home last night it all came rushing back."

"Andy, I'm so sorry." I reached for his arm. "I should have checked in before you left."

"No, it's not your fault, boss. I'm just saying it's weird how we all deal with seeing death differently. I guess that's why my grandma has always told me I should be a cop or firefighter. I was talking to her about it last night and she said I'm a natural under pressure."

"She's right. You were amazing." I lifted my mug in a toast. "Almost amazing as this . . . lemon latte?"

"Yeah, or maybe something like lemon cream supreme? Lemon dream latte?" Andy closed the sprinkle drawer and took another drink of his coffee. "It was kind of like a jolt of caffeine. A serious rush. My heart was pounding in my chest all night. At first I thought I might be having a heart attack or something, but my grandma told me it was a panic attack. Flight or fight, right?"

"Right." I leaned in. "Is there anything I can do to help? Do you want to take the day off?"

"Nah. I'm fine. Well, maybe not fine, but like I said, I talked it through with my grandma last night and then I came up with the idea for the lemon dream latte, so I got it out of my head." He clutched the coffee cup.

"You said you wanted to talk, though." I nudged him. I wanted to make sure there wasn't more he needed to get off his chest.

"Right. It's about the Wizard. You remember how the Professor told us to think about anything we may remember?"

I nodded.

"When I was up late last night I remembered something. Two things, actually. I'm not sure if either of them are a big deal or not, so I thought I would ask you about it and then you can tell me if you think I should call the Professor. I don't want to bug him, but he did say that even something small might lead to a breakthrough."

"Absolutely, and I know he meant that."

Andy finished his coffee and set his empty cup on the marble countertop. "This happened a couple of weeks ago. I was down at Railroad Park throwing the Frisbee around with some friends and our Frisbee went too far. It flew over the fence and the blackberry vines. I went to retrieve it and saw Addie and Dean on the railroad tracks."

"Okay."

"It's weird because I don't want to start a rumor or anything." Andy bit his fingernail. "They looked really shady. Like it was a drug deal or something."

This was huge news. "Maybe Addie was buying milk from Dean," I suggested, knowing how lame it sounded as the words escaped my lips.

"For her yoga classes?" Andy ran his fingers through his shaggy hair. "I don't know. She handed him an envelope and he gave her something in return from his pocket. Maybe it was nothing, but they both looked really skittish and broke apart right away."

"Yeah. That sounds like a potential drug deal. You definitely need to tell the Professor. What was the other thing you witnessed?"

"That same day, I saw Laney Lee talking to the Wizard, and she didn't sound very happy."

My heart dropped. I didn't want my friend Laney to have had any involvement in the Wizard's murder.

"The thing is, it wasn't like they were fighting exactly, but they were really deep in conversation. I could tell they were talking about something serious. My Frisbee flew in the wrong direction and landed at their feet. I guess I need to work on my Frisbee skills, huh?" Andy made a goofy face. "Anyway, they were sitting at one of the picnic tables by the gazebo. I ran over to grab my Frisbee and I overheard Laney say that she was going to have to turn the Wizard in."

"Turn him in?"

Andy shrugged. "That's what I heard. I grabbed my Frisbee because I could tell that Laney didn't want anyone listening in to their conversation. Not that I was trying to. Honestly."

"I wonder what she meant by that?" I twisted my ponytail.

"No idea. I got my Frisbee and didn't hear any more. Do you think I should tell the Professor? I mean, there's not really much to tell."

I finished off my coffee. "Yes. You should. He will want to know all of this. You heard him yesterday—his words were that no detail is too small."

"Okay." Andy picked up his empty mug, while I took another sip of my creamy lemon latte. "Good. I didn't want to be a nuisance, or accuse Addie and Dean of drug dealing if it was something else, but it looked bad. You're right. I'll call him."

"Good. He asked for our input. He can decide if the information you have is worth pursuing or not." I drank the last drop of coffee. "Please tell me this is going on the special's board."

"On it right now, boss." Andy grabbed our empty cups.

"Also, please know that I'm here if you need to talk more, okay? I'm glad that you were able to talk about what happened with your grandma, but I don't want you to feel like you're alone. We're a team." I held his gaze and patted his forearm.

"Yeah, boss." He gave my hand a warm squeeze. "I know."

I watched him bounce up the stairs. I felt grateful that

he'd been willing to admit that the Wizard's death had upset him more than he realized, and I made a mental note to keep an eye on him today. Could he be right about Addie and Dean? Was there more to Dean's milk deliveries than cream and yogurt? It would explain him biking at night under the guise of delivering. I was going to have to pay more attention to them. Andy's revelation about Laney made me even more anxious to find some time to chat with my friend. What had she meant by "turning the Wizard in"? Could the Wizard have been mixed up in drug dealing too?

Sterling, Stephanie, Marty, and Bethany arrived around the same time. I loved the frenetic energy of morning prep. Marty pitched yeast and warmed the bread oven for proofing. Sterling chopped onions, garlic, carrots, celery, and fresh herbs for a creamy chicken dumpling soup, while Steph and Bethany mixed vats of cake and cookie dough for walk-in and specialty orders.

My meltaway cookies were ready to bake. I lined a cookie sheet with parchment paper and arranged one-inch balls of the chilled dough in neat rows. They would bake for eight to ten minutes or until their centers were firm.

Then I whipped our classic buttercream with pretty pale natural food gels and a touch of the extracts I had used in the cookie batter. For the vanilla meltaways I tinted the buttercream a lovely blushing rose with a hint of vanilla. The almond meltaways would get frosted with robin's egg blue and almond buttercream, and the citrus meltaways would have fresh orange and lemon zest added to their pale yellow buttercream.

After the cookies had cooled, I filled a piping bag

with the pink vanilla buttercream and piped a delicate rose on the top. I repeated the piping technique with the blue and yellow buttercream until I had trays filled with dainty spring flowers.

"Ohhhh, those are so cute," Bethany gushed. "Let me get a pic." She took a break from spreading dark chocolate cake batter into eight-inch rounds. When she removed her apron, it revealed yet another punny T-shirt: a melting cone of ice cream and the words JUST CHILL.

"Great shirt," I said, centering the plate on the island for her photo.

"I wore it honor of Scoops." She snapped a picture of the meltaways. "These are definitely going on our social media."

I passed around a plate for the team to taste.

"What gives them the crumbly texture?" Steph asked, studying one of the cookies that she'd broken in half.

"Cornstarch." I grinned. "It's the secret ingredient. That, and there are no eggs in this recipe."

"They remind me of something," Marty said, polishing off a citrus meltaway. "Something that my mom used to buy at the grocery store during the holidays, but I can't recall the name."

"Yeah, they almost have a vintage flavor," Sterling said. He stood at the gas stove sweating the vegetables for his soup in olive oil.

"Is vintage good?" I asked.

"The best!" Bethany interrupted. "Vintage is totally on point right now. These will be a hit."

"As long as you approve, I'll take a tray upstairs. They should mix well with Andy's special. Has anyone tried it yet?"

"The lemon dream latte?" Steph asked with a scowl. "It sounds weird."

"I thought so too," Bethany replied, snapping a picture of the meltaways. "You have to try it. It's amazing. *Soooo* good. I swear. It might change your life."

"Ha!" Steph scoffed.

I appreciated that their energies were polar opposites and yet they worked together seamlessly. We spent the next few hours baking pastries, flatbreads, and running up and down the stairs to restock the pastry case. Torte was a busy rush of familiar faces through mid-morning. Andy's lemon dream lattes sold in record numbers. My meltaways disappeared faster than we could bake new batches.

It was always rewarding when new creations were well received by our customers. We stocked a variety of classic sweet and savory pastries that we offered every day, like our pesto egg croissants, sourdough blueberry bread, and salted caramel tarts. But, experimenting in the kitchen was the best part of owning a bakeshop. There wasn't a day that went by when my mind didn't drift off into a dreamland of creamy strawberry rhubarb custards or basil-and-tomato wood-fired pizzas. Creativity breathed new life into the bakeshop and kept our customers coming back for more.

The morning surge had begun to dwindle not long after ten. I went upstairs to assess the damage. Sequoia was wiping down the coffee bar. Rosa cleared tables in the dining room, and Andy manned the espresso machine. Fortunately, the pastry case was well stocked for lunch, except for one empty tray waiting to be filled with a new batch of meltaways.

"Things look relatively calm," I said to Rosa.

She set a pile of dishes in a bin. "It's been a steady stream, but we've stayed on top of it." She pointed to the front windows. "Now that there's a lull, Stephanie and I will swap out the window display."

We'd had shamrocks, shiny pieces of gold, and beautiful fake chocolate stout cakes in the windows for St. Patrick's Day. Now that the holiday was behind us, it was time to give the display a face-lift.

"Stephanie and I were thinking of using your rose cookies as our inspiration point," Rosa said. "Since things are starting to bloom, we thought we could string tissue paper roses and fill the base with flower petal cutouts." She showed me one of Stephanie's sketches. With my expanding duties at Scoops, I had given Stephanie and Rosa full autonomy over our window displays. Steph was a talented artist and Rosa had an eye for simple elegance and clean lines. Thus far they had not disappointed.

Mom and I had one goal when it came to Torte—to make sure that everyone who walked through our front door felt welcomed, like family. We arranged comfortable seating around the atomic fireplace downstairs, and cozy booths and intimate dining tables upstairs where we encouraged our guests to linger over a fresh pot of French press. For our youngest guests we kept a collection of toys, books, and puzzles in a basket along with reserving a section of our chalkboard menu for little fingers. This morning one of our preschool patrons had drawn a snow family with carrot noses and button eyes.

"This is perfect." I handed the sketch back to Rosa and glanced out the window.

Arlo was chatting with a woman I didn't recognize across the plaza by the bubbling Lithia Fountain.

This was my chance to go have a word and see what I could find out about the mystery man who seemed to have caught Lance's eye.

"I'll be back in a minute," I said to Rosa. I hurried outside and crossed the street into the center of the plaza by the information kiosk. An assortment of posters for concerts, art shows, and open-mic poetry nights were tacked to the kiosk. Arlo and the woman he'd been talking to hugged and ended their conversation. The woman headed toward Lithia Park.

He turned in my direction. "Juliet, we meet again." He beamed a welcoming smile and reached out to hug me. "How fortuitous."

"Actually, I saw you and thought I would invite you to Torte for a latte and pastry." I nodded toward the bakeshop.

He took a brief glance at his watch. "Yes please. I have thirty minutes before my next appointment."

We walked to the bakeshop together. Arlo was dressed in a pair of jeans, Chuck Taylors, and a casual V-neck sweater. He took wide steps with a steady gait.

"How was the pub last night?" I asked.

"Wild." He grinned and held the door open for me. "I don't know if you know this, but softball coaches are crazy."

"I did not know that." I laughed. "Have a seat at one of the booths. Do you have a preference? Sweet? Savory? Both?"

"Not at all. Surprise me."

"What about coffee? How do you take your coffee?"

"I take it however you want to give it to me." He strolled over to a booth while I went to plate a variety of pastries and put in an order for Andy's lemon dream latte. I didn't know much about Arlo yet, but his easygoing attitude was warm and welcoming. I was excited to learn more about him and try to deduce if Lance's love life was about to take a turn for the better.

Chapter Thirteen

"Are you trying to get me fired from my coaching job?" Arlo teased when I presented him with a plate piled high with tea cakes, meltaways, peanut butter brownies, sun-dried tomato egg-salad flatbread, and ham and Swiss croissants.

"I'll share." I sat across from him.

"How does a baker who makes a spread like this stay so slim?" He leaned against the back of the booth in an easygoing manner.

"Good genetics?" I took a brownie and broke it in half. "That and the fact that we burn a lot of calories baking, running up and down the stairs, and delivering our bread around town."

"It sounds like I could recruit you to come coach." Arlo studied the plate with wide eyes. "What should I try first?"

"I'm not a good judge. Each of my pastries is like a baby. I can't pick a favorite."

He threw his head back and let out a deep, baritone laugh. "No wonder Lance adores you. Pastries babies!"

Andy brought us coffees. A lemon dream latte for Arlo and a straight black cup of our blond roast for me.

"Lemon, huh?" Arlo said after Andy left. "That's the thing I'm quickly learning about Ashland. This isn't your standard small town."

"You're very observant."

Arlo decided on the egg salad. "It comes with the job. I've spent the last fifteen years traveling from theater to theater. You'd be surprised how the same issues come up no matter if you're in Iowa or LA. I spend the first few weeks watching and observing, and listening—listening is the key—before I begin to brainstorm solutions."

"Interesting." I bit into one of Bethany's brownies. It was the consistency of fudge with a creamy peanut butter filling. Mom and I had begged her to join our team at Torte and even offered a small percentage of profit shares after trying her brownies at Ashland's annual chocolate festival. "What have you learned about OSF so far?"

Arlo sipped his coffee. A faint smile tugged at his lips. "I can say with certainty that Lance has set a vision. He has command of his company, and expectations that exceed anything I've ever seen."

"Is that a good thing or a bad thing?"

"Perhaps a bit of both," Arlo answered honestly. "The company and community clearly revere him, but have they bought into his vision? That, I'm not sure."

I hadn't expected Arlo to be so forthcoming. His confidence allowed him an ease that made me feel comfortable.

"Don't get me wrong. I think Lance's vision for OSF

is trailblazing. He wants to revolutionize theater as we know it. Which he's already doing. It's pretty incredible actually. When I told people I was taking a job in Ashland, the response was consistently positive. Lance has a reputation for being on the cutting edge. He wants to push audiences out of their comfort zone and make them feel what it's like to walk in the shoes of people who are very different from them. He sees theater as the great educator and equalizer of our times. He sees the stage as having the most impact to bring us together. To help us understand that our worldview is slanted, no matter what our belief system is." Arlo's eyes were bright and open as he continued. "Lance doesn't want to put on yet another production of *Romeo and Juliet*. He wants you—the audience member—to become a Capulet. He wants you to walk away from a three-hour production and have it live on for days and weeks and years to come. It's an ambitious vision. I personally think he's right to use this platform to help shape understanding, but he can't pull it off without buy-in. My challenge is going to be figuring out how we engage with patrons. How we message the community—and how we fill seats in the theater, because there is a percentage of our devoted members who want to come see a show that they recognize and leave feeling happy and good. Some of what Lance wants to do isn't going to meet those patrons where they're at. It's going to leave them feeling uncomfortable. That could drastically change attendance numbers. It could sink the theater."

"Really?" I clasped my hands together. The theater, along with most businesses in southern Oregon, had taken a hit from wildfires the past few summers. Attendance numbers had been down and some of the outdoor shows at the Elizabethan had to be cancelled due to poor air quality. Ashland's bevy of bed and breakfasts, retail shops, restaurants, and outdoor recreation companies had been impacted. I didn't like hearing that Lance's vision for OSF's future might also jeopardize ticket sales.

Arlo's face was severe. "I've seen it happen before. Now, I also concede that Ashland is unique. If anyone can pull it off, I think it's Lance and I think it's here. But, it doesn't come without risk and without some painful bumps in the road."

"Have you said this to Lance?" I sipped my coffee.

"I have." The smile returned to Arlo's cheeks. "You and Lance have been close for a while now; how do you think that my input went over?"

It was a good thing I had set my mug on the table, otherwise I might have spit coffee at Arlo. "Not well."

"Nope." He snapped his fingers together to signal I had answered correctly. "Lance blew off my concerns. And, trust me, I get it. I get that he wants to do big things here, but if he alienates his base it could spell disaster."

Arlo was scaring me. If OSF crumbled, so would everything I knew and loved in Ashland. The theater was the lifeblood of our community.

"What's the answer then?"

"My answer would be to stay the course. OSF has an international reputation not only for its top-caliber talent, but also for staging new plays and works by playwrights who traditionally haven't been given a voice. I think it's about balance. Each season should have both. We should be producing revolutionary shows. We should help push the boundaries of understanding, but we also need a few feel-goods. We need big productions outside at the Elizabethan that get people up on their feet and dancing. Shows that bring down the house. Lance told me that he loves a good song-and-dance number, which is critical."

"It's true," I interjected. "Lance loves Rodgers and Hammerstein as much as he loves Shakespeare."

Arlo pressed his palm to his heart and nodded. "That's good. That's going to be my pitch to Lance and our point of balance. Those musicals draw in families and new theatergoers. They are gateway shows. They generate buzz and they help fill seats in some of the lesser-known shows. Maybe somebody comes to see *The Music Man*. They're on their feet clapping and singing through the show. They have such a great experience that they look through the season brochure and one of our more serious productions jumps out. They give that a try and it's a transformative experience."

Arlo sounded like he knew his stuff.

"But Lance doesn't agree?" I asked.

He rolled up his sweater sleeves. "I wouldn't say that. I think Lance knows that at his core, but will he admit it? That's the question."

"I don't envy you."

"Don't worry about me. I can handle it. I'd rather go head-to-head with someone as passionate as Lance than a theater director who just wants to dial it in."

The more we chatted, the more I liked Arlo. He was levelheaded and calm. Lance may have met his match. I couldn't imagine Arlo caving to Lance's every whim, and I was glad he had OSF's best interests in mind.

"Enough about me." Arlo picked up an almond melt-away. "Tell me about you. How did you come to be a baker extraordinaire?"

"I don't know if I'd say that, but baking is in my blood." I gave him a condensed version of how my parents had opened the bakeshop when I was young.

"How is it returning home? Weird? Good? Both?" Arlo's relaxed body language continued to put me at ease. It was no wonder that he excelled in his position. Like Mom, he had a natural way of asking questions designed for more than a yes or no answer.

"Both. Things have changed since my childhood, but mostly for the better. It was strange at first, but you've experienced Ashland's embrace enough to understand that you would have to be a hermit not to find your tribe here. I love that. I love living in a place where everyone looks after each other. It took traveling the world to teach me how special Ashland is."

Arlo ate two more cookies. "Ashland is lucky to have you. I've spent a fair amount of time traveling too, and I have to say these are some of the most delicious pastries I've ever had."

I felt my cheeks warm.

"As much as I would love to learn more about you, I have to run. Board meetings—the joy." Arlo made a face then placed his napkin on his plate and took one last drink of coffee. "Thank you so much for the wonderful early lunch. That sad peanut butter and honey sandwich waiting for me at the office is out of luck. What do I owe you?"

"Nothing, it's on the house." I waved him off.

He frowned. "In that case, beers on me one night this week. What do you say?"

"I'd love that."

Arlo stood. "I'm a hugger. Is that cool?"

"Me too." I gave him a quick hug and promised that I would find time for beers soon.

After he left I went downstairs to the kitchen. A family with two teenagers appeared to be locked in board game battle. They had Catan spread out on the coffee table next to plates of my rose cookies and mugs of hot chocolate with our hand-pulled marshmallows. "Can I get you anything?" I asked before going to check on my staff.

The mom held up one of the game pieces. "We're fine. Everything is delicious, but I could use a teammate. I'm getting crushed here."

"I feel you. I've been there." I chuckled. When Ramiro had visited over the winter holidays we had played Catan for hours. He'd beaten me every time.

Bethany scooted by me with a tray of cupcakes, hand pies, and macarons. I continued into the adjoining kitchen. Steph had a pair of earbuds in at the decorating station, where she was frosting a fault-line cake. The trendy cakes were so popular that there was rarely a day we didn't have at least one custom order for one. To create the contemporary look, lines of buttercream were swiped out of the middle of the cake and then filled with sprinkles, berries, cookies, or sugar geodes.

Sterling called me over to the stove. "Hey, Jules, can you come sign off on my soup?"

He ladled half a cup into one of our sturdy bright red

bowls and handed it to me along with a spoon. The one thing I had tried to impart to my staff above anything else was tasting. A chef can never taste too much. "It looks great," I noted. "And it smells even better."

Sterling tucked a dish towel into the apron tied around his waist while he waited for my input.

The chicken soup was packed with flavor and the dumplings were light and buttery. "This is incredible. I am going to need more than this little scoop in my bowl."

"Glad you approve." Sterling added more of the creamy soup to my bowl. "Speaking of Scoops, are you heading over to the new space?"

"Yeah. I figured I would take off as soon as the lunch prep is complete, and it looks like it is. What about you? Do you want to come, or skip it today? How are you feeling?"

Sterling dished up bowls of the chicken-and-dumpling soup for the rest of the team. "I'll come. I'm good. I'm not over the shock, but a routine helps, and I know Andy wants to go over the menu and Steph said she would do the chalkboard."

Marty took one of the soup bowls that Sterling offered. "Things are running smoothly. I think the rest of us can manage for the afternoon. Now once the season starts and the crowds return, we might be singing a different tune."

"I know. Mom and I are already planning for that." I clicked my fingers together. "In fact, thanks for the reminder. I need to post an ad online and in the paper for seasonal help."

After I checked in with everyone, I gathered my

things and left. The walk to Scoops revived my spirits. I stopped to chat with fellow business owners, allowing my skin to soak in the springtime sun.

I could smell Nana's food truck from two blocks away. Laney was probably in the middle of lunch service, which meant that I wouldn't be able to talk to her alone. I went straight to the garden and dropped off my things. When I walked behind the counter to put a few supplies in the refrigerator I froze.

Someone was curled up in a sleeping bag sprawled out on the ground.

Chapter Fourteen

I jumped at the sight of someone camping out behind our coffee counter. What were they doing here?

An empty feeling swirled in the pit of my stomach. What if the person was dead?

Please don't let them be dead, I prayed internally as I knelt next to the person.

"Are you okay?" I gently shook the sleeping bag. It was army green and tattered and dirty. From the condition of the bag it appeared that it had gotten a lot of use.

The person's head was buried inside.

I shook it again.

No one moved.

Oh no. I clasped my hand over my mouth. This couldn't be happening again.

I tried again. "Are you okay?"

This time the person stirred.

Whew. Relief washed over me. For a moment I wanted to be still and allow the feeling to flood my body.

The person made a mumbling sound and pushed their head from beneath the badly worn sleeping bag.

"Sky?" I'm sure my eyes must have been wide with surprise.

His upper body swayed from side to side as he tried to shuffle out of the sleeping bag. "They're after me." His eyes were glassy. They darted in every direction. He blinked rapidly, as if trying to focus.

"Sky, it's Jules. I'm the one who helped with your hand."

He had managed to sit up, but he continued to rock in circles. "They're coming for me. They're after me."

"After you? Who?" I glanced around.

Sky scrunched his face. His eyes were bloodshot and his pupils were the size of dimes. "I gotta hide. I gotta get out of here."

Was he in danger or was he on something or both?

"Hold on." I steadied him. "Take a minute before you try to stand again. You look a bit dizzy."

He swayed as he scratched his dreadlocks. "No, I gotta get out of here. They're gonna find me and if they do they'll kill me." He used his injured hand to steady himself. The cut had bled through the bandage.

"Slow down, Sky." I tried to keep my voice calm and even. "Who is following you?"

"The Wizard's killer. They think I saw something too. I didn't. I swear I didn't see anything, but they think I did and now they're gonna kill me."

What did he mean by "saw something too"? Had the Wizard witnessed something that had gotten him killed?

"Take a minute and breathe," I cautioned Sky, who wiggled out of the bag and stumbled to his feet. He clutched the countertop to steady himself, knocking off a box of silverware that Andy had brought over. Spoons scattered everywhere.

"Sorry. Sorry." Sky bent down, grabbed his sleeping bag, and bolted toward the front gate.

"Wait," I called after him, but he tripped toward the front gate, unlatched it, and wobbled down the sidewalk in a zigzagging pattern. I watched him almost lose his balance as he tried to step over a collection of plastic pots outside of the Grange and disappear behind the building.

He was obviously spooked and he looked pretty out of it. The question was why. Was his fear legitimate or was he on a paranoid drug binge? I picked up the spoons. Then I placed a quick call to Thomas. I wasn't about to take any chances. The Wizard was already dead. If there was a glimmer of truth to Sky's concerns, I wanted the police to follow up.

"Hey Jules, glad you called," Thomas said. "I was hoping to swing by Torte later this afternoon. I could use your opinion as long as you have a few minutes to spare."

"Sure, but I won't be at the bakeshop. I'm here at the new space—Scoops."

"Even better. I'm going to be in that area later. The Professor wants me to canvas the Railroad District. We need a break in this case, and maybe it will come from one of the new business owners."

"That's why I called." I explained how I had found Sky sleeping behind the coffee counter and that he'd told me about someone trying to kill him.

Thomas' tone shifted as he listened. "Thanks for letting me know, Jules. The minute we hang up I'm going to send a squad car to find him. You think he was headed north along the tracks?"

"That's the direction he went. I couldn't see him after he went behind the Grange."

"Okay. I'll stop by as soon as I can."

We hung up. What did Thomas want to talk to me about? Could it be connected to the case? I wondered about the wrench Lance and I had found last night. Had they been able to confirm that the substance on the wrench was blood? There was another possibility. One that I didn't want to think about—that Thomas wanted to read me the riot act for meddling in the case.

I didn't have time to dwell on it because Sterling, Andy, and Steph arrived. "The gang's all here, boss," Andy announced, clicking the latch on the gate.

Steph had a satchel of chalkboard pens and stencils tucked over her arm. Andy carried a box of supplies and Sterling brought up the rear with a cooler.

"Any excitement, boss?" Andy opened the front gate.

"Thankfully, none." I decide not to tell them about Sky. Andy and Sterling had been through enough yesterday. I didn't want to worry them more. "I see you all came ready to work."

Steph tugged on the strings of her black jacket. Black and purple were her signature colors. "I'm going to sketch out the menu now because I have a three o'clock class."

I moved out of her way. "The chalkboard is yours."

Andy unpacked cleaning supplies. "I thought we should probably give this place a complete wipe-down before we start putting stuff away and organizing. I found a nasty industrial cleaner that is supposed to take off anything it touches. Even your skin." He held up a pair of thick plastic gloves. "I'm going to try and get the graffiti off the fridge."

"Good plan, but be careful," I warned.

"No worries, boss. Safety is my middle name." Andy shot me a thumbs-up.

"How was the lunch rush?" I asked Sterling.

"Easy." He brought the cooler to the back area. "Everything was running smoothly when we left. Marty has it under control."

"I don't doubt that."

Andy tossed Sterling a pair of gloves. "Let's scrub this baby down before we load her up with anything." He patted the stainless steel fridge and freezer.

Sterling opened the fridge. "That's weird. There's a bunch of milk and cream in here. Did Dean come by?"

"Really?" I went to look for myself. At least a dozen bottles of milk were lined in the fridge. "I bumped into him and he mentioned that he could swing by, but I told him not to bother since we're in the middle of getting the space ready to open."

I thought of Sky. When had Dean delivered the milk? If he had stopped by this morning, he would have seen Sky sleeping. An open-concept garden space like Scoops might not work in many places other than Ashland. I'd never been worried about theft. Technically speaking we could lock the front gate at night, but it wouldn't take much effort for a would-be criminal to hop over a three-foot fence. The Professor had suggested getting locks for the fridge and cupboards to protect our inventory, which at the time had seemed like overkill, but now I wasn't so sure.

"Weird. I told him to deliver everything to Torte so we can make the concretes there and start handing out samples here. Maybe he got confused. I'll text him." Sterling reached into the back pocket of his skinny jeans for his phone.

I noticed that the line in front of Laney Lee's food truck had dispersed. Since Thomas was coming by later, I decided there was no time like the present to see if I could learn anything from my friend.

"What concretes did you bring?" I opened the cooler.

Andy had already started scrubbing the fridge. "The cinnamon oatmeal cookie is my favorite. Sterling also made a buttered popcorn that sounds gross, but it's amazing."

I searched through the labeled containers until I found both. "I'll give our new neighbors a taste of each. I know they'll help spread the word."

"Good thinking, boss. That's why you get the big bucks." Andy winked.

Whether or not he believed that was my only intention was up for debate. I scooped little tastes of the concretes into small cups and placed them on a tray. "Back in a few."

I went to Laney's first. "Hello," I called at the ordering window. "Ice cream delivery."

"Coming!" Laney replied. A few seconds later she appeared at the window, wiping her hands on a floral dish towel. "Did I hear you say 'ice cream delivery'?"

I handed her a cup of the oatmeal cookie and popcorn custards. "It's one of the perks of being our new neighbor. You're going to have to be a taste-tester."

"Never have I been happier to have forced the neighborhood on you." She set the custards on the aluminum ledge. "Let me turn off the stove and I'll come outside to eat these. I could use a break from this glorified tin can."

"Do you have time to walk down to the park?" I suggested.

"I'll make time." Laney smiled as she closed the roll-down window. A few seconds later she appeared at the narrow doorway. She shut the door behind her without locking it.

We walked along the path. It was like a different place in the light of day. The blackberry vines that Lance had pushed me into stretched along the chain-link fence as far as I could see. The sound of children's laughter filled the air. Bikers, joggers, and walkers shared the popular pathway.

Laney tasted the buttered popcorn custard as we strolled together. "This is like nothing I've tasted."

"Is that good or bad?" I matched her stride.

"Good. Surprising, but good."

We made it to Railroad Park, where a group of pre-schoolers ran through the grass chasing bubbles. At the far end of the park a Tai Chi class moved with flow, their arms opening to the sky. We found an empty bench near the gazebo and sat down. "I wanted to check in and see how you were doing after yesterday," I said, putting my hand on her knee.

Tears welled in her eyes. She kept them focused on a golden retriever fetching a tennis ball. "Honestly, I'm not doing well. I appreciate you asking. It's been rough."

"If there's anything you need to get off your chest, or if you just need a listening ear, I'm here."

Laney's face blanched. "Oh my God, is it obvious? It must be. I knew this was going to come out sooner or later." She wrung her hands as tears spilled from her eyes. "I don't know what to say. You're totally going to think differently of me now. Everyone is."

My heart rate sped up. What was Laney talking about? She couldn't possibly mean that she killed the Wizard, could she? There was no way.

I was distracted for a moment as Lars, Hunter's son, and his crew of skater friends zoomed along the crowded path on longboards, darting around a mom pushing a baby jogger and a retired couple holding hands. That kid was never in school. I wondered if Hunter home-schooled him or if Lars was perpetually truant.

"Please promise me you won't say anything about this to anyone else yet, Jules," Laney pleaded. "I know it's going to come out and I know it will be around town soon, but I just need a little more time, okay?"

"Laney, I have no idea what you're talking about."

She brushed tears from her face. "Jules, you're too nice. You don't have to say that. Look, I don't want to put you in an uncomfortable position. I know I have to tell the police. Thomas is coming by this afternoon to talk to me. I should have been honest and confessed yesterday but I couldn't bring myself to do it."

Again I wondered whether Laney was admitting that she had killed the Wizard. She was the last person I could possibly imagine resorting to violence. She was also the only one of our new Railroad District business owners who had shown any true remorse about his death.

"Laney, I don't understand. I'm not being nice. I actually have no idea what you're talking about."

I held my breath, waiting for her response.

Had I completely misread my friend?

She let out a low whimper. "I can't believe this is coming out. I've tried so hard to keep it together. To keep it a secret."

"Laney, wait. What are you saying? You're not saying that you killed the Wizard, are you?"

She tried to compose herself, but could barely speak between sobs. "God, no, no. I never would have hurt him. The Wizard was my father."

Chapter Fifteen

"Your father?" I asked, biting the side of my cheek to try to mask my shock. "Oh no, Laney, I'm so sorry."

Laney swallowed back tears. "I didn't want anyone to know. I loved him, don't get me wrong, but it was easier to let people think he was a homeless man I looked out for. Not my father. It's embarrassing."

"There's nothing to be embarrassed about. People loved your father. The entire community is grieving right now."

"That's easy for you to say. You have a normal mother. My dad's been sick for years. Mom said they never should have had me. She knew when they got married that he had struggled with mental illness. He was on his meds back then. He had pretty normal days. I mean he was always quirky—different. I knew it when I was a kid. He wasn't like the other dads, but I didn't care. That's what made him special. He would make up elaborate games and have tea parties with me. He was more like a friend."

"What happened? How did he end up on the streets?"

She used the napkin I had wrapped around the tasting cup to dry her eyes. "We lived in Hawaii when I was young. My parents met in college. He studied engineering and landed a good job that took them to Hawaii. He was working on the military base and started getting paranoid. He was sure that people were following him—watching us. He went downhill from there." She hugged her knees.

I waited for her to continue. At the far end of the park a guy wearing spandex that showcased his chiseled muscles barked out commands to his boot-camp participants. In formation the group dropped to the grass and began doing push-ups. Railroad Park offered an authentic snapshot of Ashland's eclectic community. Iridescent bubbles bobbed above the swing set where kids shrieked with laughter. The sound mingled with the harmonic flow of the slow, intentional moments of the Tai Chi class. Moms sipped coffee and gossiped while the boot camp grunted and sweated.

Laney fiddled with the watermelon-colored flower tie in her braid before continuing. "Dad got fired because the paranoia got so bad. After that he had a bunch of odd jobs. He worked in the sugar-cane fields, a surf shop, a bento restaurant. Mom was the primary source of our income. She was a school nurse. I think it's one of the reasons she was attracted to him initially—she had a thing for lost souls." Laney paused and fought back another round of tears. "We had some good years together. It might not have been a typical childhood, but I have plenty of happy memories. Then when I was in fifth or sixth grade they started fighting. Mom was fed up with Dad's mood swings. He'd check out for days at a time and lock himself in their room, and then he'd re-appear and be fine. I realize now it was typical manic-depressive behavior. He couldn't keep a job. He went off his medication. Mom had enough. She gave him an ul-timatum. Go to therapy and get back on his medication or she was done. He tried, but he couldn't do it. She divorced him. That sent him into a tailspin. He never recovered. He slipped deeper into his own imaginary world. When I moved to Ashland I brought him with me in hopes that maybe a change of scenery would help. It didn't. He's been on the streets ever since."

"Laney, thank you for trusting me with this." I tilted my head from the sun to meet her eyes. "It must have been so hard to take care of your dad like that."

Her lips trembled, threatening more tears. "It *was* hard. It's been a routine for so long now that I kind of forget he was never normal—whatever normal is. I kept an eye out for him. I fed him every day. Things are tight at Nana's. You don't open a food truck to make mil-lions, but winter sales were slow. Painfully slow. I wasn't sure I was going to survive. I didn't have much to give him in terms of money, but at least I could feed him. We maintained a relationship of sorts. It was a role rever-sal. I felt like I was the parent. I was worried about him, but Ashland is so safe, and like you said, the commu-nity really loved him." She broke down.

I let her cry, holding the space for her.

Her eyes were puffy and swollen. She massaged her temples. "I can't believe he's dead. It feels so surreal. Who would have killed him, Jules? He was sick. He wasn't a criminal."

"I know." Laney's revelation made me even more

resolved to bring the Wizard's killer to justice. "What was his real name? The police need to know so they can pull records. Maybe someone he interacted with in the street community was dangerous?"

"That could be." She smoothed her apron with her hands. "His name was Jim. Jim Lee."

I made a mental note, although I was sure that Laney would share this information with Thomas. "There's another possibility," I said, thinking about my interaction with Sky. "Do you think he could have witnessed a crime that put him in danger? Maybe he saw something on the tracks."

"Who knows? Half of what my dad said didn't make sense. The last few years he's slipped deeper into his own universe, but it's definitely a possibility. He was often mumbling about 'trouble' on the tracks, but I blew it off. I thought it was him getting looped into one of his manic fantasies. Most of the time I was never sure if he was in this world or off in some other universe in his mind. What if I was wrong? I should have paid more attention to him. If I had, maybe he would still be alive."

"Laney, you can't blame yourself. This is not your fault. Whoever killed your father is responsible—not you."

"Maybe. It was so hard to believe what was real and what wasn't. I think I'm going to second-guess myself forever now." She blinked back tears again. "Sky tried to warn me. He stopped by the food truck and told me that he was worried about Dad."

"Did he know that the Wizard was your father?"

"Yeah. Sky was his only friend. I should have listened

to him. He told me that Dad was really worked up. I blew him off. I told him that it was part of Dad's pattern. He would do that. He would go through stretches where he basically was a different person and then he'd come back to earth for a while. I'd lived with it my entire life and just assumed that Sky wasn't used to Dad's swings."

Hopefully, Thomas had found Sky. I kicked myself for not following after him. He might be the one person who knew who had killed the Wizard—Jim.

I shifted the conversation. "Laney, one of my staff overheard you say something to your dad about turning him in. Do you know, was he involved in dealing?"

"Drugs?" She recoiled at the suggestion. "No. Never. Not Dad. He wouldn't have been involved in drug dealing. That was taken out of context. I told him I was going to turn him in for a wellness check. I wanted him to get help. I was worried that things were escalating with him and some of the other business owners in the Railroad District."

Laney's concrete samples had melted in the cups. She stood and tossed them in a nearby garbage can. "I should check on the food truck."

"I'll walk with you."

We returned on the bike path. A couple of travelers (as Ashland's roving hippie population was known) strummed guitars at the entrance to the park. Their unkempt hair, stringy beards, and cardboard sign that said TRADED EVERYTHING FOR LOVE was a dead giveaway that they were part of the migratory youthful tribe that tended to travel up and down the West Coast in converted school buses. Unlike the Wizard or Sky, travelers were homeless by choice. Many of them spent the spring and summer months in Ashland, busking on the plaza and camping in the parks. They could work, but opted for an alternative lifestyle instead.

There had been many discussions at city council meetings about how to deal with the booming population of trust-fund hippies in the summer. I had learned to ignore their pleas for cash or leftovers, but many tourists were put off by their constant begging and the scent of pot that tended to envelop them.

"Woah," Laney exhaled and waved her hands across her face. "They've been partaking."

"Yeah." We picked up our pace to get past the overwhelming smell. I thought about what Andy had said about seeing what looked like a drug deal go down between Dean and Addie. "Do you know anything about drug dealing in this area?"

Laney gave me a strange look. "Why? Are you interested?"

"No. That's not my scene. I had heard a rumor about dealing on the tracks."

"Could be." Laney considered it for a moment. "It's legal in Oregon now, so it's hard to know for sure who's smoking legally. I mean, as I'm sure you know, pot can only be sold by a state licensed dispensary and smoked in private residences. You wouldn't know that around this area most days. It often lingers in the air, especially from the travelers, but I wouldn't put it past Lars and his skater friends. They're never up to any good."

As we walked toward Namaste I drank in the pastoral views of town. Houses were tucked into the forested hillsides that nestled in the plaza. The Siskiyou Mountains branched out as far as the eye could see.

Laney stopped mid-stride, gasped, and threw her hand over her mouth.

"What?"

She pointed to the end of the alleyway where someone in a long, dark cape that resembled the Wizard's made a sharp turn on their bike and sped away.

"Did you see that?" Laney clutched my arm.

"Yeah." I blinked twice as if my eyes were playing tricks on me.

"That looked like Dad." Laney's shoulders crumpled.

I helped her along the path. When we reached Nana's, I left Laney with a long hug. "Please don't hesitate to let me know if there's anything I can do."

She forced a smile. "I appreciate it. It feels slightly better to talk about it, and I know that I have to tell Thomas everything. Hopefully, they can find whoever did this to Dad."

At Scoops, Steph had finished creating the new chalkboard menu design. The red, teal, and white chalk added an extra pop of color. She had sketched ice cream cones, coffee cups, and silhouettes of cupcakes on the sides of the menu, but left space in the middle to change out our weekly offerings.

"That looks great," I complimented her.

"It's okay." Her eyes were shielded by strands of her purple hair. "Too bad we can't tear down this old structure. It's ugly."

I had to agree. Our cleanup efforts had lightened the garden, but ripping the ivy from the aging pergola above the coffee stand had revealed sections of rotting wood. In contrast to the newly stained bar, it looked gray and sad. Unfortunately rebuilding the structure would put us way over the money Mom and I had allotted for beautifying Scoops.

"Alas, that's not in the budget at the moment," I replied.

Steph tucked the loose strands of hair behind one ear. Her nails were painted black to match her lipstick. She wore a pair of intentionally ripped skinny jeans and black combat boots, and had a backpack slung over her arm. "Could we stain it?"

"We could try." I wasn't sure that the structure could be improved.

Andy chimed in. He had successfully removed any trace of graffiti and was in the process of bleaching the fridge. "Nah, I don't think it's worth it, boss. As my grandma likes to say, that would be 'putting lipstick on a pig.'"

Steph snarled at him.

He threw his arms up in surrender. "Don't shoot the messenger. Look at that thing—it's half-rotted. I think it's ugly too, but I'm more worried that it's going to come crashing down on me and Sterling."

Sterling wrapped his hands around one of the pergola's posts. He tried to shake it. "Feels solid to me."

That was a relief, but I didn't want to take any chances either. I would make a call to our contractor later to see if he could come assess the structure.

Steph shifted her backpack. "I've got to get to class."

Sterling reached for his hoodie. "Mind if I take a break and walk up to campus?" he asked me.

"Of course. Go."

Andy had finished scrubbing the outdoor kitchen. The smell of bleach assaulted my nose when he opened the fridge for me. The racks had been sanitized and arranged to accommodate the supplies we'd be bring over. Every inch of stainless steel sparkled. The cabinets looked revived and fresh. "I've started organizing supplies, boss." He walked me through his strategy for arranging cups, glasses, and plates.

"Everything looks fantastic. I can't get over how quickly it's coming together. I had thought it might take much longer."

"You put in that order for the rest of the supplies last night, right?" Andy stacked a set of our red towels near the sink.

"Yep. We should have the last of the list by the end of the week."

"Sweet." Andy gave me a thumbs-up.

We spent the next hour mapping out schedules and figuring out flow for the small kitchen. Given the tight space, there wouldn't be room for more than two staff members to work together. That should be fine since we weren't going to be baking anything in the new space. Aside from scooping concretes and blending shakes, most of the job would be packaging orders and making sure the garden dining area was kept clean. In addition to calling our contractor, I needed to place that ad for help. I made a note to do both.

Andy and I disassembled the faded and stained umbrellas. We stacked them in a pile in the center of the garden. I hated throwing them out. They weren't aesthetically pleasing for our new shop, but someone could probably get use of them. I added another note in my ever-growing to-do list to post a free ad.

I saw Thomas park his police car across the street at

Cyclepath as I tossed a pile of weeds into the yard debris bin. He waved and pointed to Laney's food truck. He must be here for their meeting. If nothing else, now at least Thomas, Detective Kerry, and the Professor would know the Wizard's real name and his connection with Laney.

Sterling returned from walking Steph to class shortly after three. I sent him and Andy back to Torte to help with closing. I used the time alone to posts ads for summer help and the umbrellas, and left a message for our contractor.

Thomas knocked on the gate. "Hey, Jules. Mind if I come in?"

"Not at all." I waved from the kitchen. I looked up to see him amble into the garden. He wore a pair of navy blue shorts that matched his police uniform, tennis shoes, and sunglasses. The badge pinned to his chest glinted in the sunlight.

He hadn't changed much since high school. I appreciated that he found a way to retain his optimistic charm in a field that had to be trying, especially at times like this.

"I spoke with Laney Lee," he said, leaning his muscular arms on the countertop.

"She told you about the Wizard?"

"She did. Although this won't surprise you, the Professor suspected as much."

It didn't surprise me. The Professor was one of the most astute people I had ever met. Not much got by his keen and discerning eye.

"Does it make a difference?" I asked.

"What? Knowing who the Wizard really was?"

Thomas removed his sunglasses and placed them on the top of his sandy blond hair.

"Yeah."

"Absolutely. I already put in a call to Kerry. She's pulling medical records now. That should give us some insight. We're still waiting for the coroner's report to see if there were any drugs in Jim's system that might have played a role in his death."

"Does that mean you don't think he was killed?"

"No." Thomas picked up a sketch of the new menu that Steph had been working on. "We're sure it was homicide, but we need to know what may or may not have been in his system. There's a possibility that the killer drugged him, or given what I've learned from Laney, that he could have been taking prescription medication that could have interfered with his cognition."

"What about Sky? Did you find him?"

Thomas tapped the sketch. "No. Not yet, but I have officers looking for him. I'm sure he'll turn up."

"But, what if he's in danger?" I expanded on our earlier conversation and repeated what Laney had told me. "If the Wizard—Jim—and Sky both witnessed something, Sky could be in trouble."

"I know." He folded his hands on the counter. "I understand why you're upset, but there's not much more we can do. I would bet that Sky's hiding, which is probably a good thing. If we can't find him, then the killer can't either."

That was a fair point.

Thomas glanced around. "It's just us, right?"

"Yep. I sent my team to Torte."

He relaxed his shoulders. "Good. There's something

I want to show you." He took one more look around the garden, then reached into his shorts pockets and removed a small black felt jewelry box.

My stomach dropped. Thomas and I had a history. We had shared many wonderful early memories together. He had been my first love, but that was in the past. When I had first returned to Ashland, I think we both felt a bit of the spark we had once held for each other, but that was fleeting. Young love burns hot, but the flame rarely lasts. Isn't that why Shakespeare penned *Romeo and Juliet*?

I had thought we both understood that. The sincere look in his robin's blue eyes made me wonder if I'd been mistaken.

"Jules, why does your face look funny?"

"Huh?" I sucked in my stomach and tried to compose myself.

"You look like you've seen a ghost. What's wrong?" He checked behind us.

"Nothing. What did you want to ask me?" He wasn't going to propose, was he? That would be crazy. He knew that Carlos and I were trying to figure things out. Thomas wouldn't put me in that position, would he?

"Jules, you've been my best friend ever since I can remember." His voice was thick with emotion.

I felt my body pulling away from him. "Uh-huh."

"I can't begin to tell you how important your friendship is to me. I guess I didn't realize it when you were gone for all those years. I mean, don't get me wrong, I missed you, but when you came home it was like no time had gone by. We picked up where we left off, and I feel so fortunate to have you as a friend."

Thomas was scaring me. Had I read our relationship wrong?

He strummed his fingers on the countertop. "Jules, you know me well. You probably know me better than anyone else in town and I'm so nervous to tell you this."

I felt queasy. Where was he going with this?

"I don't want things to change between us. I want us to be friends for life."

"Me too. I want that too." I thought about saying something like, "If you want us to stay friends then please, please don't say whatever you're about to say." But I kept that thought to myself.

"Jules, I think I'm in love," Thomas gushed. The tips of his ears turned red, a smile permeating his entire boyish face.

"Okay." My mouth went dry. How was I going to get out of this conversation tactfully?

"I shouldn't say that I think I'm in love. I *know* that I'm in love. I haven't felt like this for a long time. Maybe it's rash. Maybe I'm following my heart instead of my head, but I don't care." His words came out fast. "I'm in love and I want to shout it from the top of Ashland Springs."

I bit my bottom lip. This was terrible. What had changed? I searched my brain for any recent exchange between Thomas and me. How had our signals gotten this crossed?

"Jules, I'm ready to propose."

I held out my hand. "Thomas, wait—"

He cut me off. "No, I have to say this. If I don't I'm going to lose my nerve. I can't risk that. This has been weighing on me for too long."

"Okay." I braced myself.

"You must know how I'm feeling."

"I'm not sure I do." My stomach knotted.

"Jules, don't be like that." Thomas bounced from one foot to the other. "You do, I know you do. I can't escape these feeling. I can't deny my love and as much as I don't want to risk losing our friendship, I have to do this."

I wanted to scream, "Don't!"

He flipped open the velvet box to reveal a shimmering diamond ring.

"That's beautiful," I said, trying to think of what I could possibly do to salvage his feelings when I turned him down.

"Be honest. I value your opinion more than anything. Tell me what you really think. Do you like it?" He pushed the box closer to me.

"I am being honest—it's gorgeous." The square-cut diamond was elegant and simple. Its mirror-like shape drew in the light.

"Oh good." Thomas let out a long sigh. "I've been worried. It's been in my pocket for a couple weeks now. I've been sure that someone is going to figure out my secret because every five minutes I touch my chest pocket to make sure it's still there."

"Thomas."

"Wait, I'm not finished. I'm glad you approve. If you didn't like it I knew it would have to go back." He shut the box and tucked it back into his uniform pocket.

I ran through every scenario in my mind. Despite the fact that Carlos and I had been separated for the last two years we were still technically married. Thomas knew that. We'd had dozens of conversations about how con-flicted I'd felt. Carlos was living with me. He was here to try to make our relationship work. I couldn't believe Thomas wouldn't respect that.

"I'm so nervous, Jules." Thomas held out his hands. "Look, my palms are sweating."

Mine were too.

"Jules, there's one more thing I need to tell you."

My breath caught in my throat.

"I want you to be one of the first to know." He paused ever so briefly, as if working up the courage to continue. "I'm going to ask Kerry to marry me."

Chapter Sixteen

"What?" I threw my hand over my mouth because I was sure I had screamed so loud that everyone in the nearby vicinity had heard me. I leaned across the counter and wrapped him in a hug. "Thomas, that's so exciting. I'm thrilled for you. You don't need my approval."

His cheeks spotted with color. "I'm glad you're excited. I was worried that you might be upset."

I released him from the hug. "Why would I be upset?"

He looked at his feet. "I know you and Kerry didn't get off to the best start initially. She can be kind of tough until you get to know her. It's a coping strategy. One I wish I was better at sometimes."

"Thomas, your heart is what makes you so good at your job."

"Thanks, Jules, but you're biased, you know." He pointed to the white-and-blue squad car parked nearby. "Although they do call us peace officers here in Ashland. That's always been my slant. To keep the peace."

"You do it well." I gave him a wide smile. "I can't believe it, you're going to propose!" My joy was genuine.

For that brief moment that I had thought I was the object of Thomas's affection, the idea of hurting him felt terrible. It was validation that our relationship was exactly where it was meant to be—as friends.

"Crazy, isn't it?" He touched the pocket containing the ring.

"How are you going to ask her?"

"Tell me what you think of this." Thomas strummed his fingers on his pocket. "Kerry isn't much for big gestures. She's pretty private. I know she wouldn't want an elaborate proposal. I was wondering if I could hire Torte to make us a romantic dinner. If you're up for it, you could deliver it to my place. My mom is going to deck my apartment out with flowers from the shop, and you know Kerry loves your donuts. I thought I could have a plate of them ready for dessert and I would tuck the ring box inside the stack. Or maybe a donut cake. Can you make a donut cake? I don't know. What do you think?"

"I think that she's going to love it. You know her so well. And, whatever you need, I'm in. Donuts, donut cake, you name it." I could feel my features softening. Not only was I relieved that I wasn't Thomas's intended, but I was genuinely happy for my friend. "Do you have a specific dish in mind?"

"She loves pasta. I remember a dish your mom used to make with chicken and sun-dried tomatoes. Do you know the one I'm thinking off? It was really creamy."

"Not only do I know the dish you're talking about, but you're going to freak out when you hear its name."

"What?"

"Proposal Chicken!" I tapped my bare ring finger.

"I'm not even kidding. My dad made it for my mom on their first date, and she teased that it was the pasta that made her fall for him. In fact, it used to be an annual Valentine's Day tradition. Mom gave it up after Dad died. She said it was too painful to make it without him, but I remember they used to have a running tally of how many proposals had been done over plates of Torte's Proposal Chicken. It was a joke around town that if you ordered it, you were destined for love."

"Are you serious?" Thomas grinned.

I made an X over my heart. "I swear."

"Alright, I'll take an order of Proposal Chicken and a box of donuts—or a donut cake. Whatever you think would be best."

"Done." I gave him a huge smile. "I think both. I'll put my creative energy to work. When is the big night?"

Thomas pressed his hand to the ring box again. "Is Friday too soon?"

"Not at all."

"Thanks, Jules. I'm relieved that you're excited and willing to help."

"Anything for you, Thomas." I walked around the counter to give him a hug. "There's only one catch."

"What's that?" His brow furrowed.

"You have to promise that Torte can cater the wedding."

"I don't know if Kerry will even want a wedding. She might want to go to the courthouse and keep it simple."

"That's fine, but you'll have to have a celebratory dinner at some point."

"True." His cell phone buzzed. "I've got to go. We might have a lead on Sky. Thanks for your support,

Jules. I'll drop by Torte tomorrow and finalize every-thing."

"Deal." I watched him drive off. My childhood friend was getting married. That was if Kerry said yes, but she couldn't turn Thomas down. I'd seen the way she looked at him. They were a good match. Kerry kept Thomas grounded and he brought her out of her shell. Secretly, I hoped that she would want a wedding. There was nothing better than a wedding to bring the community together, and I was already dreaming of a donut-inspired three-tiered cake.

The sound of a door slamming behind me made me turn around. Addie stormed out of the side exit to the yoga studio. For someone who taught an ancient calming, spiritual practice, she always seemed on the verge of blowing up. Aside from her yoga attire, I would think that she worked on Wall Street.

She stomped down the stairs. "Ugh! I'm so mad! I want to hit something."

I wasn't sure if she was talking to me or herself.

"Is everything okay, Addie?"

"Jules, jeez, don't scare me like that!" She clenched and unclenched her hands. "I didn't know you were here."

She answered my question for me.

"Sorry. Just organizing." I motioned to the stack of plates on the counter.

"Before I forget, where are my cameras?"

"They're on top of the fridge."

Addie walked into the kitchen and stood on the tips of her toes to check the top of the Andy's sparkling-clean fridge. "They're not here."

"What?" I looked for myself. She was right, the cameras were gone. "Andy must have moved them when he was cleaning. I can call him."

"No, it's fine. Just get them to me later." She laced her fingers together and cracked them in one fluid motion. "I'm ready to punch someone in the face, but otherwise I'm fine."

That also didn't sound in alignment with the yoga vibe.

"Seriously, if I could punch through this wall right now, I would." Addie pounded on the counter to prove her point.

"What's going on?"

"The stupid local police. They are such idiots."

Clearly Addie wasn't aware of my connection to the Professor and my history with Thomas, or if she was she didn't care.

"How so?"

Addie blew air out her nostrils. "They've been by my studio three times now to question me. They keep asking the same stupid, idiotic questions over and over again. It's ridiculous."

I knew that if the Professor was returning to question Addie, he likely had a good reason.

"It's like they think I killed that dirty homeless guy. Why do they keep bothering me? They won't leave me alone. I've told them that I wanted nothing to do with him," she continued, her eyes fixed on the prayer flags waving in the slight breeze. "They know that anyway. I told them to look up my many attempts to get a restraining order. The Wizard was not allowed on this property. I have the paperwork to prove it."

A restraining order? Addie had taken out—or tried to take out—a restraining order on the Wizard?

"I don't understand," I said to Addie. "Why did you need a restraining order?"

"He wouldn't stop bugging me." She cracked her neck. "He hung around here all the time. All the freaking time. He was dirty and gross and he scared away my clients."

She kicked a rock at her feet. Then shot her head toward Nana's. "I blame Laney. She was constantly feeding him and checking on him. I told her that he was nuts. He was a grown adult and if he couldn't take care of himself that was not our problem."

Her callous attitude gave me pause.

"But, why a restraining order?" I pushed, not wanting to reveal Laney's secret.

"Because he was a menace. He would dig through the garbage cans and hang around outside the studio begging for money. It was a total turnoff for my clients. He would ride his bike by the studio and scream his head off to interrupt my classes. He did it every single day. I lost tons of business."

That didn't sound like the Wizard. I had never seen him panhandling. And loitering didn't equate to danger in my book.

"He was stalking me," Addie insisted. "He would follow me down the path to my car at night—not once or twice. Every night. He knew what he was doing too. He would ride just far enough behind me to creep me out."

"So you took out a restraining order?"

"No, I tried. The police declined multiple times. They claimed that the bike path is public domain and said I didn't have any evidence. He rode by here all the time to mess with me. I warned him a few days ago that if he came near me I was arming myself and he'd be sorry."

"Arming yourself?" Addie had a gun? The thought of a yoga instructor toting a gun was a complete dichotomy.

"Not with a gun, although my dad told me he would bring one of his hunting rifles up for me if the Wizard kept bothering me. I bought pepper spray and a Taser. You can't be too prepared. If he was going to follow me at night, then I would take matters into my own hands. The police were worthless. They wouldn't do anything."

I tried to digest what Addie was saying. She had threatened the Wizard. Could that be why the Professor kept questioning her?

It was like Addie had read my mind. "The police are stuck on that. They think because I bought pepper spray—legally by the way—that I had a vendetta against the Wizard. It was the other way around. He was out to get me from the start. From the first day I moved here he started harassing me. There hasn't been a day that's gone by that he didn't try something. I don't know why everyone in this town is so concerned about his well-being, when they should have been concerned about mine."

"I'm sorry to hear that you had challenges with the Wizard. I think the reason the community has responded like we have is because none of us had interactions with him like that. I never knew him to be dangerous. In fact, if anything he was the opposite—he spread joy."

"You try being followed to your car every night by someone in a black cape and see how it feels." She stared at me with fury. "And that's not true about the entire community loving him. You should talk to Hunter. He'll back me up. The Wizard did the same kind of stuff to his bike shop. Stealing bikes, begging in front of the store. The graffiti by the dumpsters. That's from the Wizard." She motioned toward the alleyway. "Hunter was fed up too. I told the detective to talk to him and stop asking me the same freaking questions."

"I'm sure that the police are following up on every lead." I wondered about the truth behind Addie's statement. When she had complained about someone following her earlier, I had gotten the feeling that she meant from a distance, like my experience. Now she was making it sound like the person was on her heels.

"Yeah? You think so? I'm not so sure. If they want to know who killed the Wizard they should stop bugging me and venture across the street." With that, she turned and disappeared into the studio.

Had I heard Addie correctly? Was she hinting that Hunter could be the killer?

Chapter Seventeen

My conversation with Addie left me more confused than ever. I couldn't reconcile the docile and kind man I had known as the Wizard with her description of him. Was she lying? Could it be the other way around? Had she harassed him because he didn't match the aesthetic of her high-end yoga studio? Why was the Professor continuing to question her? He must have some serious suspicions about her story.

And, what about Hunter? I had witnessed him threaten the Wizard in person. Was he an ally in Addie's fight or could there be more to it?

I finished stacking the last of the supplies and closed up the outdoor kitchen for the night. In the flurry of activity, I hadn't checked my cell phone since I had posted the ads. I turned it on to find I had two missed calls and a voicemail from Carlos.

"Julieta, you left me sleeping this morning. You should have woken me. I hope your day was good. I have a meeting at five this evening. Then Lance would like to meet for dinner and drinks at Alchemy. Is this okay, si? If so, I will meet you there at seven."

A meeting? The dropping sensation returned to my stomach. What meeting? Carlos seemed to be having a number of meetings, none of which he was talking to me about. Why the secrecy?

I knew what I had to do—face my fears and talk to Carlos. If he wanted to return to the ship, it would be better to have him go sooner rather than dragging out my heartbreak.

Tonight, Jules, do it tonight, I told myself as I tucked Steph's menus into a drawer and left Scoops. I had nearly two hours. That would be enough time to swing by Torte and get my thoughts together. After our dinner with Lance, I was going to sit down with Carlos and ask him for the truth.

Thoughts of him returning to the *Amour of the Seas* clouded my vision as I headed for Torte. At least we had given it a shot. That was better than not trying. I guess I hadn't realized how tightly I'd been clinging to the hope that Carlos might fall under Ashland's spell.

How can he not love this? I thought as I strolled along Fourth Street, past sweet little cottages with white picket fences. Bees hummed on wildflowers. Neighbors chatted on porches, and everyone waved hello as I walked past.

I barely remembered turning onto Main Street. Hot tears welled in my eyes as I imagined driving Carlos to the airport and saying a final goodbye.

At Torte, I stopped to get my emotions in check before going inside. The team was likely gone, but I didn't want to risk looking like a blubbering mess. Steph and Rosa's window display provided the perfect distraction. I blinked away my tears, rubbed my eyes on my sleeves, squared my shoulders, and took in a long, slow breath. The window turned out even better than I expected. They had strung paper flowers and purple and pink fairy lights from the top of the window. Cake platters in a variety of sizes had been arranged in paper grass at the bottom of the window. Each cake stand was piled with rose meltaway cookies and paper rose petals.

I smiled, feeling more centered, and unlocked the front door. Once inside, I went downstairs to find Mom in the kitchen.

"Mom, I'm so happy to see you!"

Mom wrapped me in a hug. "Me too. I told Marty that if he doesn't see me around here more, I should fire myself."

"Never." I kissed her cheek. "You have no idea how glad I am that you're here."

She sprinkled olive oil on pizza dough. "I told Doug that I would make dinner here since he's busy with the case. That way he doesn't have to drive out to the lake or settle for takeout."

"What's on the menu?" I looked over her shoulder.

She massaged the oil into the pizza dough. "A simple wood-fired pizza with fresh basil, goat cheese, tomatoes, and grilled chicken."

"Yum." I swiped a piece of chicken.

"You're welcome to stay. Carlos too."

"Apparently we're having dinner with Lance later." I watched as she brushed red sauce on the pizza dough. "Anything new with the case?"

"Not that I've heard. Doug is upset by this one. The Wizard has been part of the community for as long as I can remember."

"Did you ever think he was dangerous?" I asked.

Mom scowled. "The Wizard? No."

I told her about my conversation with Addie.

"That doesn't make sense." Her brows arched. She wiped her hands on a towel. Mom was a true beauty. She was in her fifties but could have passed for my older sister with bright brown eyes and soft features.

She sprinkled goat cheese on the pizza. "As far as I know, the Wizard never panhandled. Doug told me that was because he didn't need to. Once they discovered his identity they were able to pull old records. Jim had plenty of money. In fact his bank account had nearly thirty thousand dollars in it."

"Really?" That was huge news. The Wizard had money? Laney couldn't have known that because she had mentioned on more than one occasion that things were tight at Nana's. Could someone have killed him for the money?

We shared what we each knew about the case. Then the conversation drifted to Scoops and baking.

"I have some exciting news that is top secret," I said to Mom, knowing that I could trust her to keep what I was about to tell her quiet. Plus, I wasn't ready to talk about Carlos. I figured Thomas's news would keep us occupied. "Thomas is going to propose to Detective Kerry."

Mom gave me a strange smile.

"What?"

"Janet called earlier to tell me." Mom and Janet, Thomas' mom, had been best friends for years. "Isn't it wonderful news?"

"Yes! I'm holding out hope for a real wedding, but

Thomas wasn't sure if that's Kerry's style. However, we have been asked to make an engagement dinner." I told her about his request for Proposal Chicken.

"Many love stories have been launched with that chicken." Mom grinned.

"Let's do that along with a shaved Brussels sprout salad and garlic knots. Thomas wants donuts, so I was thinking we could make an assortment of glazed rounds and decorate them with beautiful fruit-infused glazes—raspberry, blackberry, lemon cream, chocolate orange, almond cherry. Then we could bake a tiered donut cake in our round Bundt pans—I'm thinking buttermilk with touches of cinnamon and nutmeg with a cherry drizzle and sprinkles on the top. He could tuck the ring box into the center of the cake. What do you think?"

"Ohhhh, I love it." Mom clapped. "Who doesn't love love?"

"Exactly!"

We worked in tandem, prepping her dinner for the Professor. He showed up a few minutes before I was due to meet Carlos and Lance at Alchemy.

"Baking goddesses, what smells so divine?" The Professor hung his tweed jacket on the coatrack near the basement door and came into the kitchen. He greeted Mom with a soft kiss on her forehead. Then he turned to me. "Juliet, I'm pleased you're here. Will you be joining us for dinner?"

"I'm actually on my way out the door to meet Lance and Carlos."

"Ah, excellent." He looked to the clock that hung on the far wall. "Might I beg five minutes, or will that make you late?"

I glanced at the clock. "No. I have time."

Mom shooed us out of the kitchen. "Go sit. I'll finish dinner."

The Professor and I moved to the couch near the atomic fireplace in the seating area adjacent to the kitchen.

"Did you find Sky?" I asked.

He removed his Moleskine notebook from his plaid striped shirt. "Alas, not as of yet. I'm not abreast to what you may have already learned from Thomas, but we suspect that he's gone into hiding."

"Yeah, that's what Thomas said. He also said you knew about the Wizard being Laney's father?"

"I wouldn't necessarily say that I knew, as much as I had an inclination that he was connected to someone here who had his best interests at heart."

"Laney was distraught when I saw her earlier. Mom said that Jim had money—thirty thousand dollars? I don't think Laney knows that. She's talked candidly about the financial challenges of running a food truck. Do you think he was killed for his money?"

"It's most unsettling, and frankly at this point everything is a possibility. However, it's doubtful anyone could have known his financial status. We discovered the money in a 401k that hasn't been touched for thirty years." He pressed his index fingers to his lips and turned the page in his journal. After finding what he was looking for, he returned his gaze to me. "I don't want to keep you from your engagement, but I would like to ask what your impressions are of your new landlord, Addie."

I wasn't the least bit surprised that the Professor was

interested in learning more about Addie. "Did Andy call you?"

"He did. I appreciate you steering him in my direction."

"Well, there's that. I don't know if Addie and Dean or someone else has been dealing on the tracks. Laney wondered about Lars too, Hunter's son."

The Professor made a note. I went on to explain our strange conversation and her insistence that the Wizard was stalking her. "That doesn't sound like him, does it?" I asked.

"Jim—the Wizard—may have been eccentric, but a stalker, absolutely not."

"Do you think Addie's lying?"

He considered my question for a minute. "Perhaps. Or perhaps this is a case of mistaken identity."

"You think someone was pretending to be the Wizard?" I flashed to the biker Laney and I had seen in a cape earlier.

"At this stage, I have no proof and nothing tangible to go on other than my instinct, but it wouldn't be difficult to tie on a cape and take a spin around the bike path, would it? I think there's a distinct possibility that in the dark, one could easily make an assumption that they'd seen the Wizard, when in fact they hadn't."

The Professor's hypothesis made sense to me. Addie had specifically commented on seeing her stalker in a cape. Someone could have been posing as the Wizard, but who?

Mom came toward us with a bottle of wine and two glasses.

"I must let you go, Juliet." The Professor stood and

offered me a hand. "Do give our best to Lance and Carlos."

I hugged them both goodbye and left. On the short walk to Alchemy, I racked my brain for who could possibly have pretended to be the Wizard. Someone who wanted to intimidate or scare Addie. Why? Addie had a brash personality. Was it possible that her attitude had rubbed someone the wrong way? Maybe the imposter had simply picked the Wizard as an easy scapegoat. Or, could it be connected to his murder?

Chapter Eighteen

Alchemy was a swanky bar connected to the Winchester Inn on the south side of town. Its wall of twelve-foot high windows was lined with gold rope lights. The interior was dimly lit with glowing candles and recessed soft lights on the ceiling and bar. Four dark walnut tables flanked each side of the narrow space with a bar at the far end that boasted Ashland's most impressive collection of spirits. Glass bottles in shimmering blues, silvers, and gold lined the shelves that stretched to the ceiling. A ladder on rollers hung at one end of the bar to access the top shelf. It reminded me of a Shakespearean library.

Carlos and Lance were seated at a table closest to the bar. Their heads were huddled together when I approached the table. They spoke in hushed tones.

"Hey guys," I said with a bright grin.

They jumped apart.

"Am I interrupting?"

"Interrupting? Darling, banish the thought." Lance sounded too perky.

I caught him giving Carlos a side-eye as I slid into the bench.

Carlos casually wrapped an arm around my shoulder. "You are right on time, mi querida."

"What were you guys talking about?" I looked from Lance to Carlos.

"Cocktails." Lance offered me a cream-colored, embossed drink menu. "Choices, choices."

I could tell they were holding back, but I studied the menu. Each cocktail had its own clever story on the menu, like the Drawing Down the Moon—a clove-infused gin mingled with fresh lemon, bitters, and house-made citrus syrup. The note beneath the cocktail read: "She walks amidst the shadows of night, the radiance of the moon her only light."

"Now *that* is a very romantic cocktail," Carlos said, pointing to the drink.

"I'm partial to the Don't Run in the Campground," Lance said.

We all chuckled when we read the description of the smokey whiskey: "You only ran because it's past tense."

"Clever, clever cocktails." Lance rubbed his hands together and smirked.

"What are you going to order?" I asked. "No, wait. Let me guess." I studied the menu for a minute. "I'm thinking the Persimmon Slip."

"Darling, you know me too well."

A waiter wearing a black apron and crisp white shirt approached our table.

"We're not quite ready to order," Lance said. "We're waiting for one more."

"We are?" I asked.

At that moment, Arlo strolled into the bar. Lance gave me a sheepish grin. "We are."

Lance introduced Carlos and Arlo, who immediately discovered they shared a mutual fandom for international soccer. Apparently, Arlo's sports enthusiasm wasn't limited to softball.

When the waiter returned to take our orders, I opted for the Drawing Down the Moon and Carlos went for a classic gin and tonic infused with basil and mango.

"I'll take an IPA," Arlo said.

"Same for me," Lance seconded. I caught his eye and gave him a gasp. Never in my life had I known Lance to order a beer. "It sounds refreshing, doesn't it?" He raised one eyebrow.

"My top reason for taking this job and moving to Oregon was the beer." Arlo handed our waiter his drink menu. "I'm making it my mission to sample every beer while I'm here."

"Excellent plan," Lance replied. "The choices are limitless."

"What about food?" Carlos interjected. "A cheese board and pommes frites to start, si?"

"Si, si!" Lance clapped.

Carlos put in our order when our waiter returned with drinks.

"A toast to friends new and old," Lance said raising his pint glass. It was so weird to see him holding a frothy beer.

"Cheers!" We clinked our glasses together.

"How's the softball team doing?" Lance asked Arlo.

"They are a great group of players. Have any of you followed the team?"

"Not really," I admitted. "I've read about their success in the paper, but I've never made it to a game." The SOU softball team had won the national championship the past two years. The team had become local media darlings, garnering articles and interviews.

"You have to come. They are a blast to watch. Their hitting is a thing of magic. We have a game tomorrow night, I can get you tickets if you're interested."

"How charming. I so enjoy sporting outings." Lance ran his long graceful finger along the rim of his pint glass.

If Arlo picked up on Lance's lack of sport's knowledge, like referring to a softball game as a 'sporting outing,' he didn't correct the flub.

"How was your meeting?" Lance asked Carlos.

Carlos shifted his arm and massaged my neck. "It was good. Yes, I think we are making nice progress."

Lance knew about Carlos's meeting?

I caught Carlos and Lance share the briefest of looks.

Carlos avoided my eyes. "Nothing. It was just a meeting with a vendor who may have a new bottling system for us I will fill you in later. We do not need to bore Arlo with talk of work."

"Don't mind me," Arlo said with a smile. "I have my beer and French fries are on the way, so I'm perfectly content."

Our pre-dinner snacks arrived. We noshed on creamy Rogue Valley cheeses, crusty bread, marinated olives, and pommes frites dipped in a lemon dill aioli.

"You are liking Ashland, yes?" Carlos asked Arlo after spreading a generous helping of blue cheese onto a cracker.

"Absolutely. It's the nicest place I've ever been. If I wasn't experiencing it myself, I would say it's too good to be true. The people are nice, the weather is more than nice, the views, the wildlife, and the food. I can't think of a single negative."

"Except for the murder," Lance mumbled under his breath.

"Sorry, I didn't mean to be crass," Arlo apologized. "I should have thought of that. I'm out of the loop, but I have heard a number of people talking about how much the town loved the man who was killed."

"Don't give it a thought." Lance sounded embarrassed. "You're spot-on about how idyllic Ashland can be, it just so happens that tragedy struck. Not to worry. Juliet and I are on the case. We're working hand in hand with the police to ensure that all will be made right soon."

"On the case?" Carlos moved his arm from my shoulder, so he could look directly into my eyes. "You are working with the police?"

"Not officially." I kicked Lance under the table. "The Professor, as he's affectionately known around town, is Ashland's lead detective and happens to be married to my mom," I explained to Arlo. "He's like a second dad to me. Sometimes he'll talk through a case with me, that's all."

I tried to kick Lance again, but he scooted closer to Arlo and out of reach.

"And you, Lance?" Arlo asked. "How have you become involved in the investigation?"

Lance shot me his signature Cheshire grin. "That's classified."

Carlos's deep eyes were filled with concern. "It is not dangerous for you to be helping, is it?"

"No, of course not." I reached for a fry and dipped it in the aioli sauce. "You know the Professor, he would never put me in a dangerous position."

That seemed to bring Carlos a bit of relief. The only person currently in danger was Lance. I wanted to throttle him for bringing up the subject.

Thankfully, our waiter shifted the topic by checking in to see if our drinks needed refreshing and if we were ready to order dinner. I perused the menu and decided on a green salad with pears, candied walnuts, blue cheese, and grilled chicken. Suddenly I was famished.

Arlo was a great conversationalist. He kept us engaged and off the topic of murder with stories of his various theater travels. Lance hung on his every word.

Carlos added in anecdotes of outlandish requests from passengers. "You would not believe what people will ask for. I had one lady who was furious with me because her spaghetti noodles were too long. Customers they will rewrite the menu. Can I get my sushi cooked, please? Or, I would like fish and chips with no fish." He bumped his forehead in exasperation.

"The same is true in theater," Arlo added, catching Lance's eye and giving him a sly grin. "We can both attest to bearing witness to plenty of mishaps. At one theater I literally had to tell an audience that we hear you, we see you, we even smell you—so please shower and leave your leftovers in the car. Live theater is, well—"

"Live," Lance answered for him. They had scooted closer together. "Don't get me started on patrons who show up drunk. A pre-show cocktail is always a great idea." He paused and raised his glass. "But no one wants a drunk sitting front and center."

Dinner was masterful. Carlos devoured his pork belly. He was hard to please when it came to food. That was true for most chefs, but he ate every bite on his plate.

"This is most impressive. The chef has a delicate touch. I would like to say hello."

When we finished, Carlos called the waiter over to ask if he could stop in the kitchen. Arlo excused himself to use the restroom.

"Thanks a lot, Lance. I hadn't really said much to Carlos yet," I whispered when they were both out of sight.

"Sorry. Sorry." Lance threw his hands up in surrender. "I didn't know."

My cell phone buzzed at that moment. I reached into my bag and saw Thomas's face on the screen. "It's Thomas," I said to Lance.

"You better answer it."

I answered the call. "Hey, Thomas, one sec. I'm walking outside." I stood and left the bar so as not to disturb the other diners. The air outside had gone cold. "Okay, I can talk now. What's up?"

"Jules, where are you?"

"At Alchemy, why?" I didn't like the solemn tone in Thomas's voice.

"I'm at your new space. You better get down here quick."

"Why? What's wrong?"

Were those sirens in the background?

"It's okay, Jules, no one else has been hurt, but someone has set your kitchen on fire."

Chapter Nineteen

"Wait, Thomas, it sounded like you said that Scoops is on fire."

"It is, Jules. You should get down here."

I nearly dropped the phone. "Okay, I'm on my way." I hung up and ran inside. Lance and Arlo, who had returned to the table, were considering the dessert menu.

"What's wrong, Juliet? You look like you've seen a ghost—or worse—Richard Lord." Lance chuckled at his own joke.

"It's Scoops. Someone has set a fire. Thomas is there he wants me to come right away." My hands shook as I spoke.

"Sit down." Lance took charge. "I'll settle the bill and get Carlos. We'll get you there. You shouldn't drive in your state."

I wanted to protest, but followed his advice.

Arlo modeled slow and steady breathing. "Do this with me. In . . . and . . . out. In . . . and . . . out."

Panic tried to fight its way to the surface, but I breathed with Arlo. All of the hard work we had put in prepping the new space only to have it go up in flames. Who would do this? And why?

Carlos and Lance hurried to the table.

"Let's go, Julieta. Lance will drive." Carlos laced his fingers through mine. "It will be okay. It is just a kitchen, si?"

"Yeah." I squeezed his hand as we left the restaurant. He was right of course. The important thing was that Thomas had said no one had been hurt, but still we were so close to being ready to open. What if we had to start over?

Lance flew down Pioneer Street. We made it to the Railroad District in less than five minutes. My heart thudded in my chest as we pulled up in front of the shop. Two fire trucks were on the scene, along with Thomas's squad SUV and the Professor's unmarked sedan.

"Juliet!" Mom waved from the sidewalk. She was standing near Nana's Food Truck.

I ran over. "What happened?"

"We don't know yet, honey." She hugged me. "Doug and the fire chief are sure that it's arson. Someone lit a garbage can on fire and set it right in the middle of the counter."

"How bad is the damage?" I could smell smoke, but didn't see any flames. From my vantage point all I could see was a pile of rubble and clouds of thick smoke.

"Doug's in there now. He's going to give me a report. As you can see, the pergola has collapsed. I don't know about the rest of the kitchen yet. One of the firefighters I was talking to said he didn't think it was as bad as it could have been." Mom pointed to Cyclepath, where Hunter was talking to Thomas and Detective Kerry. "Hunter was working late and smelled smoke. If he hadn't been here, who knows? The entire kitchen and most likely the yoga studio would have burned. The firefighters were on the scene quickly. I know that there's some damage, but I don't think the kitchen is a complete loss."

"That's a relief." I let out a sigh. Then I glanced at the bike shop. Thank goodness Hunter had alerted the fire department.

The Professor came over to us. He coughed and cleared his throat. "Apologies. It's certainly smokey over there."

"How bad is it, Doug?" Mom asked.

"The counter and the far wall of cabinets have been badly burned, most likely beyond repair. The pergola is not going to be salvageable, but the equipment appears to be in functional shape. The fire crew is mopping up now. Once they've finished you can go have a closer look for yourselves."

"And they're sure the fire was intentional?" I asked.

The Professor folded his hands together and frowned. "They are. There is no question about that. Whoever set the fire used your highly flammable paint stain. It was spilled on the counter and splashed on the cabinets to ignite the flames. Without the fast-acting response from the fire crew, the attached studio would have been next. The culprit doused the entire adjoining wall with paint stain."

"Why?" Mom voiced what I was thinking. "Who would want to sabotage our little ice cream shop?"

"It's too soon to say, but I highly doubt that you were the target." The Professor's eyes traveled across the street. "I need a moment with Thomas and Kerry. I'll be back shortly."

He walked away.

"What do you think that means?" I asked Mom as Carlos, Lance, and Arlo approached.

"Addie's studio?" Mom turned around and looked at the building.

"That's what I was wondering, too." I didn't say more, as Carlos gave Mom a hug. If someone had targeted Addie's studio, it couldn't be a coincidence. There had to be a connection with the Wizard's death. I felt like there was something obvious I was missing. It was like the pieces were laid out for me, I just couldn't put them together in the correct way.

"Helen, you are okay?" Carlos asked Mom.

She pressed her lips to his hand. "I'm fine. Everyone is fine. In fact, it sounds like the fire was contained quickly."

"That's good news," Lance said.

Arlo hung back.

"Mom, have you met Arlo yet? He's the new managing director at OSF."

"I don't believe I've had the pleasure." Arlo extended his hand. "I'm sorry that we're meeting under these circumstances though."

"It's wonderful to meet you, regardless." Mom smiled broadly.

"Is there anything we can do to help?" Lance asked.

"That's so kind of you, but no. We have to wait for the fire department to finish cleaning up and inspecting the scene. You should go home. It's late," Mom said.

Lance looked to me. "Do you want company, Juliet?"

"No. Mom's right. Go home. I'll check in first thing in the morning and let you know where things stand."

"If you're sure?" He hesitated.

"Go, Lance." I stepped forward and kissed his cheek.

He pressed his hand on the spot. "I'm never washing this again."

Mom tossed her head back and laughed. "Oh, Arlo, you have your work cut out for you with this one, don't you?"

Arlo didn't miss a beat. "You have no idea." He threw a palm to his forehead.

"Hey, I'm your ride home. You better watch it." Lance swatted him.

They left together. I surveyed the scene around us. Flashing lights made it hard to focus. Puffy white smoke—or maybe it was steam—rose from what was once our outdoor kitchen.

The Professor came over again. This time with Thomas and Kerry.

"Well, any more news, Doug?" Mom asked.

"One interesting fact has emerged. Hunter is sure that he saw someone matching the Wizard's description earlier. He's reporting that he saw a man in a cape, riding a bike near the shop not long before the fire broke out."

"So someone is still pretending to be the Wizard even though he's dead?" I asked out loud.

"It appears that way." The Professor rubbed the rust-colored stubble on his chin.

Could it be Sky? It made sense on one hand since he had disappeared and before that he'd been hiding out in our kitchen. The sticking point was motive. Why would Sky want to impersonate the Wizard? That didn't make sense. If anything he had seemed scared to me.

Addie showed up. She must have been stirred from her bed since she was wearing a pair of Uggs slippers and a bathrobe. "What happened?" she shrieked. Her nostrils flared.

"There's been a fire."

She glared at the Professor. "Obviously! I mean who did this?"

The Professor explained the strange turn of events in his calm and steady manner. "I often turn to the Bard at times such as this. I find his words insightful. 'Wisely, and slow, they stumble that run fast.'"

The veins in Addie's thin neck bulged. "What does that even mean?"

"It means that we must do our duty and investigate with careful consideration."

"You need to figure out who did this—now!" She jabbed her finger in the air. "I want a name and I want them behind bars tonight." Addie's outburst made Mom take a step back.

"I understand your frustration," the Professor responded in an even yet authoritative voice. "Alas, I'm afraid that's not exactly how things work in the real world. Perhaps on television, but not here. We have procedures we must follow and an investigation to complete."

Addie folded her arms across her chest. "That's unacceptable. Just because I'm a millennial doesn't mean that I'm an idiot, old man. You obviously need to put a team of people on this now."

I cringed. That was uncalled for. What Addie likely didn't understand was that this *was* Ashland's team. And, the Professor was hardly an old man, and Addie had some nerve berating him like that when his sole purpose was to help us.

He took it in stride. "I too wish that things were different, and yet they aren't. As the Bard would say, 'Things done well and with a care, exempt themselves from fear.'"

"I'm not afraid," Addie shot back. "I'm pissed. Someone tried to burn down my studio. I want them found and in jail. If you're not going to do it, I'm going to find someone who will." She didn't bother to hang around to hear the Professor's response.

We watched her march toward a group of firefighters.

"She's not happy," Mom noted.

"That's an understatement," I agreed. "Although, the longer I spend with Addie, the more I think that's the way she operates in the world. She has a short fuse."

"Which is so odd given that yoga is her chosen profession."

The Professor was quiet. I noticed that he was carefully observing Addie's interactions with the fire crew.

Carlos looped his arm around my waist. "It is late. I think we should go. Let the police and fire complete their work and we can come first thing in the morning. It is too dark to see much tonight, anyway."

"Wise advice." Mom gave him an approving smile.

"Indeed, might I beg your help in escorting Helen home," the Professor asked. "I have the sense that it may be a late night."

"Of course." Carlos extended his free hand to Mom. "We will gladly give you a ride."

Mom turned to the Professor. "Do what you need to do, Doug."

They shared a sweet kiss. I appreciated their relationship in so many ways, but one of them was how they allowed each other autonomy while still offering support.

"Shall we reconvene here tomorrow?" the Professor asked before we left.

"Sure." I wanted to see the damage firsthand, but Carlos was right. I needed sleep. Hopefully by the light of a new day things would be clearer.

Chapter Twenty

As promised, we returned to Scoops early the next morning to assess the fire damage in the daylight. Carlos and I arrived before Mom and the Professor. The smell of burnt wood hung heavy in the air. Only one beam of the rotting pergola was still standing. Everything else was a piled mess of charred debris and muddy water.

"It's bad," I said, staring at the yellow caution tape that stretched from the side gate around to Addie's studio.

Carlos kissed the top of my head and rubbed my shoulders. He smelled of fresh mint, Italian lemons, and cedar. I recognized the subtle scent of his cologne and leaned into his solid embrace.

"Should we wait for the Professor?" I asked, pulling away from him after a minute.

"No." He stepped forward and lifted the tape for me to crawl under. "This is your space. I think it is fine for us. We will not touch anything, but you need to see what repairs will be needed. We will need to file an insurance claim, si?"

I was glad that Carlos didn't have any reservations about crossing the police boundary. We surveyed the garden first. It looked like a war zone. Foamy residue coated the old sun umbrellas. It mixed into the grass like soapy snowflakes. A muddy path had been carved from the kitchen to the side gate where the firefighters had stomped back and forth in their boots to put out the fire. Fire retardant had dusted the bistro tables, but at least they were still intact. That was a relief and one less thing we were going to have to replace.

We squished through the mud to get a better look at the kitchen. Our hard work the past few days had literally gone up in flames. Stephanie's chalkboard was a total loss, as was the new awning and sign. The long bar and cabinets were black and sooty.

In addition to the fire damage, the kitchen looked as if it had been hit by a mini tsunami. Water pooled in muddy puddles on the ground and dripped from above.

"This isn't good," I said to Carlos through clenched teeth.

"No, but it is not terrible either." He kicked a piece of singed wood that had once belonged to the pergola.

I could tell he was trying to be positive for me. When the Professor and Thomas had said the damage wasn't as extensive as it could have been last night, I guess I had gotten it in my head that maybe Scoops wasn't a complete loss. Seeing how the fire had scorched the kitchen changed my definition of "extensive damage." Yes, the building had been salvaged, but the majority of our kitchen was in bad shape. We were likely going to have to start from scratch.

Carlos tapped the blackened post above the pile of rubble. "This is not stable. It must go."

I moved away, starting to make mental notes of everything that would need to be repaired.

"Julieta, you are too quiet." Carlos grew still and watched me.

"It's hard to see," I admitted. "I guess I sort of thought it wasn't going to be this bad. We're going to have to start over, aren't we?"

His blue eyes pierced mine. "Si. It is true."

I let out a long sigh, wishing I had never agreed to try something new in the space. I had thought building out the ice cream shop would be relatively easy, inexpensive, and painless. The thought of spending hours on the phone with the insurance company, waiting for payments to come in, and negotiating a settlement made me want to call Addie and say forget it.

"Mi querida, it will be okay." Carlos kissed the top of my head.

"But it's so much work." I hated the whiny tone in my voice. I should have been grateful that no one had been injured, and that the firefighters had been able to put the fire out before it leapt to Namaste.

"Si, but the work it is always worth it, no?" He tugged me away from the kitchen. "Look, up here you can create something that is entirely you. You will make this space your own. I know it is a setback, but it is also an opportunity. You don't have to force yourself to fit in a box that belonged to someone else. We will make this space belong to you—it can now become a true evolution of Torte."

His words touched me. The expansive sky above reminded me of the sea. He was right. What if we could truly create an open-air experience? What if we brought touches of the turquoise ocean waters here?

An idea began to form in my mind. Everyone had wanted to tear the pergola down. Fate had intervened for us. Instead of closing the kitchen in with the heavy vines, we could pull down the sky.

"I know that look, Julieta. You can see it, no?"

"Yes!" I threw my arms around him. "Yes. I can see it. Sun drenched and dreamy with wispy clouds as soft and delicate as our creamy concretes stretching above, the earthy grass at our feet."

"And we could install a retractable awning for cover in the rain or shade if it is too hot, like the sails of a ship."

The images that were starting to take shape were even more exciting than our initial designs. Carlos was right. I had been trying to piece together someone else's space. Now I could create my own.

By the time Mom and the Professor arrived, Carlos and I had come up with an entirely new plan for the out-door dining area. Mom was a bit taken aback by our burst of energy.

"How much coffee have you had this morning, Juliet?" She gave me her best Mom side-eye.

"Not enough. Listen, when we saw the damage it was like a punch to the gut, but Carlos reminded me that this space has never felt quite right. Maybe the fire is a blessing in disguise."

Carlos explained our ideas. I took a minute to myself. I had forgotten how his unyielding positivity permeated everything he did. It was a rare gift. One I had relied on often in my early years in the ship's pastry kitchen.

Carlos always found a way to shift my perspective, to evolve my frustration over a soufflé that had fallen flat or a guest's off-handed criticism into a learning experience.

"Do not let this get under your skin, Julieta," Carlos had said one night when I returned to our cabin with puffy eyes because a guest had complained that the dessert was so sweet it made her seasick. "Dessert, like life, it is our own interpretation. This is not about you or your dessert. This is about the guest. She is looking for someone to blame for her misfortune. Do not take responsibility for her. She must do this for herself."

Why had I forgotten this side of Carlos? His positivity came from a place of genuine joy. It wasn't forced or fake. It didn't involve an agenda. His intention when trying to build someone up was simply that. It was one of the reasons I'd fallen in love with him.

I watched him talk with Mom and the Professor. His casual stance and easy mannerism balanced his addictively charming smile and dazzling blue eyes. Other men as handsome as Carlos might come across as self-centered, but his spirit broke through his exterior. It was impossible not to feel a zest for life when Carlos was around.

But what if he wants to leave?

How could I ever be happy, if he's not happy?

The thought sent an ache of pain burning through my chest. I should have asked him last night. I knew I was only dragging out the inevitable, but part of me wanted to live in the happy bliss of denial a little longer.

Did he sense it too?

He caught my eye and motioned for me to come over.

I squared my shoulders and pushed the unsettling emotions stirring within me aside.

"Did the fire chief discover anything new last night?" I asked the Professor.

His hazel eyes were narrowed on the side of Namaste where the fire had started to spread. If the firefighters hadn't arrived when they did, the building would have gone up in flames too. "Nothing as of yet, aside from the fact that this fire was absolutely intentional. The arsonist took advantage of your highly flammable paint and stain and they weren't subtle about it. Which is of interest."

"How so?" Carlos asked, zipping his puffy black vest and tucking his hands in his pockets.

"I'll say this, I don't believe we're dealing with a professional. More likely a crime of opportunity or something to that effect." The Professor trailed off.

"Has Addie calmed down?" I asked.

"Excellent question." He cleared his throat. "I didn't see her again after our exchange, but that's not to say that she didn't give my colleagues an earful."

"It is upsetting," Mom replied, staring at the charred remains of the outdoor kitchen. "I can't blame her for being out of sorts, but that doesn't give her an excuse to be awful to the very people trying to help her. It's so hard to watch." She looked to the Professor.

"Comes with the territory, my dear. I have thick skin. Or at least a thick jacket." He patted the sleeves of his tweed jacket. "Trust me, over the course of my career I've dealt with people in much more frenzied states than Addie."

Mom didn't look convinced, but she changed the subject. "The insurance adjuster should be here any minute. They'll need to take pictures and document the scene, but once they're done are we okay to start tackling cleanup and demolition or is there more to be done with the investigation?"

I had wondered the same thing. Given the yellow caution tape, I assumed that the police and fire crews still considered our space to be an active crime scene.

"Let me place a call to my colleague. Don't quote me, but I believe you should have the green light to commence with cleaning once the insurance inspectors have had a chance to examine the scene. That is unless something changed after I left last night." He walked to the side gate to make the call.

"I wonder how we start to clean up this mess." I glanced at the residue on the countertops and charred cupboards.

Mom frowned then made a funny face. "Sledgehammers?"

I chuckled. "Yeah, you might be right on that."

Carlos's phone buzzed. He glanced at the screen. "I need to take this and then I have an appointment at Uva soon. I will check in later, okay?"

"Sure." I forced a smile as he left me with a quick kiss on the forehead. More secrecy.

"How are things going with you two?" Mom asked after Carlos was out of sight.

"Good." That was fair. Things were good between us.

"And?" She pressed.

"Mom, that's not fair."

"What?"

"That look. I can tell you don't believe me."

"Honey, those words never left these lips." She put her index finger to her lips.

"I know. Things are going well. We're good. We're great." I paused. "It's different now though. I can't exactly explain how. There's nothing tangible. We have a lovely, easy relationship. Carlos seems to be enjoying spending his days at Uva. Honestly, I see him less than I thought I would. We have our separate focuses, which I think is good."

"It *is* good," Mom agreed. "I think it's healthy and important in any partnership that you each have your own interests and activities."

"Right. We do."

"Then, what's the problem?"

"I think he wants to leave."

Mom's lips parted. "Really? He seems so happy here."

"Yeah. He hasn't said anything, but just like that he keeps getting calls and sneaking away for mysterious meetings. I think he's talking to the *Amour of the Seas* about a new contract." Saying it aloud made me even more sure.

"The worst part is that I love having him here. I hadn't realized how much time I've spent the past two years pining for him while he's been at sea. It felt like he was Odysseus and I was trying to keep the home fires burning for his return. I spent large chunks of time daydreaming about what it would be like to have Carlos here in Ashland. I imagined long, leisurely days like the ones we're experiencing now, where we swapped stories of our day over a bottle of wine and a plate of pasta at night. I imagined jogs through Lithia Park, strong shots of espresso, and cooking in the kitchen together."

"That hasn't happened?" Mom's forehead scrunched.

"It has. That's the problem. It's been wonderful. Perfect. Too perfect. I don't know what's wrong with me. This is what I wanted. I wanted Ashland and Carlos. I have both now and yet it doesn't feel right. If feels too easy, like it's just an illusion. It's not real. He's going to leave."

Mom nodded, but didn't say anything.

I sighed. "Maybe I've changed more than I realized."

"You have changed, honey."

"I know, but what if Carlos hasn't? What if this isn't the right place for him?"

"That I can't answer for you."

She didn't have to. Saying the sentence aloud made it true. Was that the problem? I had changed. I had left the ship. I had dramatically altered the course of my life. He had stayed behind. He had stayed the same. Not in a bad way. He was the same, solid, impish chef who had sent my heart aflutter a decade ago. But *I* wasn't the same. Ashland had changed me. Or maybe Ashland had reminded me of who I really was. What if I had been trying to be someone I wasn't on the ship? What if coming home had ignited cellular memories buried deep within? What if telling myself I left that life on the ship behind was actually true? What if Carlos didn't love the new me?

Carlos didn't need to change because he was happy, confident, and content with who he was and is. I wasn't sure I could say the same for me. When I had packed my things and booked a one-way ticket to Ashland I had felt broken in places, and not just because of the secret he had kept from me. I was beginning to understand that now. His betrayal was a catalyst for an evolution that I never knew I desperately needed. Yet, that evolution might end up being the very thing that could tear us apart for good.

Chapter Twenty-One

"Juliet, are you okay?" Mom's voice broke the moment.

"Yeah. I'm fine." I meant it. I knew what needed to be done. I had to talk to Carlos. I was ready to face my future.

"The insurance adjuster just arrived." She waved to a woman stepping out of a sedan.

We showed the agent around the space. It didn't take long for her to snap photos, confirm our policy information, and complete the necessary paperwork for our claim. "We won't be able to pay out on this until the fire chief completes his investigation," she cautioned as she left. "It could take a few weeks. Maybe longer."

Depending on how long that took, we might have to push back our grand opening. In the scheme of things it could be worse.

The Professor came over as the insurance agent drove away. "Sorry for the delay. I placed a call to the chief. Alas he's in a morning meeting. I had hoped he might return my call, so I took the opportunity to check in with Addie while I waited. Unfortunately, I'm due at the station and have yet to hear. The minute I do, I'll be in touch." He turned to Mom. "Would you like a ride into town?"

"I think I'll stretch my legs and walk up to Torte. Are you going to stick around here?" she asked me.

"For a little while." I nodded. "If we get the okay, at least we can start demo today. If we can clear out the debris and I can have Andy and Sterling break down the arbor, we'll have a blank slate once the insurance sends us a check."

"Don't worry, honey. Everything is working out as it should." Tiny wrinkles formed in the creases of her eyes when she smiled.

Her words made my eyes water. I knew she wasn't only talking about the fire.

"See you later." I wanted to start ripping things down, but instead wandered to Laney's food truck where she was prepping for lunch. "Good morning," I called.

"Juliet, how are you?" She peered down from the open window. "I heard about the fire. Things are getting worse by the minute. Nothing like this has ever happened in the Railroad District and now it feels like things are falling apart."

"The good news is that no one was hurt." I didn't want to burden Laney with my problems when her father had just died.

"I guess, but if Hunter hadn't called the police last night, we all would have been screwed. Can you imagine if the flames had crossed the gate and made it to my truck? This baby has enough propane for a nice explosion. The whole block might have gone up."

The thought made me shiver.

"You haven't seen anyone riding a bike with a cape like your dad's again, have you?"

She organized sauce bottles on the ledge so that every label was facing out. Each bottle had a pink flower label in the center—BARBECUE, HULU HULU, TERIYAKI, and SPICY LAVA. "No. Not this morning anyway. The police asked me the same thing. But I can't see much from the stove. My back is turned the other way most of the morning while I'm prepping and cooking. Once I open, my view is pretty limited from this window. The person with the best view is Addie. She has a wall of windows that face the tracks."

Laney was right. Addie had a bird's-eye view of the railroad tracks and the bike path. Could she be lying? What if she had seen the Wizard's killer? And what about Sky's fall? She could have been watching the entire time.

"Did you hear about Hunter?"

"No, what happened?" She placed a tip jar covered in hibiscus flower stickers on the counter.

"There was another theft last night. That's how he saw the flames. He got a notification from his alarm company that there had been a break-in and he came to check it out."

"Really?" I hadn't heard anything about a break-in. Why hadn't the Professor or Thomas mentioned anything? But then again, last night was such a blur. They probably didn't want to worry me more. "Was anything stolen?"

"More bikes, and I guess the thieves spray-painted graffiti inside. I talked to him briefly this morning and needless to say he's furious." She cleared space on the aluminum counter for straws, napkins, and plastic utensils.

I was beginning to wonder if someone had a vendetta against the Railroad District business owners. "I'll go check in with him. I'm trying to fill time until we hear whether we can start tearing down the kitchen. Mainly, I wanted to see how you were doing."

Laney forced a smile. "I'm upright for the moment. I don't think I can ask for more."

"Let me know if there's anything I can do," I said.

"The same to you. It looks like you have some serious repairs ahead."

"I'm trying to think of it as an opportunity to create something entirely new."

"That's the spirit, sister." Laney leaned down to give me a high five. "We have to try to keep our heads up. Otherwise, I don't know about you, but I might crumble."

"Well said."

"Come by in about an hour. I'll make you a shoyu lunch plate with teriyaki rice and my world famous macaroni salad."

"Sold. I'll be back." I gave her a thumbs-up and crossed the street to Cyclepath.

The bike shop catered to the Rogue Valley's active biking community. There were two types of bike enthusiasts—tourists who rented day-use bikes with baskets to cruise around town and the serious mountain bikers who burned insane amounts of calories biking up the vast network of trails for the serious fast-paced pay-off of the downhill ride.

I stepped inside. The front of the shop was a showroom. Road bikes, mountain bikes, electric bikes, joggers, recumbents, and kids' bikes were on display everywhere. They hung from the ceiling, were mounted in the windows, and were grouped by style throughout the large room. The bright white epoxy floor and sterile white walls reminded me of a chemistry lab.

It smelled like bicycle grease and paint thinner. The grease made sense, but the thinner not so much. I realized it was because Hunter was scrubbing spray paint from the far wall, which had been tagged in black, purple, and red spray paint.

"Hi Hunter."

He dropped a rag and turned around. "Jules, I didn't hear you come in."

"Sorry to startle you. The door was open." I pointed behind me.

"I guess I forgot to lock it." Hunter reached for the rag.

"Laney told me that you were vandalized last night." I fixed my gaze on the graffiti.

"Vandalized and had two of my most expensive bikes taken. This is starting to get old." He wiped his hands on a towel and pointed behind him. The back of Cyclepath housed Ashland's largest bike repair shop. Wrenches, tubes, tires, and chains dangled from a pegboard wall. "They took a bunch of tools, too."

I thought back to his heated exchange with the Wizard. Hunter had been convinced that the Wizard was responsible for bike thefts, but since he was dead that didn't add up.

"Do the police have a suspect? Did they happen to catch anyone on camera?"

"I know who did this. The police do too." Hunter wrapped his burly arms around his chest.

"Who?"

"Sky. That other homeless guy who used to hang around with the Wizard. I know it was him. He's taking up his old friend's gig. Ruining my business and every business here in the Railroad District." Hunter sounded convinced.

"Did you see him? Laney mentioned you have an alarm system."

"I do." His eyes briefly shifted up above the cash register where a small white camera was tucked into the corner of the ceiling. "The guy was smart enough to hide his face so the camera couldn't pick it up. He had the Wizard's cape on though. It's obvious that it's Sky. I thought I had taken care of the problem, but apparently not."

What did that mean? Taken care of the problem? Was he alluding to the fact that he had killed the Wizard? I took a step backward.

Hunter knelt down and dabbed a rag into paint thinner again. "Sorry about the smell. It burns the nostrils but it's the only thing that has a chance at taking out this graffiti."

I studied the scribbled paint. "Does it mean anything?"

"What?" He scrubbed the stained paint with such force I wondered if his hands would start to bleed.

"The graffiti—I read that taggers have a signature style. Do the police have any idea if it's a specific tag or whether those jagged lines mean anything?"

"Who knows? The police are worthless." He stopped

scrubbing for a minute. "Sorry, I know that you're tight with Doug, but the only thing they tell me is that their hands are tied and there's nothing they can do. Why do I pay taxes? These vagrants are destroying our town and the police do nothing. Nothing. You know what I mean?"

I didn't respond because I doubted he would agree with my answer.

"I say it's up to us as small business owners to take up arms. If the police aren't going to do anything to stop this, then we can."

"How?" I thought of Addie and her pepper spray. Had Hunter gotten it into her head that she had to arm herself?

Hunter returned to scrubbing the wall with furry. "I'm working on a few ideas. I'm not ready to talk about them yet, but you'll hear from me soon. Everyone will."

I didn't like where this conversation was going. My phone buzzed, giving me the perfect exit. "Good luck with the graffiti."

"Thanks." He made a gun with his finger and thumb, along with a clicking sound. "Like I said, I'll be in touch."

I let out an involuntary shudder and stepped outside to answer the call. There was no hard evidence to prove that Hunter had killed the Wizard, but the way he spoke about taking action made me want to steer as far away from him as possible.

Chapter Twenty-Two

I answered the phone. It was the Professor. "Excellent news, Juliet. You have been cleared to proceed with cleanup and demolition. The fire chief will likely drop by at some point with an update, but in the meantime, break out your rubber gloves and purge."

"That is good news. Thanks." I almost ended the call, but I had to tell him about my unsettling conversation with Hunter.

"I see." The Professor sounded pensive. "Many thanks for sharing. As you stated, I would honor your inner compass and keep a safe distance from Hunter in the short term."

When we hung up I wondered if that was the Professor's veiled attempt to let me know he considered Hunter a top suspect too.

I crossed the street, taking in the amazing smells coming from Nana's food truck. Was it too early for lunch?

Sterling and Andy were waiting for me in the garden. "Hey boss, Mrs. The Professor filled us in on what

went down last night, but man the kitchen is torched."
Andy's cheeks flushed with anger.

"Seriously." Sterling clenched his jaw as he tried to
lift a section of the burned pergola. "It's messed up."

I appreciated that they shared my angst. "It's pretty
disturbing," I agreed. "Did Mom tell you about our plan?
The glimmer of hope in this is that now we can design
the space completely according to our own wants and
needs. You two have carte blanche. The sky is the
limit—literally. What do you think about truly embracing an open-air concept?"

Their energy shifted as I explained my vision to re-
structure the kitchen.

"Totally. I feel you on this, boss." Andy's freckled
face broke into a grin. "Yes. We can bust this out, can't
we, Sterling?"

Sterling rolled up the sleeves on his dark hoodie.
"Give me a sledgehammer. Let's do this."

It was surreal to tear down the kitchen we had spent
the past week laboring over. Yet I found it more than
slightly cathartic to rip down charcoaled branches on the
ivy vines and trash the old countertops. Sweat poured
from my forehead as the three of us used our collec-
tive strength to demolish the cabinets and countertop.
Within an hour we had a heaping pile of wood and debris in the center of the garden.

"It's kind of a bummer that tearing everything down
took us no time." Sterling used the sleeve of his hoodie
to brush dust from his face. "We spent days getting this
place ready for business and not even an hour to gut it."

"Yeah, and now we can't even have java to fuel us,"
Andy complained, pointing to the pile of rubble.

"That is a tragedy," I teased. "I do have a consolation prize for you. It's not cold brew, but Laney told me earlier she was making chicken shoyu platters for lunch. You should both go grab one from her before there's a line. My treat."

"Thanks, boss!" Andy sprinted toward the food truck with Sterling at his heels.

It didn't take much to appease them.

While they were occupied with Laney's handcrafted lunch plates, I made a few calls to the Ashland recycling center, the insurance company, and to the contractor we had hired to remodel Torte's basement. Most of the basic redesign we could handle ourselves, but I needed a professional to build a new arbor, counters, and cabinets. The build-out of the kitchen was nothing close to the scale of our basement renovations. However, the challenge in Ashland and the greater Rogue Valley was supply and demand. Contractors were in short supply and high demand. Luckily, I had a personal relationship with our contractor, who agreed to fit us into his tight schedule.

"Jules, Laney made a plate for you," Sterling said, handing me a paper plate piled high with beautifully grilled chicken, rice drenched in teriyaki sauce, and macaroni salad.

We gathered around one of the bistro tables and savored the traditional Hawaiian fare. Laney's creamy mac salad was the stuff of dreams. It had the perfect balance of mayo with sweet onion, brown sugar, and garlic.

"This is one of the best things I've ever tasted," Andy gushed through a mouthful of the tender chicken. "How have I never had this before?"

"Working right next to Nana's this spring and summer should remedy that," I said, stabbing a piece of chicken along with a scoop of rice.

"Or it could be dangerous. I have to keep my boyish figure trim." Andy pinched his waist. Until recently he had played football at Southern Oregon University. Ultimately, he had opted to give up football to work at Torte full time and immerse himself in the world of artisan coffee with the goal of opening his own roasting company one day. At first I had worried about his decision to drop out of school. The statistics of students returning to college after dropping out weren't in his favor. Andy had made a calculated risk. A risk that in his opinion came with fewer side effects than one too many hard hits on the football field. I couldn't argue with him there.

"Hello! Hello. Milk delivery."

We turned to see Dean standing at the side gate holding a crate of glass milk jugs.

"Come in," I called.

Dean unlatched the gate and came into the garden. "Yowza! What happened here? Looks like you had an explosion."

"You didn't hear about the fire?" That was shocking given that it was nearly noon. I would guess the entire town had heard by now.

"No." Dean puffed out his cheeks and set the crate on the grass. "An accident?"

"Arson." I watched his reaction. It was almost too exaggerated.

"Arson? In Ashland! It can't be!" He shifted his weight from side to side as he took in the pile of wreckage. "They must have had it wrong. I bet you had an accident. With the painting and staining you've been doing, I bet a bunch of rags spontaneously combusted. You can't be too careful."

Odd reaction, I thought to myself. "Well, the police are saying it's arson."

"The police are known to jump to some crazy conclusions. I bet you had a burner go bad or maybe an electrical problem. I've seen it in this line of work. Lots of commercial kitchens have had similar issues."

Why was Dean insistent that it wasn't arson?

Sterling's wary look seconded my opinion.

"Last week the same thing happened out in Eagle Point. One of my clients put a stack of towels hot out of the dryer on the counter. Left for the night, and *poof!* They ignited. Burned the kitchen to the ground. Nothing left. A total loss. It's a shame. You can't be too careful," he repeated.

"We *were* careful," Sterling interjected. "The fire was intentional."

Dean shrugged. "I guess that means you won't be wanting milk anytime soon." He tapped the top of the glass bottles. "Looks like the homeless camp over there is going to get a bounty today. Should I take this stop off my delivery list for a while?"

"Yeah." I nodded to the demoed kitchen. "We're going to have to push back our grand opening until we can rebuild."

"Sorry to hear it." Dean sounded anything but sorry. He stood and picked up the crate. "You be careful now."

Was he genuinely worried about us? His words almost sounded like a warning.

"That was weird," Sterling said once Dean was gone.

"I'm glad you think so too. He completely dismissed the fact that our space was intentionally set on fire."

"And what did he mean that the police in Ashland exaggerate things?" Andy's eyes wandered to my plate. "Are you going to finish that?"

"It's all yours." I pushed him my half-eaten plate. "I have no idea. The Professor is the last person to jump to conclusions when it comes to an investigation, or anything for that matter."

"I feel bad for recommending Dean," Sterling admitted.

"Why?"

"I don't know. He seemed really great when we were first interviewing potential vendors, but the more I get to know him the less I like him."

If Sterling had reservations about Dean, I wasn't about to blow them off. One of Sterling's best assets was his ability to read people. The more interactions that I had with Dean, the more confused I became. On one hand he seemed untrustworthy, and yet he was heading out to give away the milk we couldn't use to the homeless. There was something about him that didn't add up.

"Maybe this is a natural way to break ties," I suggested. "We can use this time to look into other vendors."

"Okay. I like that idea." Sterling nodded.

Andy polished off my lunch plate. "If we're done with demo I'm going to head back to Torte. I have an idea for a new coffee that I have to go try."

"Do tell." I rubbed my hands together with anticipation.

"Nope. It's a secret. I have to go experiment and see if I can pull it off. If I can, I'll tell you this much. It will be an ode to the fire."

"Interesting. Like spicy chili and cinnamon."

"Not even close, boss." Andy clapped Sterling on the shoulder. "You coming?"

"I'll be there in a few. I want to take a few pictures for Steph."

Andy left. "Meet you guys back at Torte later then."

"Jules, you remember our conversation the other day?" Sterling asked while taking pictures of the gutted kitchen. He didn't make eye contact.

"Of course."

"I made a decision." He clutched his phone in his hand. "I'm going to do it. I'm going to ask Steph to move in with me."

"Sterling, that's amazing." I stepped over a charred paint can.

"Don't get too excited. She hasn't said yes yet."

Unlike Detective Kerry and Thomas, I wasn't as sure about Steph. She could go either way. It was obvious that she had a deep connection with Sterling, more so than with anyone else on staff, but given how fiercely private she was, she could also want to maintain her own space.

He stuffed his phone in his pocket. "Can I ask a favor?"

"Sure."

"It's kind of cheesy, but Steph is a huge fan of the baking shows."

"Oh, I'm aware of that." It was one of her most surprising and endearing qualities. She was obsessed with reality baking shows.

"We were watching the Cake Debate last week and

this guy had one of the bakers design an engagement cake. I was wondering if you could do something like that for Steph? I would do it myself, but you know me, I'm a chef, not a baker. She loves black and purple, so maybe a cake with those colors?"

"That is the sweetest idea. I would be honored to design a cake for you."

"I'll pay." Sterling's face was earnest.

"Never. Wipe that thought away. I would love to make a special cake for you and Steph!"

"You don't think it's too cheesy, do you?"

"I'm the wrong person to answer that. I'm a hopeless romantic, like you. And I suspect that secretly Stephanie is too."

"Right?" He nodded with relief. "Cool, thanks, Jules."

An engagement cake, a let's-move-in-together cake—I had some serious baking to do.

Chapter Twenty-Three

The remainder of the day was refreshingly uneventful. We'd done as much as we could at Scoops for the short term. Now it would be a waiting game for the insurance payments and contractors. With things on hiatus at the new space, I spent the afternoon at Torte.

The bakeshop's busy kitchen grounded my nervous energy. I baked alongside the team, happy for a distraction from the Wizard's murder, the fire, and Carlos. Before I knew it, it was time to close. I said goodbye to Marty, who was the last staff member to leave, and turned the sign on the front door to CLOSED. Then I returned to the basement to bake cakes for Thomas and Sterling.

Baking a cake in a professional bakery is different than baking at home for many reasons. The most notable being how much more time is required when baking professionally. At Torte we have a flow sheet for the many steps involved in our custom cakes. The first is baking the actual cake. Then we cool the layers, cut and trim them as needed, stack the cake, frost a crumb coat, chill completely, frost the base layer, chill completely again, frost again, pipe, and decorate. Most of our custom cakes are built over the course of a couple days. For larger cakes and more intricate design work like wedding cakes, the timeframe can extend to a week.

For the donut cake, I began by creaming butter and sugar together in our industrial mixer until it was smooth and silky. Then I added in vanilla, eggs, buttermilk, baking soda, flour, and a touch of cinnamon and nutmeg for the donut spice. I baked the cake in round Bundt pans shaped to resemble a donut with a hole in the center.

Once the donut cake was in the oven, I switched gears to a cake for Steph. I knew the perfect flavor—black velvet. The deep black color in this cake was achieved with dark chocolate cocoa powder. When baked it would resemble the night sky. I mixed oil, sugar, eggs, sour cream, and the cocoa powder together, slowly adding in the dry ingredients. The black batter made me smile. I knew Steph would love the moody vibe of the image I had in my head. I would stack the cake with dark chocolate ganache and blackberry buttercream. Then I would frost it with more of the blackberry buttercream and pipe it with black royal icing. It should be a dramatic statement cake.

"Julieta, are you here?" Carlos unlocked the basement door. The site of his impish smile brought a rush of blood to my head.

"I'm baking away," I called in return.

He took off his coat and moved with style toward me. I noticed a large envelope tucked under his arm. The other held a bottle of wine from Uva. "Would you like a glass?" He rested the envelope on the marble decorating station and held up the wine.

"Sure." My hands were coated in flour. I brushed them on my apron and reached for baking spray. "How was Uva today? Anything eventful?"

Carlos expertly twisted the cork out of the bottle. He poured us two glasses of the burgundy wine. "No. Not so much. We had visitors from New Zealand and South Africa."

Ashland had a presence on the global stage thanks to OSF. It wasn't unusual to hear a variety of international languages spoken in the plaza. Theater lovers ventured to our tucked-away corner for Shakespeare. They stayed to experience the Rogue Valley's lush wine and outdoor culture.

"I'm sure you loved that," I said, coating baking pans with nonstick spray.

"Si. We talked so much about our travels and of course the food. I have a new recipe for a South African stew that we must try." He pulled a piece of paper from the pocket of his khaki slacks. "I wrote it down exactly as they told me; their grandmother made this dish."

"You won't get any resistance from me." I spread the pitch-black batter into eight-inch rounds.

Carlos walked over to hand me a glass of wine. He swiped a taste of the batter with his finger. "It is very good. Very dark, no?"

"That's the goal." I told him about Sterling's plan.

"Ah, young love." He raised his wineglass. "To the young lovers who set the world on fire. We were like that once, you remember?"

His eyes were full of emotion.

"I do." I fought against the warring sides of me. What was holding me back from fully embracing having Carlos here? Was it that I had changed? Or was it that I was scared?

"We were lucky to have had a life together on the sea. How many places have we seen? How many sunsets have we stood watching as the sun dropped below the horizon? How many times have we sipped espresso under a scarlet pink sunrise?"

"Not as many sunrises for you as sunsets," I teased.

It was true that we had had a charmed life floating on calm waters. Busy ports of call, crowded farmers markets, empty black sand beaches—we'd seen so many places that I had never dreamed of visiting. I could almost feel the ocean breeze on the back of my neck and taste the salty air.

But, then again, the reality of our day-to-day life on the *Amour of the Seas* wasn't quite the glossy picture that Carlos or my memories tried to paint. That was the thing about memories, they couldn't always be trusted. With a bit of distance we tend to toss out the less glamorous pieces of our past and hold onto the more pleasant parts.

Yes, the ship was romantic and full of opportunity for adventures. It was also arduous work with long, grueling hours in ship's kitchens. It was an unrelenting churn of pastries, cakes, éclairs, and custards. There was little rest. Most nights I stumbled to bed with blisters on my heels and aching fingers from molding fondant and pressing cookies by the hundreds. I suppose if I had learned anything being away from the ship it was that both were true. It was an experience for the ages *and* it was exhausting.

Being in Ashland had taught me the importance of relationships and community. Seeing friends and neighbors in the bakeshop enjoying what we were crafting with love every day was the most rewarding part of the job. Yes, running a small business came with long hours and stress, but it was a different kind of stress. I knew that, ultimately, I was the captain of my ship. I could steer Torte in any direction.

"That is unfair. I had no choice. My shift it did not end until after midnight." He pretended to be hurt.

"I know." I slid the cakes into the oven. Then I took a sip of my wine. "Be honest, Carlos, do you miss it?"

"Ah, not so much." He caught my eye. "Okay, maybe I miss the hum of the kitchen and the intensity of getting dinner out to the guests on time."

"I understand. What else?"

"I miss the rhythm of the sea. I have not slept on land for so long. My sleep, it is not as good, but I'm sure my body will learn."

"Mm-hmm."

"There is that flow of being in motion, like the sea is still beneath me, and of so many moving parts on the ship. It is like a conductor bringing every instrument into perfect tone. That melody. That song of the sea. It becomes part of you, no?" He stopped himself. "No, no. Don't look at me with those sad eyes, mi querida. I did not mean that I'm not happy with you. I am. I will do anything to be together with you. You asked about the sea, that's all."

I put my wine down. Then I moved closer and rested

my head on his shoulder. "Carlos, this isn't going to work. I can't keep you here. I know that you'll do anything for our relationship. I love that about you. I love you—deeply, madly, and because I love you, it's clear that it's time we set each other free."

His hand clutched my head. "No, mi querida. We have a chance to make this work."

"We did. We tried." I lifted my head and looked into his eyes. "It's okay. This time apart has taught me that we both know who we are at our core and who we're meant to be. I can't thank you enough for trying. There's no doubt in my mind that you would stay for me, but I can't live with that. This place, it's small, Carlos. It's not intense. It's not frenzied and moving. It's solid and stable. It's like us. I need to be grounded in one place. You need change and the energy of somewhere new."

"Julieta, you don't understand. I am happy. Very happy." His eyes filled with tears.

I pressed my fingers to his lips. "We were lucky. You were right about that. We still are. If we end this now, we can end as friends."

"Julieta." He leaned in and kissed me slowly. "I love you."

I returned his kiss. Sadness welled inside me.

"Me too." I kissed him again. A tear streamed down my cheek. Carlos brushed it away with his hand.

"Julieta, you must listen to me. We do not have to say goodbye."

The oven timer dinged. I jumped up to remove the donut Bundt cakes and check on the black velvets, happy for a brief moment to try to collect my thoughts. "What's in the envelope?" I asked using oven mitts to place the Bundt pans on cooling racks. I set the timer for ten more minutes.

His face lost color. "It is nothing."

I could tell from his reaction that it was definitely something. "What? Tell me the truth, Carlos. You've been having secret meetings and taking phone calls. It's okay. I can handle it. What I can't handle is feeling like I'm in limbo. If this isn't going to work, let's deal with it."

His shoulders slumped. "I do not want you to see, because it will only make you more sure that Ashland she is not right for me."

I took off the oven mitts and came back to the island.

Carlos sighed and handed me the envelope.

I recognized the logo—Royal Bateau. It belonged to the parent company of the *Amour of the Seas*.

"Go ahead. Open it."

The seal had already been broken. I opened the envelope and removed a letter with the same navy Royal Bateau logo embossed on the top. The letter was from the president of the company complimenting Carlos on his years of service. The first two paragraphs were glowing about Carlos's work ethic, exquisite menus, and numerous awards and accolades.

"Wow, this is really impressive."

"Keep reading."

I continued on. The third paragraph included an offer. An offer that made my jaw drop. The president wanted Carlos to be the executive chef for their new flagship luxury European line—El Lujo, headquartered in Spain. Carlos would receive an extremely generous salary, bonus, and vacation package.

"Carlos. This is an incredible opportunity."

"Si." He sounded devastated.

"Is that why you've been having so many meetings? You didn't want me to know about this offer, because I would tell you that you had to take it."

"No. It is not. I have not accepted the offer. Si, it is a wonderful opportunity but it is not with you, Julieta." His voice was thick with resolve.

"Carlos, you have to accept. Offers like this don't come often. And, you would be based in Spain, near Ramiro. It's perfect."

"Perfect." Carlos scoffed. "What is perfect? I have made many mistakes over the years. Hurting you was the worst." He gave me a pained smile. "I have learned that perfect, it is nothing more than what we make it."

"No, but this is what you've dreamed of. Executive chef for the entire cruise line. You can create all of the ship's menus, and you'll be working with some of the best chefs in the world."

It was as if the job description had been written specifically for Carlos. His kitchen would be based in Madrid, allowing him to spend more time with Ramiro and balance the rest of his time traveling from ship to ship on the line. It was as if the universe was steering us toward our futures, but did that mean futures without each other?

Chapter Twenty-Four

"Julieta, you are too stubborn." Carlos sipped his wine and stared at me with a gleam in his eyes. "I am not taking the job. I am meant to be here in Ashland with you. I understand now. I see what you mean when you say you have been captured under her spell. I have too."

"But—" I tried to speak.

Carlos shook his head. "No, you must listen. It's true that I didn't know what I would think when I came to stay for this long. I was worried. I was not sure how I would feel after being away from the sea. Would I be bored? Would I be lonely? Would I miss it? Sí, yes. Like I said, there are things I miss. I will not lie. And, this is very important." He reached for my hand, gently caressing my palm with his finger. "You must hear this, Julieta. I would not, and I will not, sacrifice my own happiness. Do you understand?"

I bit my bottom lip.

"This is my choice. I want to be here. It is not boring. It is so alive. I was meant for being with the vines and I have many, many ideas that fill me with such excitement. Uva she is ripe and young and rich. I want to do dinners amongst the vines and teach classes, and keep wild honeybees. Every day it is different at the vineyard. It is a chef's dream. I can cultivate the vines. The wine it will be unique because of what I do. It is art in my favorite form. The winemakers I have met have been inviting and I have much to learn. We are in the heart of what will be the world's best wine scene. We have a chance to shape how the Rogue Valley is seen around the globe. It fills me with so much creative energy. We will be part of something new and cutting edge."

"Carlos, are you sure?" I wanted to believe him. The timer dinged again. I stopped him to remove the black velvet cakes from the oven.

He grasped my hands tighter. "Julieta, I have never been more sure. It is not just the vines. It is you. It is Helen and Doug and Sterling and Andy. This team. This family that you have created. I feel lucky to even be allowed to be part of it." His eyes misted. "It is the evolution of us. It is a love story, no? We had to be apart to understand where we are meant to be. And, Julieta, I know now in every cell of my body, that I am meant to be with you—in Ashland."

Were my dreams within my grasp?

I was acutely aware of every sensation in my body as Carlos leaned in and cradled my head in his heads.

"Julieta, will you let me stay?"

I didn't trust myself to speak. I nodded.

Carlos kissed me through my happy tears.

"You're sure?" I pointed to the offer letter.

He brushed the letter off the table. "Si. I have already declined. They do not take no for an answer. They have asked if I might come help with trainings and special workshops every so often. For that I might say yes. You could come with me, or I will go and see Ramiro."

"Of course." I couldn't stop a silly grin from forming on my face. "As long as you're really sure. I don't want to hold you back."

"Hold me back? We are just beginning, mi querida." With that he swept me into his arms and we held each other for what felt like hours. At some point in the blur of the magical evening, we meandered home, our hands intertwined, slightly tipsy from the wine and the knowledge that Carlos was staying.

Sleep was futile. Visions of my new life with Carlos played like a movie all night long, so, I gave up before dawn, snuck out, and headed for the bakery. The plaza was plunged in deep slumber. I didn't give it much thought until I started down the stairs to unlock the basement door and heard the sound of a man's voice.

"Hey!"

I dropped the keys and nearly tumbled down the steps.

Stay cool, Jules. I placed my hand on my stomach and turned toward the sound of the voice. It was coming from around the corner on the Calle Gaunajuato. I reached into my puffy jacket pocket for my phone.

"Who's there?" I called, getting ready to hit 911.

"Hey!" the throaty voice repeated.

I stepped away from the stairwell. A single golden antique streetlamp cast a hazy glow on the cobblestone path. The only other sound was of Ashland Creek rushing with spring snowmelt.

A figure crouched in the darkness near the waist-high wall that divided the path from the creek below.

"Who are you?" I squinted in an attempt to get my eyes to focus.

"It's me, Sky." He stood and tossed off a blanket he'd had wrapped around his shoulders.

"Sky. Everyone's been looking for you."

His body trembled. "I know. I've been hiding. It's not safe."

"What do you mean?" I asked, taking a step closer.

"They're watching." His head twisted from side to side.

"Come on, let's go into the bakeshop and talk. You look like you could use a coffee."

"No. It's not safe."

"Sky, it's me. I'm not going to hurt you." I reached a hand out to him. "You're shivering. You're probably on the cusp of hypothermia. Come inside with me and let's get you warmed up."

I could tell that he wanted to come with me.

"I promise. You'll be safer inside than out here."

That did the trick.

He wrapped the blanket tighter around his shoulders and shuffled toward me.

I retrieved my keys and unlocked the basement door. After flipping on the lights, I directed him to the couch and lit the gas fireplace. "You stay right here by the fire and warm up. I'm going to make us some coffee."

He sat without protest.

I made a pot of dark roast. While the coffee brewed, I sliced day-old baguettes, slathered them with butter, and placed them in the oven. Once the coffee was ready I took Sky a mug along with cream and sugar. "Sip this. I'll be right back with something for you to eat."

His hands quaked as he tried to cradle the cup. The bandage I had used to seal his injury the other day was dirty and dried with blood.

I wondered if I should call EMS.

The baguettes had toasted to a beautiful golden brown and the butter had melted. I grabbed jars of our raspberry and blackberry preserves and brought them out to the seating area.

"Sky, are you sure you're okay? You look pretty cold. Maybe I should call a doctor."

He clutched the coffee. "No. No doctors. No police. They'll take me. They'll kill me."

"Who? The police?"

"No." Sky shook his head but wouldn't say more.

Maybe food would help. "Would you like some toast? I have raspberry or blackberry jam."

"Blackberry. Thanks." He stared at his feet, which were stuffed into shoes that appeared two sizes too small.

I spread a generous heaping of jam onto one of the baguettes and handed it to him.

He ate it so fast I wondered if he had even swallowed.

"Would you like more?" I pointed to the second buttery loaf.

"Yeah." His fingernails were black with grime. His khaki pants were frayed on the seams and splotched with stains. The poor guy needed a shower.

After he had devoured the second helping and more of the coffee, the trembling seemed to slow.

"Sky, can you tell me what's going on? This is about the Wizard's death, isn't it?"

He stared at a hole in his tennis shoe.

"Do you know who killed him? Is that why you're scared?"

He dragged his foot in a small circle on the floor. "Yeah. If they find me, they're going to kill me too."

"That's why we should call the police. The Professor can help you. He can protect you."

"No!" Sky shook his head with force. "They can't protect me. They will want me to talk and that's going to get me in more trouble."

"I don't understand."

"Go there now. You'll see. They tried to kill me when I was sleeping."

"Where?"

"Your place."

"You mean, you were there when the fire started? Did you see who did it?"

"Yeah, and he's hiding it. He's trying to cover it up."

"Who?"

Sky looked like he wanted to tell me but clammed up. He picked at his bread and used a finger to lick jam from his plate. We didn't have long before my team would arrive. I needed to find a way to get him to relax.

"Please, Sky. I promise, I will do everything I can to keep you safe, but you have to tell me who started the fire."

"Talk to the bike guy."

"Hunter?"

He held out his empty coffee cup. "Can I have more?"

"Sure." I stood to refill his cup in the kitchen. "Do you mean that Hunter started the fire?"

"I'm not saying anything else. Talk to him."

"Okay." I returned with a fresh cup. "I'll do that."

"You should go now. They're there. I saw them. They're doing nothing good."

"Who? Hunter and who else?"

Sky was silent.

I glanced at my watch. Andy, Marty, and Steph would be arriving soon. "Do you want to come with me or stay here?"

"I'm not going down there."

"Okay. My staff is going to show up. Are you comfortable staying here until I get back?"

He clenched the coffee cup. "Yeah."

I left him and shot off a text to the team to give them a heads-up that Sky was warming himself by the fire. Then I texted Thomas and told him I was heading to Cyclepath, just in case. Sky was skittish and paranoid. I wasn't sure if it was warranted or not, but there was only one way to find out.

Dawning purple light guided me to the Railroad District, which was a ghost town at this hour. I hurried down Water Street, following the gushing sounds of Ashland Creek and a single crow that flew overhead.

What was I going to do if I saw Hunter? I couldn't confront him by myself.

No, Jules, not a smart move.

What I could do is document whatever he was up to.

I had my phone on me and Thomas had been informed, so I crept along the edge of the sidewalk, staying in the shadows.

Sure enough Hunter and Lars stood outside of the bike shop. Hunter screamed at his son. "I'm done covering up your messes. This is the final straw!"

"Whatever." Lars tossed something on the ground.

"Go ahead. Talk like that. If anyone finds out about this—you're going to do jail time. They're not going to care that you're a minor."

Jail time?

"I'm so scared," Lars retorted, with a scoff.

"Lars, this is serious. I've tried everything to get through to you. If it hadn't been for these cameras I installed yesterday, it would be the cops here now. Not me. You're out of chances, kid."

Lars must have been unimpressed with his dad's lecture because he shrugged and reached for his longboard, which was propped against the side of the building.

"No way. You're not taking off. Get inside right now. We're calling your mother and we're ending this once and for all."

Hunter dragged his son inside the bike shop.

Lars? Had Lars killed the Wizard?

I waited until they were inside, then hurried across the street to see what Lars had dropped.

My hand flew to my mouth when I got a closer look at the discarded item—a cape exactly like the Wizard's.

Chapter Twenty-Five

I stood in the middle of the street, holding the cape and unsure what to do next. Lars had been the person imitating the Wizard? Why? Was it some sort of prank, or could he be involved in the Wizard's murder, and setting Scoops on fire?

I had no idea how long I'd been standing there, holding the cape, until a voice shook me into reality.

"Jules, Jules!"

I looked up to see Thomas sprinting toward me. Detective Kerry was right behind him.

"What are you doing here? Did you get my text?"

"I did, but we were already in route. We got an anonymous tip that there was an altercation here." He stared at the cape. "What's that?"

"A cape that is exactly like the one the Wizard used to wear." I handed Kerry the cape and told them what I'd just seen.

"Let's go," he said to Kerry without hesitation. "Stay here, Jules."

Just as they began to move toward Cyclepath, the front door swung open and Hunter appeared in the doorway, yanking Lars behind him. He stopped in his tracks at the sight of Detective Kerry and Thomas.

I inched closer, not wanting to miss out on what they said.

"See Lars, I warned you." Hunter pushed Lars forward. "You take him. He's out of control. I can't stop him."

Neither Kerry nor Thomas moved.

"Tell them, Lars. Tell them what you've done. Or should I?"

Lars folded his arms across his chest and gave his dad a defiant look.

"Fine. I'll tell them." Hunter pointed to Kerry. "You might want to take notes. This kid is going to end up with a rap sheet longer than a tandem bike."

Thomas removed his iPad mini. "I'm happy to take your statement."

"Fine. I just got off the phone with his mother and we agreed that we're not going to protect him anymore. I didn't want to believe it was you." He shot Lars a look of disgust.

Lars didn't react.

Hunter picked up the longboard that was propped against the side of the building. "He's done. I'm over it. I'm ready to take this board and burn it. The kid needs to face serious consequences for his delinquent behavior."

Did Hunter know that Lars had killed the Wizard and had kept it quiet?

Hunter smashed the longboard on the sidewalk. "See what you've done, Lars! Your mother is at home crying right now. Lock him up, officers."

Thomas held up a hand to try to calm Hunter. "We're not going to lock anyone up, sir."

"Why? You're looking at a vandal. This kid and his friends have been ditching school for the last three weeks. They tagged my store, stole my bikes, and set fire to the space across the street."

Lars had started the fire? I felt my jaw drop.

Hunter continued to rant, rattling off a variety of crimes his son had committed. I was shocked.

"Do you have anything you'd like to say?" Thomas asked Lars after Hunter had finished.

"Nah. I don't know why my dad's being lame as always." He snickered. "It's no big deal. Me and my friends were just having fun."

"No big deal?" Kerry replied, unable to hide her incredulous tone. "Vandalism, theft, and arson. Those are major crimes."

"No one got hurt." Lars smirked. "I don't see why everyone's freaking out. It was just stupid pranks. We didn't set the fire. We smashed some bottles and tagged a couple buildings. What are you going to do? Make me and my friends do community service for a week? Ohhhh, I'm shaking."

Lars showed no remorse for his deeds.

Thomas reached to his waist and proceeded to handcuff Lars.

"Good, get him out of my sight." Hunter grabbed the longboard and stormed back into the bike shop. He slammed the door behind him.

Thomas took Lars to the squad car.

I walked over to Kerry.

"Did you hear everything?" she asked.

"Yeah, but I don't get it. Why?"

"Who knows?" She frowned. "A kid with too much time on his hands probably."

"What about the Wizard? I didn't hear him say anything about being involved in his death, unless I missed it."

"You didn't miss anything. We're going to take him in for questioning. Let's hope he's not connected to the murder or the arson at your shop. He already has a deep hole to crawl out of." Her phone buzzed. "We've got to go."

I watched them drive away.

How sad for Hunter. To have his own son target his shop and steal bikes. The question was whether Hunter had known all along. Had he protected Lars initially? It certainly sounded like that from what he'd told Kerry and Thomas.

Before returning to Torte, I decided to stop in to Cyclepath. I knocked softly on the door. Hunter came to answer it and looked surprised to see me. "Jules? You're here early."

"I could say the same about you."

Hunter's shoulders slumped. "The alarm woke me."

"I was there when everything went down with Lars," I confessed.

He rubbed his temples. "I don't know what else to do. Turning in your own kid is the worst thing. Let me tell you, I feel sick right now, but when the alert came in this morning, I saw him on camera. This entire time I've been harassing the police for not going after the Wizard and his friends, when the whole time the criminal was living under my own roof. Why? We have given Lars everything. He doesn't want for anything."

Except maybe attention, I thought to myself.

"I'm sorry about your place. We'll see that the damages get covered. I don't know how yet, but we'll figure it out."

"It sounded like Lars said he and his friends didn't set the fire."

"You trust him on that?" Hunter pounded his fist into his palm.

I was careful in how to word the next question. "Hunter, you don't think that Lars and his friends could have had anything to do with the Wizard, do you?"

"You mean in his death?"

I nodded.

"No. They're stupid kids. Don't get me wrong. Lars made terrible choices but he would never kill anyone." Hunter didn't look as convinced as he was trying to sound.

"I'm sure you're right."

"Why, did you hear something?"

"No." I thought about Sky, who I hoped was still huddled by the fireplace. Could he have seen Lars and his friends start the fire? Or maybe he witnessed them stealing bikes or spray-painting Cyclepath too.

Was Hunter to be trusted?

Sure, he had turned Lars over to the police, but what if he'd been protecting him? Or, another possibility formed in my mind. What if Lars had been acting on his father's behalf? Hunter had been extremely vocal in his dislike of the Wizard. What if Lars killed the

Wizard to stay in his dad's good graces, or to pay for Hunter's silence about his other crimes?

Why was Sky scared?

Could Lars or Hunter have threatened him?

Suddenly, I wanted to get out of the bike shop. I glanced at my wrist. "I should probably get to the bake-shop. My team is likely wondering why I'm not there rolling out bread dough with them."

Hunter pointed to the door. "You can let yourself out."

"I'm sorry about Lars," I said as I walked to the door.

"Me too," Hunter said, before taking a bike wrench and throwing it against the wall.

Chapter Twenty-Six

My mind played through dozens of scenarios on the walk to Torte. Did Detective Kerry and Thomas have the Wizard's killer in custody? Lars didn't strike me as a killer, but then again I couldn't image damaging Torte or trying to set it on fire. Hunter seemed genuinely upset and yet I wasn't entirely convinced that he hadn't covered for his son.

"Hey, Jules. Your guest is still here." Marty greeted me as I started down the stairs and he came up holding a box of bread.

"How is he?" I asked.

Marty shifted the box into his right arm. "Jumpy."

"I know. I can't figure out if that's normal or if he's really scared."

"Well, it could have to do with the caffeine. I think he's on his fifth cup of java."

"Oh boy."

"I'm off to deliver the bread. Good luck." Marty continued upstairs.

I knew that Sky would be upset, but it was time for me to call the Professor. Before I went inside, I put in a quick call. The Professor didn't answer but I left him a message explaining that we would keep Sky at Torte until he could get here.

"Sky, I have some good news," I said, once inside. "They've arrested Lars."

"Lars?" Sky looked confused. The shaking had subsided, though.

"He confessed to stealing the bikes among other things."

"Lars?" Sky repeated.

"Yes. Hunter's son. You know, the kid who hangs around Railroad Park with his friends. The police have him at the station now. You're safe."

He tapped his forehead as if trying to force his brain to process what I was saying. "Lars?"

"Lars admitted to stealing and tagging," I said again, hoping to appease him.

"Lars?" He repeated, rocking back and forth.

"Yes."

"Okay." He stood up.

"Wait here for a minute. There's something else I want to make for you."

"I need to go. It doesn't make sense." He gnawed on his filthy nails.

"Give me five minutes." Hopefully the Professor had gotten my message. I wasn't sure how much longer I could keep Sky in the bakeshop.

"Morning," I said to Steph, who removed one earphone.

"Huh?" She was already piping pastry cream into cooled croissants.

"I just said good morning."

"Oh. Morning." She put her earphone back in and returned to filling the pastries.

Bethany and Rosa were up to their elbows in bread dough. I scooted into the walk-in and gathered supplies to pack Sky a hearty lunch. I tucked savory hand pies along with carrots, olives, and Sterling's lemon garlic hummus into a bag. Then I added an apple, three cookies, and two day-old pastries. When I returned to the seating area, Sky was already on his feet, the blanket hanging from his shoulders.

"Here. Be sure you eat today, okay?"

"Thanks." He took the lunch sack.

"Are you sure you won't stay longer? The couch is a comfortable spot to rest. We don't open for business for another hour."

"No, I gotta go. I gotta figure something out." He rubbed his forehead.

At that moment Mom and the Professor walked in. Thank goodness. Talk about the eleventh hour. The Professor deftly swept over to Sky with a nod of thanks to me. "What a wonderful coincidence. You are just the person I want to see."

Sky rounded his shoulders and started rocking again.

"It's okay. The Professor is on our side," I said to Sky.

"Might we step across the street?" The Professor asked. I knew that it wasn't really a question, but Sky agreed and they left together.

"Fill me in," Mom said, warming her hands in front of the fire. "Spring in Ashland means my hands never warm up in the morning."

I told her everything.

She sighed. "What a shame about Lars. I hope he'll

get the emotional help and support that he obviously needs."

"Unless he's the killer."

"True." She paused. "There's more. What is it? You look lighter this morning."

"You were right, Mom." I couldn't contain my smile. "Carlos is going to stay."

"Oh, Juliet. I'm so happy!" She wrapped me in a tight hug and stood on her tiptoes to kiss my cheek. "For the record, I'd like it known that I never had any doubts. I've seen the way he looks at you. You've found the real thing and I couldn't be more thrilled that Carlos is going to be a part of our family. Tell me every detail."

She nursed a cup of Andy's dark roast while I relayed the details of last night's conversation.

"He's a keeper, Juliet. And, he's right about Uva. You've seen the newspaper articles touting Ashland as the new Napa. I think you're smart to invest in the vineyard. It reminds me of when your dad and I started Torte."

"Thanks, Mom." Both of our eyes got misty. "I think I need to bake. I have some specialty cakes that got left unfinished last night and I have way too much eager excitement built up inside." My bouncing left foot was evidence of my newfound energy.

"Good plan. I'll join you." Mom blew me a kiss. "You know my philosophy, baking is the antidote for everything."

With that we returned to the kitchen and I immersed myself in designing Thomas's donut cake. The cakes had cooled overnight, so I started by stacking them with layers of luscious raspberry preserves and fresh raspberries.

Then I frosted them with a thin layer of buttercream and returned the cake to the walk-in to allow the frosting to set.

Decorating the cake with donuts would be a challenge. I didn't think the airy, fried treats would be structurally sound, but I wanted the cake to look like a donut. I thought through possibilities until inspiration struck—macarons. I could make batches of colorful berry macarons in the shape of mini donuts to adorn on the cake.

Macarons require patience and delicate care. A few simple ingredients—powdered sugar, almond flour, and egg whites—were the building blocks for the French confection. If done correctly, the result would be a delectable Parisian meringue cookie sandwiched with jam and buttercream. After folding egg whites into the almond flour and sugar, I scooped the dough into a piping bag, and piped round donuts onto a parchment-lined baking sheet. One of the mistakes that novice bakers make when attempting the ethereal delicacies is not allowing the cookies enough time to dry. Macarons need close to an hour to harden before baking.

While I waited for them to set, I used a flat spatula to frost another layer of buttercream on the cake. Once the macarons had baked, I piped raspberry, blackberry, and cherry jam along the rims and sandwiched them together. Then I finished the donut effect by piping chocolate and vanilla royal icing on the top and dusting them with sprinkles. Finally I used more buttercream as glue to press the miniature donuts onto the sides of the cake and pile them on the top, like a stack of Sunday morning donuts.

"That is adorable, Jules," Bethany said as I placed the last of the pastel donut on the tiered cake. "I've got to post that on our social."

"You bet. Just wait a couple days to post them. This cake is for a surprise proposal."

"I love weddings!" She clapped with delight and snapped pictures before I returned the cake to the walk-in to keep it cool until Thomas picked it up tonight.

I had to be more sneaky when it came to working on Steph's cake, so I stuffed the last jar of our pearl-bead sprinkles into my apron pocket. "Hey, Steph, can I ask you a favor?"

Steph had finished the last of the custom cake orders. Her workstation was filled with six-inch, eight-inch, and twelve-inch round cakes meticulously decorated with fire trucks for a boy's fifth birthday, gold and white beading with delicate sugar feathers for a Great Gatsby bash, and a fault-line cake filled with green buttercream succulents.

"We're out of pearl sprinkles. Could you run up to Medford and restock the sprinkle drawer? There are quite a few jars that are nearly empty and you have the best eye for what's on trend."

"I guess." She sounded disinterested but I caught a tiny curl of her lip at my compliment.

"Take petty cash and I'll pay for your gas too."

Once she was gone, I took the black velvet cakes out of the walk-in and layered them with deep purple blackberry buttercream. Then I frosted the stacked cakes with midnight black frosting and trimmed the sides and top with gothic purple swirls of blackberry buttercream.

"What do you think?" I asked Sterling when I finished.

"That's awesome, Jules. It's like Steph in cake form." He spun the cake on the stand to see every angle. "She's going to freak when she sees this."

"I'm so glad you like it. I'll hide it in the walk-in behind the produce. Take it whenever you're ready."

"Thanks." He bit his bottom lip. "Wish me luck."

"It'll be great," I assured him. I boxed Steph's cake, tucked it behind a box of apples, and took a break upstairs. The bakeshop was alive with vibrant morning energy. I loved watching customers perusing the pastry case, trying to decide on which delight to order, and listening to them chat with Andy and Sequoia as they poured creamy shots of espresso and foamed milk.

Addie stood at the end of the line. I was surprised to see her at Torte.

"What brings you to the bakeshop this morning?" I asked, walking over to join her at the end of the line.

"I needed a chai latte." Her eyes were on high alert. They darted from the espresso bar where Sequoia foamed oat milk to the booths by the front windows.

Was she looking for someone?

Addie rolled her neck in a half circle. "I have to spend the morning with the insurance agent and I'm not looking forward to it."

We stepped closer to the counter as the line moved.

"Did you hear about Lars?" I asked.

Addie wrapped her cashmere shawl tightly around her narrow shoulders. "Who's Lars?"

"Hunter's son."

"No."

She didn't sound particularly interested, but I filled her in about Lars getting caught breaking into Cyclepath and how he'd been pretending to be the Wizard as we waited in line.

Addie made it to the pastry case where Rosa waited to take her order. "What? You mean the kid? The teenager who skates around the neighborhood with his friends when they should be at school?"

"Yep. You got it. That's Lars." I motioned toward Rosa. "Did you want a chai?"

Addie pressed her hands to her cheeks. "Wait, what are you saying? That skater kid was impersonating the Wizard?"

"Apparently. It sounds like he and his friends took advantage of the Wizard being a known entity around town. They committed a variety of crimes, pretending to be him."

"Oh my God! I have to go." Addie slapped a five-dollar bill on the counter.

"Did you want to order?" I asked. Rosa looked at me, unsure what to do with Addie's money.

"No. I've need to go. I can't believe this. I've been so wrong. God, I'm so stupid. It totally makes sense now. He used to hang around the studio. I told him and his friends to stop loitering. This entire time I thought the Wizard was following me at night. I bet you anything it was Lars. I have to get back to the studio and check my cameras and files."

"Your files?" I reached for the five-dollar bill and handed it back to Addie.

She stuffed it in her sports bra. "I made a file documenting everything when I was trying to take out the restraining order. I have pictures and videos. Some of them aren't the best resolution because they were taken at night, but the police might be able to enhance them. My surveillance cameras have hours of footage. The police can probably tell based on height and build whether whoever was following me on the bike path was Lars or the Wizard." She stepped out of the line. "I feel terrible. What if I was wrong?"

"It was an honest mistake. I think that was Lars' intention—to try and blame his crimes on the Wizard."

"That's terrible." Addie practically ran out of the bakeshop.

If nothing else, Laney might get some relief in knowing that her father wasn't a stalker, assuming that Addie's documents proved that Lars was the one following her.

"Darling, over here!" Lance's singsong voice turned my attention away from Addie.

Lance waved his fingers. He sat at one of the front window booths. "Don't be shy. Come sit."

When had he snuck in? I scooted behind the bar and poured two cups of coffee. Then I took a seat across from him.

"Coffee?" I offered him a cup.

"Always, darling." Lance blew me a kiss. "I must know everything about the investigation, but first I have a special request."

This is becoming a trend, I thought to myself, fully expecting Lance to want a "surprise" cake.

"I have the absolute best idea for this weekend's Sunday Supper theme."

"What's that?" I cradled my coffee cup.

"Romance. A spring in your step as they say. Think springtime in the south of France. Beautiful budding flowers, wine, and something decadent for dinner."

"How does Proposal Chicken sound?"

"Uh, let's not get ahead of ourselves, darling!" Lance shot me a look of horror.

"Eating the dish does not mean you have to propose. It's simply a lovely, romantic dish infused with flavor, and every so often it might spark getting on a knee and popping the question."

Lance snapped fingers on both hands in unison. "You won't be seeing me on a knee, but a romantic lovely dish does have a nice ring to it. What do you say? Time for a Torte supper? Sunday?"

"Sure." The south of France reminded me of my wedding day. "Why the inspiration?"

"No reason. No reason." Lance strummed his fingers on the table. "Put me down for two."

"Oh really, and who's your guest?"

"You'll have to wait and see." He winked. "Now, on to the good stuff. Do tell, what is the latest?"

Yet again I repeated what I knew about Lars' arrest.

"An imposter amongst us. Do you think he did it? Killed the old man?"

I shrugged. "Not really. I guess it's possible, but he doesn't seem like a killer to me."

"A killer kid. Shudder. Let's leave that level of drama for the stage." He pretended to wipe his brow.

"Fine by me. I saw the whole thing evolve this morning and Lars swore he didn't have anything to do with the fire. I don't know why, but I believe him. I feel like pieces of the puzzle are right in front of me but I can't make them fit. The fire has to be at the center of it. But what are we missing? If the fire was intended to burn down Namaste Yoga, then what's Addie's connection?"

Lance's gaze drifted to the window where Arlo was chatting with a woman near the bubblers.

"Are you listening?"

He drew his eyes away from the window. "Yes, yes. You are definitely on the crux of a breakthrough, but I must run, darling. Duty calls. Let's book that spring-time in Paris dinner. Ta-ta."

He left with a spring in his step. I couldn't blame him. I felt the same. I wanted to run through the plaza and sing at the top of my lungs. Carlos was staying. Thomas was proposing. Lance was gushing. And Sterling and Steph were moving in together. Love was winning. Everything would be perfect if I could just figure out who killed the Wizard.

Chapter Twenty-Seven

As the afternoon wore into the evening, I finished my baking duties and started on Thomas's dinner. The Proposal Chicken would marinate in a base of olive oil, garlic, onions, and sun-dried tomato pesto. I started by dicing the savory onions and garlic and tossing them in a cast iron skillet. Then I added the sun-dried tomato pesto, chicken breasts, and fresh chopped basil. After I had browned the breasts on both sides, I added heavy cream and Parmesan cheese, and placed the skillet in the oven to bake for thirty minutes.

Donuts are best served fresh, so I saved those for last. Sticking with the romantic theme, I wanted to bake our signature raised donuts with an assortment of fruit-and-berry-infused glazes. I warmed milk and yeast. For fluffy donuts it was critical to activate the yeast without killing it with scalding hot milk. I set it aside to rise and mixed melted butter, eggs, flour, salt, and a touch of sugar together. Once the yeast was bubbling, I incorporated it and turned the dough onto a floured cutting board. There's nothing quite as cathartic as kneading dough. My mind wandered as I punched and pressed the dough until it became thick and soft while still slightly sticky.

I added oil to the fryer and turned the heat to medium high.

My thoughts drifted to Addie's studio as I rolled the dough and began cutting out donuts. If my gut feeling about Lars was right and he hadn't set the fire, then who had? Hunter had been on the scene. He claimed to have been working late, but what if that was a lie? What about Sky? I'd caught him sleeping in the outdoor kitchen. Maybe the fire had been an accident or a burst of outrage.

I dropped the first few donuts into the grease. They had to be watched closely so as not to burn. After about a minute and a half I flipped them with tongs. The donuts were a beautiful golden brown.

I lined cooling racks with paper towels to soak up any grease and transferred the first batch from the fryer. As I repeated the steps with the remaining donuts, I considered other possibilities. What if Addie had set the fire herself? She didn't act as if money was a problem, but I had learned over the years that appearances could be deceiving. Or, what about Dean? What was his relationship with Addie? Was he dealing more than milk or was it the other way around? Was Addie *his* source?

It felt like I was so close to an answer, yet nothing quite made sense.

I flooded the donuts with citrus and berry glazes. Then I boxed them up along with the donut-themed engagement cake, salad, and bread.

Thomas texted a little after six. "Running late from

the case. Any chance you could bring dinner to the park? Kerry's meeting me here in thirty."

I texted back a reply right away. "Of course. See you soon."

The chicken had cooked in its cheesy, garlicky base. I finished it with more fresh chopped basil.

When I arrived at Railroad Park, my breath caught in my chest. Thomas had wrapped tiny yellow and pink twinkle lights around the gazebo. A silky cream tablecloth was draped over the picnic table. Two place settings, a bottle of champagne, and dozens of votive candles were arranged on the table. Janet, his mom, trimmed yellow and pink roses that were bundled with wildflowers and herbs.

"Hi Juliet, isn't this beautiful?" She set one huge bouquet of flowers in the center of the table.

"Incredible." In the distance the summit of Grizzly Peak was barely visible as the sun sunk behind us. The sepia-toned range, warm breeze, and scent of budding blackberries was an unequaled backdrop for a proposal.

"Hey, I'm here," Thomas called from the path. Instead of his uniform he was wearing black slacks, a crisp white shirt, a suit jacket, and a simple black tie. His pace was quick as he approached the gazebo.

"Can I help you with that, Jules?" He fiddled with his tie.

"No way. You'll get your suit dirty." I set everything on a bench and began unpacking the feast.

He paced back and forth. "You haven't seen Kerry yet, have you?"

"No sign of her yet," Janet replied, resting a dainty

bouquet on Kerry's plate. "Don't worry about us. I'll help Juliet."

It took us only a few minutes to set up dinner. To make sure everything would stay hot, I'd brought warming trays. I tossed the salad, arranged loaves of bread in a basket, set out ramekins with herbed butter, and uncorked a bottle of Uva's cabernet. Next I propped the box of donuts open to reveal the glossy glazed sweets adorned with sprinkles, drizzled chocolate and caramel, and fresh-grated orange, lemon, and lime rinds.

Saving the best for last, I unboxed the cake while Thomas and Janet gushed over my shoulder.

"It's so adorable," Janet said. "The macaron donuts are so clever."

"I'm glad you like it." I pointed to the pastry box with the actual donuts. "Those are the real deal."

Janet steadied an antique platinum cake stand while I slid the cake onto the center. It had turned out better than I had expected, with a touch of whimsy and elegance.

"Jules, you've outdone yourself. There's enough food for the entire police force. Man, we're going to be stuffed." Thomas grinned. A car pulled up near the children's play structure.

"That's our cue," Janet said to me. She kissed Thomas on the cheek. "Good luck. I can't wait to hear the details tomorrow."

"Same here." I waved.

Janet and I hurried down the path as Kerry got out of her car. Part of me wished I could stay and watch as Thomas got down on a knee. Proposals were so romantic.

"That was kind of you to cook for them," Janet said as we parted ways on the path.

"I'm excited for them. They're a good match."

Janet gave me a long hug. "They are. And you are a dear friend. I hope you know that."

I squeezed her hand. "I do."

Since I was near Scoops, I decided to stop by and see if Addie had learned anything new from the insurance inspector.

Namaste was dark. I was surprised. Addie's evening classes were always packed with the after-work crowd.

Even stranger than not having class was the fact that the porch door leading to the studio was halfway open. I went up the stairs to the front porch and tapped on the door. "Addie, are you in there? It's Jules."

There was no answer, but I could have sworn I heard a whimper.

The tiny hairs on my forearm stood at attention. I reached into my pocket, pulled out my phone, and called the Professor.

He answered right away. "Juliet, to what do I owe the pleasure?"

"I'm at Namaste. I think something's wrong," I whispered. My brain told me to back away, but I stood frozen on the porch. "The front door is open, the studio is dark, and I think I heard whimpering."

"Stay there. I'm on my way and I'll car a squad car."

"Okay." I hung up as a loud thud sounded inside the yoga studio.

"Addie?" I pushed the door open farther.

Another whimper sounded.

Was it a cat?

"Hello?" I stepped all the way inside.

The lights were out but the sound of meditative music was playing in the next room. Maybe my imagination was getting the best of me. Could Addie be teaching a new form of yoga in the dark?

I tiptoed toward the door, and turned the handle slowly so as not to disturb a class—if there was one.

The music grew louder when I opened the door—as did the whimpering.

My worst fears turned into reality. There wasn't a yoga class. Addie was tied to the ballet barre that ran along the far wall. Dean was in the process of gagging her.

"Tell me where the footage is now! I'm going to finish you off the same way I did that crazy old man." Dean's back was to me, but he loomed large over Addie, holding a milk bottle in one hand.

She tried to move her head away from Dean's grasp, but he was much stronger.

I could feel my pulse throbbing in my neck. What should I do?

I glanced around the studio for anything I could use as a weapon. If I snuck up on Dean from behind, maybe I could take him out.

That's not smart, Jules, my inner voice tried to reason.

The Professor was on his way and sending a squad car. They would be here any minute. My best bet was to sneak back outside and wait for the police.

"Where is the footage, Addie?" Dean shouted again. He had managed to get the gag around her mouth.

As Addie threw her head to the side she spotted me.

I shook my head and placed my finger to my lips.

Her eyes widened. She attempted to scream through the gag.

Dean whipped around and spotted me.

My stomach dropped.

"Hey!" He hurled the milk bottle at me.

It shattered against the wall.

My adrenaline kicked into high gear. "I'm going to get help, Addie!" I shouted as I made a break for the door.

Dean thudded after me.

I raced through the reception area and out the front door. My breath sounded like it had been amplified in my head.

"Stop!" Dean was right behind me.

I flew down the porch steps and glanced around me. There was no sign of the Professor or a squad car.

The front door banged shut.

Dean was outside.

I didn't have time to think.

I needed to run—now!

Chapter Twenty-Eight

"You're dead!" Dean bellowed as I sprinted toward the bike path.

I didn't remember his voice sounding so evil before. He had killed the Wizard and was about to do the same to Addie. What would stop him from killing me?

There was only one solution. I had to get to Thomas and Kerry—fast!

The muscles in my chest squeezed like a tourniquet. I kept my strides as long as I could to try and keep distance between Dean and me.

Railroad Park wasn't more than a quarter mile away, but it felt like I was running forever.

I could hear Dean's heavy steps and panting gasps behind me.

"Help!" I shouted, flying toward the narrowing part of the path.

"Thomas! Kerry!"

Was Dean about to tackle me?

His wheezing breath felt like it was hitting the back of my neck.

Using every ounce of reserves I quickened my pace.

"Help!" I shouted again.

A flashlight beam pierced the sky again and again, like a bolt of lightning.

"Who's there?" Kerry's voice reverberated in the air.

Thank goodness.

I ran over the small stream as the playground came into sight.

Kerry and Thomas raced toward me, their flashlights blazing a stream of light on the pathway.

"It's Dean!" I screamed, ready to collapse. "He's behind me."

They sprang into action.

My knees buckled. I sank onto the dewy grass as they went after Dean.

Dean's tall frame came into the beam of Kerry's flashlight.

"Stop, police!" Kerry shouted.

Dean came to an abrupt halt. Then he started jogging backward.

He was no match for Kerry, even in her short red dress and three-inch heels. She reached for her gun and commanded him to stop.

Dean froze.

Everything happened in a whirl of motion. Thomas tackled Dean and Kerry cuffed his hands behind his back. I heard the sound of sirens nearby, but stayed on the grass, trying to catch my breath and make sense of what had happened.

A squad car sped toward the park with its lights flashing. Thomas gave them orders to secure Dean in the back of the car until the Professor arrived.

"Hey Jules." He strolled in my direction with his hands in the pockets of his slacks. "How are you doing?"

I stood. "I'm fine, but what about Addie?" I wiped dew from my hands and pointed to Namaste.

"What about her?"

"Dean tied her up and gagged her. He was threatening to kill her when I walked in." I licked my lips, suddenly desperate for a glass of water.

Thomas's phone rang. "Hold that thought, Jules," he said, taking the call.

I swallowed hard, trying to get rid of the dry feeling in my mouth.

Thomas hung up the phone. "That was the Professor. He's on his way. Another team of officers have already gotten Addie. They're bringing her here. She's okay."

That was a relief.

I waited while the site of Thomas's romantic proposal turned into sea of glaring lights and police activity.

As Thomas had mentioned, Addie appeared a few minutes later, escorted by a uniformed officer. She was wrapped in a blanket.

"You two hang tight for a second," Thomas said. "We're going to need to take both of your statements." He conferred with the police officer who had found Addie.

"How are you doing?" I touched her shoulder.

She wiggled her fingers. Deep red marks lined her

hands from where Dean had bound them. "I want to kill him, but otherwise I'm fine."

"He set the fire, didn't he?" I asked, already knowing the answer. "Does this have to do with the fact that he was your dealer?"

She touched her finger to her throat and cleared it. "How did you know?"

"I heard a rumor. Everything sort of clicked right now."

Addie wrapped the blanket tighter around her shoulders. "It's not like it's a huge deal. I mean marijuana is legal in Oregon."

"Right, but through the proper channels. Not when you're getting it from some dude out of the back of a milk cart on the railroad tracks."

"I know. I'm an idiot. Dean saw me smoking behind the studio one day a few months ago. He told me he'd make me a deal. He said he had a secret grow lab on the farm. His stuff is really pure and cheap."

"Then what happened?"

"The cameras. He freaked out when I installed the cameras. I was hoping to catch the Wizard, who I now realize was Lars, but they have footage of Dean. I wasn't his only client. He took my laptop, my phone, everything digital. I think he was going to try to erase it and take off."

"You're okay?" I surveyed her body for any signs of serious injuries. I thought of the missing cameras and the milk suddenly appearing in our fridge. Dean had used his delivery service as a way into the building. He must have stolen the cameras and then tried to set Namaste on fire.

Thomas returned. He removed his phone from his suit jacket and asked me to take him through everything that had happened, while Kerry interviewed Addie.

Shortly after I finished, I spotted the Professor's unmarked car pull in front of the basketball courts.

"Duty calls." Thomas crossed both fingers. "Let's hope I can salvage this night."

"Thomas, I'm so sorry. I didn't know what else to do."

He patted my shoulder. "Jules, we caught a killer. That's a win, and it comes with the territory. What can you do?" He glanced at Kerry. "She won't ever be able to say that the night of our engagement was dull or uneventful."

I waited near the gazebo where Thomas's romantic dinner sat untouched.

"Juliet." Mom hurried toward me. "I came with Doug. I'm so glad you're okay, honey." She exhaled and hugged me.

"I'm fine, but I feel terrible for Thomas. His proposal was ruined."

We watched the other squad car take Dean away. Kerry finished interviewing Addie. She, Thomas, and the Professor huddled near the swing set.

Addie breezed past us. "I'm going to my studio. The police said they'll need to do a search and will have more questions for me. Do you want to come with me?"

"I'll wait here for a few. As long as you're okay?"

She knotted the blanket around her waist so that it didn't touch the ground. "I'm fine. Dean should be worried though. I can't wait to testify against that creep." She stomped down the path and into the moonlight.

Thomas, Kerry, and the Professor came over to the gazebo.

The Professor bowed to Thomas. "Many apologies for the interruption. I shall take it from here, you two."

Thomas laughed. "Ah, it's kind of perfect isn't it? Right, Kerry?"

Kerry beamed a smile in return.

"This is better, actually." Thomas handed Kerry the box of donuts. Then he dropped to one knee. Mom pressed her hands together and grinned. The Professor placed one arm around Mom's shoulders and the other around mine. "Ah, the sweet twist of fate," he whispered.

"Kerry, we met on the job. We're going to spend our lives on the job, so it's only fitting that I ask for your hand in marriage, while you're doing what you do best—tackling a criminal in that red dress." He lifted the lid to the donut box.

Kerry clasped her hand over her heart in a rare show of emotion.

"Will you eat donuts with me every day, Kerry?" Thomas pointed to the ring box tucked in the center of a glazed donut.

"I will!" She reached for the box, opened it, and gasped.

Thomas stood and slid the ring on her finger. Then they kissed.

We clapped and cheered.

They laughed. Kerry held up her finger to show us the dazzling ring.

We left them to finish their romantic dinner in peace. I was happy—thrilled—for Thomas and for Kerry. They were starting the beginning of something new. I smiled knowing that I was too.

Chapter Twenty-Nine

A few days after Dean's arrest, I found myself at the tasting room at Uva. Carlos told me to meet him at the winery because there was something he needed to share with me that was sure to resolve the limbo we'd been living in for good.

"Mi querida, I'm so happy you came. I have something for you." Carlos laced his fingers through mine. He looked debonair in his well-cut khaki slacks, white shirt, and khaki jacket. "Julieta, I will always cherish our time together. You have my heart forever, and now I want to give a symbol of my love to you."

He pressed his hand over his heart.

"Okay." I had no idea what he was talking about.

"Close your eyes, and trust me." He led me outside onto the deck that looked out to the organic vineyard. "Go ahead, open your eyes." Sunlight streamed on the grapevines giving them an angelic glow. Mount Ashland rose like a massive green wave in the distance. Honeybees buzzed along the neat rows. "Isn't she spectacular?"

"Yes," I agreed. "I'm still not sure I understand though."

A trace of delight crossed Carlos's face. "This is my gift to you, mi querida. A way for us to hold a piece of each other, of the land and the sky together."

"Okay." I raised one eyebrow.

"You do not understand?"

"No."

He kissed my forehead so tenderly that it was hard to breathe.

Carlos bent down and reached into a leather satchel. He removed a bundle of paperwork held together with a large rubber band. "My gift."

I took the papers. It looked like some kind of a contract. "What is it?"

"Uva. It belongs to us now."

"What? How?" I was having a hard time forming words.

"Let's say that I made Richard Lord a deal he couldn't refuse. You and I and Lance own it completely. The vineyard it is ours."

"Carlos." Words failed me.

He beamed. "I knew this would make you happy. It is the right thing. Uva should belong to us—to you. I feel you in the earth every day I'm here. When the light hits the vines like this in the mornings and they glow, it makes me think of you."

I couldn't believe what he was saying. Spots danced in my vision. I wasn't entirely sure if it was from the sun or my shock. "Thank you. But, how? I can't believe Richard would give up Uva, even for a good price."

Carlos studied my face. "Everyone has a price. Even Richard Lord."

"You bought him out? Really?"

"Si."

I threw my arms around him, soaking in the scent of his woodsmoke aftershave and the soft caress of his lips on mine. When we finally broke apart, he pressed his hands together. "You are happy, si?"

"Yes. Shocked, but definitely happy. I don't know how you did it."

"They say it is good to have some mystery in a marriage." Carlos winked.

"What about Lance?" I watched as a red-tailed hawk circled overhead.

"Lance is on our team. He will continue to be a partner. I think this is okay with you?"

I thought back to the night we went out to dinner. Is that what Carlos and Lance had been plotting? Carlos's meetings hadn't been about getting a new contract on the ship. He'd been working to buy out Richard Lord.

"That's perfect. I don't know what to say other than thank you."

"Your face right now is the only thanks I need." Carlos trailed a finger along my cheek. Then he turned my head toward the vineyard. "This is our future, Julieta."

If a heart could burst from happiness, mine was in danger of exploding.

We spent a while savoring the views and mapping out plans. I was so caught up in the moment that I nearly forgot I was due at the bakeshop. "Carlos, I have to go. We'll talk more tonight." I left him with a hug.

In a daze, I drove to Torte, barely noticing the blooming purple and yellow vetch on the hillside and the lingering snow on the summit of Mt. A.

"Morning, boss," Andy greeted me when I walked in the front door. "I made a special drink for you that you're either going to love or hate."

"Well, when you sell it like that, I can't wait to try it."

"I don't know if you'll think that once you taste it." Andy grinned. He handed me a milky black latte.

"What is this?" I stared at the dark drink.

"Smell it."

I took a deep inhale of the steamy latte and immediately smelled notes of toasty coconut. "Coconut?"

"Yep. It's a charcoal latte. You remember how I told you I was inspired after the fire?"

"Yeah?"

"This is my inspiration. Charcoal. It's hot right now—pun intended by the way."

"Nice." I chuckled. The drink was jet-black and had the slightest hint of a smoky aroma.

"Bethany gave me the idea a while ago. A bunch of social influencers are baking with charcoal. I'm sure you've seen it around, but I couldn't figure out a way to put it in coffee until the fire. Give a try and tell me what you think."

I took a timid sip. To the delight of my taste buds, the latte wasn't gritty or bitter. It had a lovely coconut flavor mingled with a touch of earthiness. "Wow, it's delicious. Who knew? Charcoal."

"Right?" Andy pointed to the specials board. "As long as you're cool with it, we're going to put it up today and see how it does."

"Go for it." I took the charcoal latte and went downstairs.

To my surprise, Mom was in the kitchen, wearing our signature-red Torte apron and rolling out shortcrust. "You're here early," I noted, taking off my jacket and tying on an apron.

"I thought you might want some company." She gave me a knowing look. "I hear you might have some news."

"What? You know?" I looked around the kitchen. "Does everyone know?" Marty was out on bread deliveries, Steph had her headphones in at the decorating station, and Sterling was either distracted with a soup on the stove or doing a great job pretending to be completely occupied.

Mom squeezed my hand. "No, honey. Carlos asked Doug and me our opinion."

"How did he do it? Richard Lord never budges for me."

"No idea. He didn't tell us that part." Mom shrugged.

"And I thought that Carlos was going to leave."

"Did you?" She raised an eyebrow. "Have I ever told you what Dad used to say?"

"About what?"

She brushed flour from her hands and traced the crust with a pastry knife, cutting a perfect freehand circle. "He said that optimists get a bad rap."

"How so?"

"You, like your father and myself, are an eternal optimist."

"Am I?"

"Yes. Trust me on this one, honey, you are. That's not my point, though. Dad always felt like there was this pervasive idea that sadness and melancholy were reserved for pessimists. It's not true. You can be both. You can be heartbroken. You can be sad, lonely, filled with grief, and you can still be an optimist."

"What's the difference?"

"The difference is that optimists—like us—know that the sadness, the grief won't consume us. They'll likely change us. Maybe those feelings will stay with us, but they won't define us. What I'm trying to remind you of is that you know who you are and how strong you are at your core. Even if Carlos had left, you would have been fine. You're fine exactly as you are, which is one of the reasons Carlos loves you so much."

Her words resonated on every level.

"Thanks, Mom. I needed to hear that." I gave her a quick hug and got to work on cake orders.

The Professor dropped by around lunch to give us an update on Dean. "Afternoon, my favorite ladies. I thought you might like to know that Dean will be arraigned tomorrow. He has made a full confession not only about killing the Wizard—Jim—but also about his involvement in drug trafficking. It should be—knock on wood—an open-and-shut case."

"That's good," I said.

"Indeed. A confession makes the prosecution's case much easier. The team was able to recover the digital files. We have video evidence of Dean dealing on the tracks. Our team seized over six-thousand marijuana plants from his property. That's nearly three tons. It will be destroyed. Dean has been growing and selling on the black market for six months. He's been charged with murder, illegal manufacturing, delivery, possession, and money laundering."

"What about the cows? What's going to happen to his farm?"

"There is no farm. He confessed to purchasing milk from the grocery store and repacking it in glass bottles."

I could feel my mouth hang open. "No wonder his milk didn't taste particularly special."

"Why was he so desperate to break into Namaste?" I asked. "Was he worried that the surveillance cameras were going to show him dealing?"

"That and more." The Professor stretched one leg over the other. "There's also footage of Jim's murder on the files. It was quite disturbing to watch, but the footage shows the assault that led to Jim's death. He confessed that Jim had planned to come to us with proof of his drug dealing. Dean will be spending many, many years behind bars."

"What a relief." Mom offered the Professor one of her spring lemon tarts.

"I'm sure Laney will take some comfort in knowing that you've caught her dad's killer."

"Oh, I'm glad you mentioned Laney. There's been an interesting development there. Laney will be receiving his 401k in its entirety."

"That's great news." I was relieved for my friend. No amount of money could bring her father back, but the cash would certainly ensure that Nana's Street Food would continue to thrive.

"What about Lars?" Mom asked.

The Professor nibbled on the lemon tart. "His fate

will rest in part in terms of who decides to press charges. Hunter, Addie, you. He did confess to tagging the buildings in the alley and your fridge, and stealing a variety of items from his father's shop."

"I have some thoughts on that," Mom said. "There is going to be plenty of manual labor to be done on the new space. It seems like a fitting opportunity for some volunteer labor."

"But can he be trusted?" I asked.

"I spoke with Hunter about that very thing. I think with some direct supervision and his father's watchful eye, we can feel confident in that."

"Fine with me. I'd much prefer not to have to press charges, as long as he never does something like that again."

"As the Bard said, 'They whose guilt within their bosom lies, imagine every eye beholds their blame.' I do believe Lars will feel the weight of community eyes upon him, and I choose to hope that those watchful eyes will steer him forward on a new course."

I appreciated that they were both willing to give Lars another chance.

"Was Lars the person Lance and I saw digging in the dumpster?"

"Ah." The Professor held up a finger. "I have another favorite quote for this, 'A little more knowledge lights our way.'"

"That's not Shakespeare," Mom said.

"No—Master Yoda. Although one could argue that Star Wars has much in common with the Bard." He brushed his hands together. "I digress. We'll save that discussion for another day. I too believed that Lars must have been the person you saw, but in new light—hence information from a very scared Sky—I came to realize that Sky was indeed in danger. He saw Lars imitating Jim but unbeknownst to him, he saw Dean too."

Mom and I looked at each other.

"Sky searched the dumpster in hopes of finding the cape—proof that someone was impersonating his friend. What he didn't realize is that he crossed paths with a killer. Dean was at Scoops that night. Our footage from Addie's front cameras show him sneaking in the side entrance. We believe that he intended to set the fire that night but Sky and then you scared him away. Sky camped out in your kitchen to try and catch the killer."

I pressed my hand to my heart. "Poor Sky. He really cared about Jim. What's going to happen to him?"

"We've connected him with social services, so my hope is that he'll find a new path forward." The Professor finished his tart. "This is a treat for the tongue. I should move along as there is a hefty pile of paperwork awaiting me, but I hear that a Sunday Supper is in order tonight. I'll see you beauties later this evening." He gave us a bow and took his leave.

Making a romantic dinner had new meaning for me. I threw myself into chopping onions and mincing garlic, leaving the decorating to Bethany and Steph.

When I came upstairs with an armful of wine, before we were due to open the doors to our guests, the dining room brought more happy tears to my eyes. Steph and Bethany had strung twinkle lights in a crisscross pattern across the entire ceiling. There were garlands of spring flowers dangling from above and lining the center of the long table. Each place setting had a votive candle and single pink rose. If Thomas and Kerry wanted to, they could tie the knot at Torte tonight. It looked like a scene from *Romeo and Juliet*.

"You've outdone yourselves," I said to the team.

"Thanks." Bethany blushed. "We went super girly, didn't we Steph?"

Steph nodded. "I guess."

"Did you hear her news?" Bethany interjected.

"No, what?" I played along while I set the bottles of wine on the table.

"Should I tell her, or do you want to?" Bethany asked Steph.

"Go ahead." Steph pretended like she didn't care, but I saw a spark of excitement in her purple-lined eyes.

"She and Sterling are moving in together. He asked her in the most romantic way. He gave her a custom cake and a key to their new apartment. Isn't that the cutest?"

"It is," I agreed, catching Steph's eyes. "Congratulations."

She shrugged.

A knock sounded on the door. I looked up to see Lance standing outside, holding a bouquet of pink lilies.

"You're early," I noted as I let him in.

"I know. It's quite embarrassing, actually. You know I like to be fashionably late, but I made an exception for you, darling."

"Me?"

He handed me the flowers. "You. Don't give me that look. I know that you and that dashing Spaniard have had a tête-à-tête by now and I must hear details."

I sniffed the fragrant lilies. "There aren't many

details. Carlos didn't tell me much, but obviously I'm thrilled."

"Me too, darling. Me too." He kissed each cheek. "So what did he tell you about Uva?"

"Not much. How did you guys convince Richard?"

Lance shook his finger at me. "Not so fast. That secret will stay with me for a while. I'll give you all the gory details once you've had some time to settle in. It's a good story, and one you'll enjoy. You've seen that hideous yellow Hummer he's been tooling around town in?"

"Yeah." Richard's choice of vehicle, like his personality, stood out like a sore thumb.

"Here's one juicy tidbit I'll give you to tide you over. Let's just say the Hummer didn't actually belong to Richard and now it does. Thanks to a stroke of genius on Carlos's part. Clever, clever, man."

"Huh? I don't understand."

"You don't need to right now. I'm personally enjoying that look of utter bewilderment."

The thought of Carlos secretly working with Lance to make sure Uva would stay in our hands stirred my emotions.

"Don't wrinkle that brow. We have to keep that radiant skin youthful. And angles, darling. Never forget your angles." He tapped two fingers under my chin. "I know you have a party to host, but you have to promise me one thing before everyone arrives."

"What's that?" I shifted the bouquet of flowers in my arms.

"Don't forget yours truly now that your devilishly handsome husband has decided to stay. We make a fierce team, Juliet Montague Capshaw. Pinkie-swear that nothing is going to change between us." He held out his pinkie.

"Lance, never. I would be lost without you."

"Banish the thought." He pointed to my hands. "Go put those flowers in water, and let's celebrate with a little vino."

Love was definitely in the air as the rest of our guests arrived. I circled the dining table with bottles of our Uva rosé and merlot. Kerry and Thomas were huddled at one end of the table, chatting with their seatmates about wedding ideas. I overheard Kerry mention Lithia Park as a potential site. Steph and Sterling looked young and in love, as they served platters of Proposal Chicken, herbed flatbread, and chopped spring salads. Lance and Arlo were cozy on the opposite end of the table. I wasn't sure if my eyes were playing tricks on me in the flickering candlelight, but I thought I spotted their hands intertwined.

Mom and the Professor offered a toast.

"If music be the food of love, play on." The Professor held out his wineglass, quoting Shakespeare.

"In other words," Mom added, raising her glass, "let's eat."

Everyone cheered and clinked their glasses together.

After dinner, Bethany and Steph brought up a birthday cake for Andy. It was a two-layer coffee cake with mocha buttercream and twenty-one candles.

"To the birthday boy." Bethany planted a kiss on Andy's cheek.

Even in the candlelight I could tell Andy was blushing. He blew out the candles. Carlos, who had arrived late, popped open a bottle of champagne and offered another toast.

"Arriba!" He motioned for us to lift our glasses up.

"Abajo!" He motioned for us to touch our glasses down on the table.

"Al centro!" He motioned for us to clink our glasses in the center of the table.

"And now, this is the best." His eyes danced with delight. "Al dentro!" He took a drink of the champagne. "That means 'to the inside'—or 'drink down.'"

Everyone laughed and took a sip of the champagne.

The evening went late. We stayed until the last of the candles had melted and the wine ran empty. I wanted to pinch myself as I nestled into Carlos's arms, taking in the love that surrounded me. I had found myself in Ashland. I had created and expanded my family and my understanding of who I was meant to be. For so long I had thought that Carlos and I were destined to be star-crossed lovers. But I was wrong. The gift of my time without him had taught me innumerable things about myself. Most importantly, that love is everywhere if we let it in.

Recipes

French Toast Bake with Mascarpone Cream

Ingredients:
For the French toast:
1 cup heavy cream
6 eggs
2 tbsp honey
1 tsp vanilla
1 tsp fresh lemon juice
1 tsp cinnamon
1 tsp nutmeg
1 loaf of brioche, sliced
½ tsp salt

For the topping:
1 container mascarpone cheese
1 tbsp honey
1 tsp vanilla
2 tsps fresh orange and lemon juice plus zest of each
Fresh berries—whatever is in season

Directions:
Preheat the oven to 350 degrees. In a medium bowl, whisk the heavy cream, eggs, honey, vanilla, lemon juice, cinnamon, nutmeg, and salt. Slice the bread into cubes and arrange them in an 8 × 8 baking dish. Pour the egg mixture over the bread and bake for thirty minutes. Meanwhile, add the mascarpone cheese, honey, vanilla, and orange and lemon juice and zest to an electric mixer and whip on medium high for 3 to 5 minutes.

Remove the French toast from oven. Top with the mascarpone cream and fresh berries.

Spring Meltaway Cookies

Ingredients:
For the cookies:
1 cup butter
½ cup powdered sugar
1 teaspoon extract such as: fresh orange or lemon juice, almond extract, or vanilla extract
½ teaspoon salt
2 tablespoons heavy cream
¼ cup cornstarch
1 ½ cups flour

For the buttercream:
½ cup butter
1 tsp of the same extract you added to the cookies: orange or lemon juice, almond extract, or vanilla extract
2 ½ to 3 cups powdered sugar

1 tbsp heavy cream
Food coloring, if desired

Directions:
Preheat the oven to 350 degrees and line a baking sheet with parchment paper. To make the cookies, cream the butter and sugar together with a mixer on medium in a medium bowl. Add the peppermint extract, salt, and heavy cream. Slowly incorporate the cornstarch and flour with the mixer. Roll the dough into 1-inch balls. Place on the prepared baking sheet. Bake for 8 to 10 minutes or until centers are cooked. Allow to cool completely.

To make the buttercream, whip the butter and extract together in a medium bowl with a hand mixer on medium high. Slowly incorporate the powdered sugar and heavy cream. Whip for 3 to 5 minutes, until light and fluffy. If desired, add a couple of drops of food coloring and whip for another minute. Spread the buttercream onto the cooled cookies.

Donut Cake

Ingredients:
For the cake:
1 ½ cups butter
2 cups sugar
4 eggs
1 tsp vanilla
1 tsp nutmeg
1 tsp cinnamon

6 tbsp cornstarch
2 tsps baking powder
1 tsp salt
3 cups flour
½ cup milk
½ cup sour cream

For the glaze:
1 ¼ cups powdered sugar
1 tsp almond extract
4 tbsps heavy cream
1 tsp cherry syrup

Directions:
Preheat the oven to 325 degrees and generously coat a bundt pan with baking spray. To make the cake, cream the butter and sugar together in a medium bowl with a hand mixer on medium speed until light and fluffy. Add the eggs, vanilla, nutmeg, cinnamon, cornstarch, baking powder, and salt. Use mixer on medium until well combined. If using an electric mixer, alternate adding the flour with milk and sour cream. Spread the cake batter into the prepared bundt pan and bake for 40-45 minutes. Test to see if cake is done by inserting a toothpick into the center. If the toothpick comes out clean, the cake is done.

Remove the bundt pan from oven and allow it to cool for 10 minutes. Invert the bundt pan onto a cake plate and continue to cool. The bundt should be dense, like a cake donut. While the cake is cooling, make the glaze. In a small bowl, whisk the powdered sugar, almond extract, cream, and cherry syrup. Drizzle over the cooled cake and serve immediately.

Curry pasties

Ingredients:
For the dough:
1 cup butter (plus 2 tbsps melted)
1 cup hot water
1 ½ tsps salt
4 cups flour
½ cup cornmeal

For the filling:
1 tbsp olive oil
1 onion
1 large bunch cilantro
1 red pepper
1 yellow pepper
1 tbsp olive oil
1 tsp ginger
1 tsp coriander
1 tsp cumin
1 jar Korma
1 can light coconut milk
2 large chicken breasts, cooked and shredded

Directions:
Preheat the oven to 350 degrees and line a baking sheet with parchment paper. To make the dough, add the butter, water, and salt to a medium saucepan and bring to a boil. Off the heat, stir in the flour until a dough begins to form. Cover and chill while you make the filling. For the filling, dice the onions, cilantro (stalks and leaves), and peppers. Add the olive oil to a Dutch oven

and sauté the onions, peppers, and cilantro on medium heat until the onions are translucent. Add the ginger, coriander, cumin, Korma, coconut milk, and shredded chicken. After bringing to a boil, turn the heat to low and simmer for twenty minutes.

Roll the dough out onto a floured surface until it's about ¼ inch thick. Cut out 10 to 12 5-inch circles. Add two heaping tbsps of filling to one half of the circle, then fold the other half over the top. Pinch the sides. Brush with melted butter and sprinkle with cornmeal. Bake on the prepared baking sheet for 30 minutes, until golden brown.

Proposal Chicken

Ingredients:
2 large chicken breasts
1 tbsp olive oil
1 small yellow onion, diced
2 cloves garlic, minced
1 jar of sun-dried tomato pesto
5-6 sprigs fresh basil, chopped
½ cup of heavy cream
½ cup Parmesan cheese

Directions:
Preheat the oven to 350 degrees. Add the olive oil to a cast-iron skillet and warm on medium-low heat. Sauté the onion and garlic for 3 minutes or until the onion is translucent. Add the chicken. Brown both sides—approximately 2 to 3 minutes per side. Add the

sun-dried tomatoes, chopped basil, and heavy cream. Sprinkle each breast with Parmesan cheese and bake for 30 minutes, until chicken is cooked through and sauce is bubbling.

Brain Freeze

Andy's latest coffee craze involves a refreshing shake sure to please your taste buds. Fair warning, sip slowly to avoid a brain freeze.

Ingredients:
2 shots of espresso
1 generous scoop of coffee ice cream
Whipped cream, for garnish
A drizzle of dark chocolate sauce and espresso bean shavings as garnish

Directions:
Add the shots of espresso and coffee ice cream to a blender and blend until thick and creamy. Pour into a glass and top with the drizzle of dark chocolate sauce, whipped cream, and espresso bean shavings.

Read on for a look ahead to

MOCHA, SHE WROTE

—the next engaging Bakeshop Mystery
installment, coming soon from Ellie Alexander
and St. Martin's Paperbacks!

Chapter One

They say that love is the answer. After years of searching for answers about my future and where I was meant
to be, I was inclined to believe that statement. My world
had expanded dramatically since my husband Carlos
had arrived in Ashland. Following a two-year separation,
we had finally reconciled, and there wasn't a day that I
woke up without a giddy feeling in my stomach. It was
almost too good to be true. The pessimist in me worried
that something was going to go terribly wrong. All of
my dreams had come to fruition. Carlos was in Ashland and managing our growing boutique winery, Uva.
Things at our family bakeshop, Torte, were running
seamlessly and we had recently opened a seasonal walk-
up ice cream shop, Scoops, where we served luscious
hand-churned concretes made with fresh local berries
and drizzled with dark chocolate and dulce de leche.
As if that wasn't enough to keep me occupied, Carlos
and I were settling into my childhood home, making
it our own by installing an outdoor oven and hummingbird feeders in the backyard and hanging collections of
photos from our travels together.

What more could I want? I asked myself as I turned onto the plaza. A lazy spring had given way to a busy summer. It was nearing the end of June, which meant that Ashland's idyllic downtown was bursting with activity. Tourists had arrived to take in shows at the Oregon Shakespeare Festival and kids lounged in Lithia Park, soaking up the warm sun and a well-deserved break from their studies. Adventure lovers waited in line at the outdoor store to take advantage of the region's abundant outdoor opportunities from rafting on the Rogue River to hiking Grizzly Peak. The eager buzz of activity brought a smile to my face as I walked into Torte.

The bakeshop sat at the corner of the plaza across from the Lithia bubblers, offering my team and our loyal customers a perfect view of all the action. Our bright red-and-teal awning, outdoor tables, and window display complete with strings of rainbow bunting, paper-mache popsicles, and colorful beach balls gave the space a welcoming vibe. A symphony of delectable flavors greeted me as I stepped inside. Andy and Sequoia, our two topnotch baristas, slung shots of espresso behind the coffee counter. We had positioned our state-of-the-art shiny fire-engine red La Pavoni Italian espresso machine next to the exposed brick wall so that our baristas could chat with customers while grinding beans or frothing milk.

The long wooden bar transitioned into the pastry case where a line of people waited for one of our summer berry tarts, mango cream buns, or roasted red pepper and turkey sausage breakfast sandwiches oozing with melted manchego cheese. Rosa, who had taken on the role of a woman of many trades, punched orders into our point-of-sale system and doled out chocolate croissants and slices of cinnamon coffee cake. She floated between the pastry counter and kitchen most days and was willing to lend a hand wherever needed.

As was typical, the booths by the front windows were occupied. The same was true for our patio seating—picnic tables with matching bright red-and-teal sun umbrellas. Finding a spot to linger during the busy season required having an eagle eye. Fortunately we had expanded our seating options with comfy couches and chairs downstairs and additional bistro tables along Ashland Creek on the backside of the building.

I paused to hold the front door open for a woman balancing a plate of pastries and a steaming mug of coffee. She scanned the busy dining room. I recognized the familiar look.

"I believe that table outside is just leaving." I pointed behind us. "If you want to grab it, I'll have someone come out and wipe it down for you."

"Thank you." She shot me a relieved smile before hurrying outside to snag the table.

I adjusted the stack of mail beneath my arm and continued inside.

"Hey boss," Andy said with a wave as he deftly poured two shots of espresso over a scoop of ice cream. "Is that the mail?"

I had stopped by the post office on my way back to the bakeshop after delivering a box of bread and cookies to Scoops. "It is, and there just might be something in this stack with your name on it." I grinned and handed him a large envelope.

"It came! It finally came?" Andy's boyish face broke out into a wide smile that almost immediately turned into a worried scowl. "I don't know, though. I'm too nervous. I don't know if I want to look. No. No. I can't look. I can't do it." He clenched his teeth and thrust the envelope to me. "Maybe you should open it."

"No way." I pushed the envelope back across the counter.

He placed a drink order on the bar and waited for a customer to take her affagato and iced latte before picking up the envelope again. "Ahhhh. Look at my hands." He held out his trembling fingers. Andy was in his early twenties with broad, muscular shoulders, sandy hair, and height that he was finally beginning to grow into. He had taken on the role of head barista and had been invaluable in getting Scoops up and running. I wasn't used to seeing him rattled.

His fingers quaked. "I don't even know if I can open it with my hands shaking like this. I'm dying to know what's inside, but then again, what if it's bad news? It might be bad news, Jules, and I'm not sure if I can handle that right now. I've practiced for months for this. If I don't open the envelope then it's not a no, right?"

"But what if it's a yes? You would never know." I tapped the envelope. "There's one easy way to find out."

"Okay." Andy sighed, then ripped the envelope open.

Sequoia and I waited, watching his face for any indication of whether the news was good or bad while he scanned the contents.

Andy read the letter with serious intent. After a minute his smile evaporated.

A sinking sensation swirled in my stomach, and not just because I had already consumed copious amounts of coffee.

Oh no! He worked so hard for this. I had been sure that he would be selected, I hadn't even considered the alternative. I pressed my lips together.

"Well, read it yourself, boss." He bent his head forward, hunched his shoulders, and offered me the paper. "It's not good news."

Sequoia put her hand on his forearm. "Sorry, Andy. You should have had it. You're the best barista I've ever worked with, and you know that is high praise coming from me."

"I know." He let out another heavy sigh.

I couldn't believe it. How had they not chosen Andy? Sequoia was right, he was the best barista I'd ever had the pleasure to call a colleague, not only in Ashland and the surrounding Rogue Valley. I'd worked with many baristas in my years at sea and no one had natural talent like Andy. He didn't have to spend hours laboring over ratios or recipes. His creative palate guided him. I knew without a doubt that one of the reasons for Torte's success was due to Andy. Locals and tourists returned again and again for his whimsical creations like his chunky monkey coffee, banana chocolate blended coffee shake, or his simple Americano with his exquisitely blended custom roasts.

I glanced at the paper. It took less than a second to realize that Andy was messing with us. The first words on the page were: CONGRATULATIONS!

"Andy!" I swatted him with the paper.

"What?" Sequoia stared at me with wide emerald eyes.

"Look." I handed her the paper. "He's been selected! Andy's in!"

Andy gave us a sheepish grin. "Sorry, I couldn't resist. I had to mess with you, at least for a minute. Blame Carlos. He's constantly telling us to add more play into our work."

Sequoia let out a whoop and began clapping. "Barista Cup, baby!"

"Congratulations, Andy!" I seconded her applause. "This calls for a celebration. Our own little Andy is going to be competing in the West Coast Barista Cup. Now the pressure's really on. You have to win. I want a plaque right up there on the wall." I pointed to a spot on the exposed brick.

"This is awesome." Sequoia gave him a fist bump. "You've got some serious practicing to do. Isn't there a crazy time limit on how fast you need to get the judges their drinks?"

"Yeah. Fifteen minutes—exactly. You have to give the sensory judges a cappuccino, a latte, and a custom signature drink in less than fifteen minutes, all while being judged on your technical skills and explaining the origin of each coffee and your personal connection to the cup." He stuffed the papers back in the envelope.

"Sensory judges?" Sequoia asked.

Andy clutched the letter to his chest. "There are four judges who actually drink your offerings and score them and then there are two technical judges who watch every move you make while pulling shots and steaming milk."

"That sounds like way too much pressure for me." She twisted a dreadlock. Sequoia was one of our newer hires and was polar opposite of Andy in nearly every way. She was laid back and exuded a chill vibe with her flowing attire and dreadlocks. Her coffee style included alternative drinks like dirty Chai lattes and matcha lavender infused cold brew.

Andy could have been a poster boy for dairy farmers with his all-American style. Until recently he had played football at Southern Oregon University, but he decided to opt out of school to focus on his coffee knowledge, improve his latte design skills, and immerse himself in the art of roasting. He tended to push the envelope when it came to pairings but his style was more in line with modern coffee shops and traditional Italian high-end espresso drinks. When he and Sequoia had first started working together it had been a disaster. In fact, at one point I had thought that I might have to let one of them go. But, they had worked things out and found common ground. Their very unique approaches were actually a beautiful balance.

"I can't believe that the competition is here this year," I said to Andy. "You're going to have a massive cheer squad."

He blushed, his cheeks matching the color of the espresso machine. "Thanks, boss. Sequoia is right. I'm going to have to put some hours in behind the machine to get ready. Don't worry, I'll do it on my own time. Off the clock. I mean, in some ways I'm way behind. There are baristas who train year-round for this. I'm going to have to pull all-nighters from now until the start of the Cup, but I swear I won't let it impact my work here."

"No way. You are representing Torte. We want our star barista to shine." I adjusted the stack of mail under my arm. "Not to mention that I want to sample whatever you're making. Plus it's summer. We're open late anyway.

We'll prop open the front door, and you can give away samples like we did at Scoops. Think of it as part of our summer marketing plan."

"Cool. I'm down with that."

"I'm heading downstairs. Anything I need to know?"

"Nope. We've got it under control." Andy shot me a thumbs-up. "When there's a lull, I have an idea for my signature drink. I've been playing around with some new flavors but I didn't want to jinx anything until I heard for sure. I'll bring a sample down for you and everyone else to taste. I want honest feedback though. That's the only way I'll improve. If anyone says, 'it's great' they don't get to taste anything else I make, got it?"

"Got it." I saluted him with two fingers and continued downstairs. The West Coast Barista Cup was a big deal. The event drew the best baristas from the region along with hundreds of coffee enthusiasts. The winner would advance to the U.S. Championships with a chance to compete in the World Barista Cup. There were cash prizes for first, second, and third place, along with bragging rights and the potential for future sponsorships. To my knowledge, no barista in the Rogue Valley had had the honor of competing in the Cup. Andy deserved to be recognized. He had put in a tremendous amount of effort at Torte and I wanted him to know we were all behind him.

This year The Hills, a swanky mid-century hotel on the east side of town, was hosting the competition. It would take place in two weeks, which meant that I intended to give Andy as much free time as our staffing schedule would allow to prep for the competition. I was thrilled for our young coffee aficionado to get to go head-to-head with some of the top baristas from up and down the West Coast. I was also excited to get to watch the action myself. It had been years since I'd attended a coffee competition. I knew that the industry was constantly evolving and I couldn't wait to learn some new techniques and see the latest in brewing and roasting equipment.

I passed a group of teenagers who were drinking iced shakes and playing trivia in the cozy seating area in the basement next to retro atomic-style fireplace. I said hello and continued into the kitchen where there was a flurry of activity. Sterling, our sous chef, was assembling rows of sandwiches. He spread cranberry orange cream cheese on baguettes and layered them with thin-sliced turkey, tomatoes, lettuce, and Swiss. Marty, our head bread baker, kneaded a vat of dough with his muscular arms. Bethany and Steph, my two cake artists, were piping buttercream onto cookies and cupcakes.

"How's it going?" I asked, tossing the mail on the counter.

"Good. Just prepping our internal order for Scoops. We'll get these over to the shop before we open," Sterling replied. He finished assembling a turkey sandwich and wrapped it in brown paper.

"Excellent. I stopped by earlier with the pastry order, so that's waiting for you." We had limited hours at the new walk-up ice cream shop. I had hired four high school and college students to run the seasonal counter. Unlike Torte, we offered a small menu at Scoops. In addition to our concretes, our version of gorgeously creamy ice creams, we served cold brew and coffee shakes, and pre-made sandwiches and pastries. Thus far it had been a great addition to the bakeshop. Not a day went by where there wasn't a line of customers waiting for a dish of our Marionberry concrete or a peanut butter blossom shake.

"Did I hear excitement upstairs?" Marty asked. "I could have sworn I heard happy applause."

"You did." I glanced above us. "Hang on a sec. Let me get Andy. I want him to be the one to share the news."

I hurried back upstairs and yanked Andy away from the coffee bar. "You have to tell everyone."

He pretended to be embarrassed, but I could tell from his wide toothy smile that he was proud of his accomplishment, as he should be.

"Andy has a big announcement, everyone," I said, dragging him into the kitchen.

"It's not *that* big, boss." Andy brushed off my compliment. "I am psyched, though, because I just learned that I'm going to be competing in the West Coast Barista Cup in a couple of weeks."

Everyone clapped and cheered.

"Congrats, man." Sterling patted him on the back.

"That *is* a big deal," Marty concurred. "I attended the competition when it was in San Fran a few years ago and the judges were cutthroat." He shivered. "They were so tough, they were scary."

Andy nodded. "I know. It's intense. I was just reading through the rules and regulations and Benson Vargas, who is *the* guy in the world of coffee, is the top judge again this year. I've heard he's super intense and he's one of the managing members of the entire compe-

tition. So there's a touch of pressure there, no problem."
He stuck out his tongue and rolled his eyes.

"Ohhhh, I remember him." Marty let out a visible
shudder before wiping flour from his hands on a dish
towel. "He made one of the competitors cry and I heard
one of the baristas claim that she'd rather die than ever
have to make a drink for him again."

"Great." Andy clutched his neck. "I'm toast."

"No, no, I don't mean to scare you." Marty sounded
genuinely concerned. "You make the best coffee in the
world. You'll have Benson Vargas and all of the other
judges eating out of your hands like puppies."

"Hope so." Andy crossed his fingers and returned to
the coffee bar.

I wondered if Marty was exaggerating. I was thrilled
for Andy, but I hoped that his coffee dreams weren't
about to get crushed before they'd had a chance to come
true.